William T   s
Redemption

an exposé of the malign forces in the world

Russell John Connor

Rose,

Big hugs

Russell

Published in July 2022 by emp3books Ltd
6 Silvester Way, Church Crookham, Fleet, GU52 0TD

Copyright © 2022; Russell John Connor

ISBN: 978-1-910734-49-0

Disclaimer
This is a work of fiction. Any resemblance to characters living or deceased is entirely unintentional.

CONTENTS

Fun Reviews and Media Reports

Well, I never thought he had it in him!
Hazel Knut, Psychiatric Nurse

Sad, poignant and, at times, laugh-out-loud funny.
Grauniad Literary Section

Great characters and fabulous scenes. There are overtones of Mikhail
Bulgakov's, *The Master and Margerita.*
Moscow News

It is a strange mixture of Bertie Wooster meets Doctor Faustus - but it
works wonderfully.
Time In

In his absence, William Taylor Findler was fined £520 for failing to
produce a TV licence on demand.
Camden and Kentist Town Gazette

The Day After

A distant, fuzzy, celestial light disturbed the infinite dark. It grew in intensity and coalesced to resemble a moon and penumbra.

Slowly, the penumbra shrank and the image transformed itself into a bare, light bulb.

This single bulb hung over a small wooden table, and I found myself sitting back on a plastic chair looking up at the bare, unshaded light.

A shiver started at the top of my head and quickly worked its way down to my toes. I was in what could only be described as an interrogation room. My legs were weak and jittery, but I managed to get up and take a few paces around the dimly lit space. The walls were pale grey and there was no furniture except a table and four chairs together with a large mirror flush against one of the walls. I looked into it and was actually pleased with what I saw. My thin, gaunt face had returned to its normal flaccid state and my deep sunken eyes now had their normal, some would say, pig-like appearance. I swept back my locks of hair and couldn't remember the last time they had looked so lustrous.

I was gratified to see that I looked well but it was odd. *Surely,* I mused *I can't look so fit after the previous day's untold excess? And who has dressed me in my favourite blue shirt and grey trousers, ironed and pressed?* I hadn't ironed a shirt in almost four years.

I slumped forward and put my head in my hands. I must have dozed a little, because I didn't hear the door open. Yet, when I

1

looked up, there was a man standing in the room with me wearing an almost dazzlingly white suit, which was odd considering the only light reflecting on him was from the weak overhead bulb. His beard was of a similar radiance and, at first, its intensity made it difficult for me to see his face. I presumed he must be a doctor of some sort.

He didn't say anything but simply walked to the table and placed a laptop onto it. He then took hold of the chair next to mine and sat down, crowding my personal space a little as he did so. A fragrance of the Mediterranean wafted over me; a mixture of lemon and olives. When he started to speak, his first words didn't make sense. 'At one time in your life we would have let you in without question. Now we need to review your case.' His voice was deep and resonant, impressive even, but I detected a hint of utter boredom.

'Let me in where? Hospital?' I asked. After the day before, it was the only place I could think he meant. He didn't reply as such but sniffed in what I took to be an amused way.

The man opened the laptop and fired it up. I looked more closely at his features. He had intensely chestnut-brown eyes and his unblemished sun kissed skin was clearly testament to a good diet and keeping out of the midday glare. His grey hair had receded on top but was swept back over his ears and bunched at the back of his head in little tight curls. Close to, his beard really did radiate an intense white fire. Overall, the words that best describe his look are cool, debonair and sophisticated. The combination of white suit, black shirt and white tie was pure nineteen eighties – to my way of thinking, the best decade ever! Well, that is in terms of the clothes. The best decade for music was the seventies and, Mamma

Mia, there really was one band head and shoulders above all the rest.

I couldn't see the screen of the laptop but it was obvious it wasn't doing what the man had hoped as, in evident frustration, he kept jabbing at the keys in a very unskilled manner. I looked at his hands and marvelled at how slim and dextrous they were. You can tell a great deal from a person's hands, and it was apparent that he had never done any manual work in his life or at least not for a long while. What is more, judging by the state of the pared cuticles and buffed and shaped nails, it was clear that here was a person who had plenty of spare time and frittered it away on personal care.

The man slammed the laptop shut and said, 'Technology! It was so much easier in the past.' I knew then that, whoever this man was, he was a kindred spirit.

Rising up, white and bright, like a cloud brushing the top of a mountain peak, the man said rather politely, 'Apologies, I will have to fetch the manual records.' He then straightened-up and walked out of the room.

I had virtually no time to wonder what records he was referring to; it seemed that no sooner had he left the room than he was back clutching three, rather large box files. Placing them on the table, he addressed me. 'Right, now let's get the admin side done. Name?' He took a fountain pen out of his jacket pocket, opened a box and took out a file. 'Name?' He repeated.

'Sorry, William Taylor Findler'

'Good! Now, shall I call you Willy, Wills, Billy or Bill'

'My name is William.' I reckoned that a show of strength on my part might even up the power balance.

'William Taylor Findler. Interesting initials.'

I'd never considered my initials to be of any particular interest and now wondered if my interviewer was a little crazy. I felt that he should, at least introduce himself, so I ignored his comment about my initials and asked, 'Before we start, would you mind telling me who you are?' The man laughed, creating a deep resonant sound that made the light bulb vibrate.

'Who am I? Who were you expecting to meet?' I shrugged. 'I am St. Peter. Who else?'

'St. Peter…. Does that mean…?' The hairs all over my body sprang to attention as if I had been electrocuted.

'I am afraid it does.' Somehow, I knew that I couldn't have got away with what had happened the day before. My heart banged against my chest as if it were about to jump out.

It seemed that I was looking at the room through a kaleidoscope and it took quite a while before all the pieces formed back into a coherent image of St. Peter sitting in front of me, looking less than happy. He leant forward and asked, 'One more question, just to make sure I am talking to the right person, are you the one who signed a contract with the Devil?'

'If you mean that old devil, Nicholas De'Ath, then yes.' I answered sincerely but at that time I had no idea St. Peter was referring to the actual Devil.'

'I have the right file. That's good. You wouldn't believe how many times Human Resources messes up. Ok, let's get on with it then.' St. Peter sounded weary.

I didn't know what getting on with it meant but he opened one of the box files, lifted out a dog-eared paper file, licked his index finger and began flicking through its pages. His only comment was, 'Oh dear, oh dear.' I peered into the box as discreetly as I could and was surprised to find that it contained a collection of diaries in various sizes and colours. I immediately recognised them as being my own and I wondered how they had come into the possession of St. Peter.

Turning towards me, he said, 'Fortunately, you have been a writer of diaries since you were quite young and have developed the easy habit of chronicling your experience, albeit sporadically and in an untrained hand. For a forensic examination of your life and to help with enabling the granting of entry or not, there is no better form of evidence available.' I didn't ask him to elaborate, but I held out little hope that this evidence would lead to an entry stamp being franked on my celestial passport.

St. Peter continued, 'For most of your early life, this report concludes, the content of these diaries is unremittingly mundane; the usual mixture of angst, descriptions of what was partaken for dinner and afternoon sports activities; that is until June 1st, 1974. On this date there is a simple insertion, *Met Jesus.*'

That simple sentence immediately brought back a memory of the singing of the congregation, the imploring voice of the evangelical preacher and the intensity of the bright, dazzling, pure white light that flooded my head as I chose to be born again.

I didn't say anything and St. Peter continued, 'This evidence of rebirth would normally be enough for you to gain admittance, but it seems that you have rather deviated from the path.' I immediately experienced a wave of regret slamming into my soul, unsettling me even more.

'I was a good follower.' I said. I knew I was clutching at straws, but I desperately wanted to establish some rapport with St. Peter. I should have added, 'For a while,' but thought he probably knew that.

'Certain people have already informed me that for a while you were a zealot, that is, you were obsessed with trying to convert the heathen to your beliefs.' 'Certain people' sounded sinister, but I didn't ask him to explain.

It was true, I had particularly liked evangelising about the joy of heaven, which to my mind included the opportunity to sit with other chosen ones and watch the suffering of the damned.

I had stumbled on Christianity by accident. The class bully was singlehandedly perpetrating a reign of terror at school, and I seemed to be his principal victim. To hide from his unwelcome attentions at break times I attended the meetings of the Scripture Union. At first, it was simply a useful safe haven, but I soon found that I was attracted to the main theme underlying the meetings – eternal hellfire for the damned. I was certainly hoping that the never-ending fire would latch onto the blighter who had been making my life a misery.

A queasy feeling arose from the pit of my stomach as I contemplated that I might be in for a good deal of wailing and

6

gnashing of teeth. I wanted to cut in with something clever or pertinent like a quote from the bible promising eternal life for all. But my synapses were strangely sluggish and no useful connection was made, no relevant file referenced. I only registered a mounting urge to be sick, which I resisted, being mindful that spoiling St. Peter's suit would hardly help my case. I let St. Peter continue. 'I see a sense of mission didn't totally subvert your self-interest. For a while, you harboured ideas of becoming a priest. What sort of priest would you have been I wonder?' This was undoubtedly a rhetorical question, but I answered it in any case.

'The Church of England sort – obviously.' St. Peter looked at me directly and I thought that his piercing chestnut eyes were looking into the depths of my soul. I wondered if he was old school and, just in case, I added, 'Mind you, I am non-denominational these days.' I was met with a stony silence and to push my point home I said, 'Differences in liturgy or ritual just bore me.' I'm not sure why he raised his eyes skywards.

'Why,' he asked, 'was this conversion so short lived? If only you had kept the faith, this interview would have been a mere formality. Think carefully before you speak as your eternal life depends upon your answer.' I was not sure what to say, but I knew I had to plead my case.

Stalling for time, I asked to see my diary for 1977. When St. Peter passed it over, it seemed that just through touching the dog-eared specimen, I was transported back in time so that I was once again the teenage author poised to capture the pure anguish of adolescence. I flicked through the pages, and memories flooded back as if the events described were from the recent past. I have to admit to wanting to linger over some of them that mentioned

7

Louisa XXX (surname withheld – data protection). However, I knew I couldn't afford to be distracted, even by memories of the beauty and magnetic sexual attraction of my first (unreciprocated) love. Passing on, I quickly came upon the entry I was looking for, which was dated 15th October 1977. *'So soon after the funeral, but I can't bring Dad's face to mind or hear his voice. All I can now think about is that I'm the owner of his brushed-cotton check shirts. Am I so heartless?*

My father had died, slowly and painfully. After his cruel death, I was shocked by the limited extent to which God intervened in my hour of need. So much for the power of prayer!

With the realisation that God might not be as bothered as all that about my suffering I had to re-evaluate my relationship with the Big Man.

I didn't feel able to be quite so honest or expansive with St. Peter. I just said, 'Look at my entry on November 20th 1977. *If God is so cruel, I don't want anything to do with Him.'*

'As it turns out, that was a rash decision.' He looked over, his tone was matter of fact, and I didn't detect any signs of pity.

'Yes. Quite possibly.' I had the feeling I had entered some sort of compression chamber as my chest tightened and my breath was squeezed out of my body.

St. Peter stood up, placed his hands on his lower back and lent back gently as if trying to get rid of some lumbago. He was tall and slender and as he arched back I thought he looked a bit like a long, wilted piece of celery. He turned towards me but seemed to

8

be talking to himself, 'I thought this might be a clear-cut case…' He hesitated.

'Of?' I asked.

'For.' He corrected.

'For…?

'Damnation.'

'Damnation!'

'Do you repeat everything?

'Sorry, how do you mean.'

'I think you know exactly what I mean. Eternal conscious torment.'

'Eternal conscious torment!' The hairs on the back of my neck prickled.

Despite the ringing in my ears and the sense the floor had just tilted I managed to ask, 'Is there an appeals procedure?' St. Peter laughed.

'I am the appeals procedure.'

'Good.' I started thrashing around for ideas like a poor swimmer trying to find a rubber ring. I presumed that establishing a more personal relationship would help so I started with, 'Pete, mate…' but after he shot me such a stern look I knew that such familiarity wasn't going to work. I continued with his formal name, 'St. Peter, please, before coming to a decision, look at my life in detail. You will see I am a victim of circumstance.' He raised his eyes.

'Victim! Do you know how many times I have heard that?'

St. Peter looked like he was just about to sit back down when he was interrupted by a buzzing sound. He reached for his belt and unclipped a pager, looked at it and then said, 'Sorry, we've been waiting for this one for some time.' With this cryptic comment, he walked out of the room, leaving the three box files on the table. My first thought was, *Pager, who uses those anymore?* Then I looked towards the pile of box files and wondered if I had been set a test. Surely it was a two-way mirror on the wall and it would be used to check whether I sneakily opened and looked inside the box files. Then, I experienced a spark of anger and told myself that I had every right to look at my own life, especially if I was to mount a credible defence and avoid the fire that was surely being stoked-up somewhere below my feet.

I opened the box file containing my early years' diaries. I saw that it also held a collection of certificates and noted with some pride that the top one was for the Twenty-five Yards Breaststroke. The first, I may add, that was awarded to anyone in my year at school. Unfortunately, it was not a portent of further success to come in my life.

I picked up the pocket diary for 1976, the year I went to university, much to my teachers' surprise, and opened at a page referencing my old tutor, Professor Dixon. I was immediately transported back to an occasion when I was sitting in his stuffy basement office.

Professor Dixon sat in his tatty armchair surrounded by a group of greasy undergraduates, myself included, in awe of the man who had so recently published a book. Yes, a real book and one that we all had to buy! And they weren't cheap in those days. On this occasion, he had strayed from his favourite topic of subliminal perception onto the subject of the afterlife. Despite the clear description I had shared with him, and the tutor group, of both heaven and hell, Professor Dixon was clear; there was an impersonal darkness on both sides of his life. He said something like, 'What gives me comfort is the thought that I should not be bothered about the silence and blackness of eternity that lies ahead of me, any more than I am about the eternity that preceded me.'

I then recalled how, when my father died a year later, I had taken comfort in Professor Dixon's assertion that all that was ahead was a comforting nothingness. At least my father being wrapped in a warm, black blanket was better than his keeping eternal company with thieves, blackmailers and politicians.

Dragging my wandering mind back to the trial I was facing, I berated myself for losing focus at such a crucial time. *This is not the time to get caught up in memories prompted by reading my old diaries,* I thought. *It's clear I can't concentrate on one train of thought for long, even if my eternal life depends upon it.*

With the self-admonition duly delivered, I returned to the task of scanning the diaries. However, their contents, an idiosyncratic mixture of big ideas and comments about what I had for tea and other trivia, didn't immediately help me to assemble a coherent

11

argument justifying why I should be granted an unlimited supply of peeled grapes forevermore or pass eternity somewhere considerably cooler than Hades. Sitting back in my chair, I tried desperately to think of a story that would help me secure a pass to the upward leading stairs and eternal harp muzak.

Despite straining the synapses, a coherent argument for salvation failed to materialise. I hoped the other files would offer me some better ideas. However, when I opened the next box, I was disappointed to see that it was full of my most recent diaries. I winced. I was not looking forward to St. Peter picking up the latest one and trying to decipher the text scrawled in crayon.

In recounting my tale, it seems, even to me, the meeting with St. Peter is fantastical; it is hard to believe it actually happened. But it all happened and I have proof. Equally, it's amazing to think that I played a part in breaking the banks and unleashing the financial crisis. If my sorry history is ever published as a book, I might even entitle it, *Capitalism; My Part in its Downfall*.

Now, two questions clamour in my brain. How the hell did I end up in this metaphorical melt down and who is responsible for all of this? Thinking about it, I can see how I was played like a puppet on a string by powers much greater than myself.

But, maybe, I'm too close to the action to really understand it. Dear reader, can you help me develop some perspective? Perhaps it was meant to be? Was it written in the stars or pre-printed in my genes? Was it inevitable? Or was it down to personality, which, as we all know, is largely formed by how well we handle breastfeeding?

I am hoping that, once you have heard me out, you will be able to help answer these questions.

I'll explain what St. Peter found out about me and how he concentrated on the most embarrassing episodes of my life. I'll supplement it with my diary entries to give you the whole picture – warts 'n' all. As I am asking you to help make sense of all that has happened, I might as well be honest.

My obsessive relationship with H, chronicled over the last few years in my diaries, is particularly important. So, let me start here.

H

Perhaps you are already familiar with H's beatific qualities, but I don't want to presume anything so I will describe her attributes. Probably the best way is to start by comparing H with a friend I'm sure you are familiar with; Aqua Vitae, or as more commonly known, Booze, Booooze. You just have to repeat the word a few times to understand its effect.

I am not much of a drinker. Even at university, a couple of halves and I was like a giddy kid off a merry-go-round. But I have enough experience to know that in excess, the initial pleasure given by alcohol and its calming of the mind, is overtaken by a disordering of the mental faculties and the revelation of the true character lurking within. While some men after copious ales shake hands, hug, shed sentimental tears and swear eternal friendship, others are driven to punch, rip and kick.

H, on the contrary, brings serenity to all the faculties and provides the sort of vital warmth and glow of health that even a yogi on a spiritual retreat would be hard pressed to feel.

To borrow a medical classification, Booze is an acute pleasure whilst H is chronic.

If they were fireworks, Booze would be a Catherine Wheel casting out its sparks, while H would be a Roman Candle emitting a steady glow and drawing your attention to the brightness of its centre. One is a centrifugal force that radiates and spreads, casting thoughts hither and thither; the other stimulates the mind and at the same time it calms the mind and brings forth the diviner part of human nature.

15

H creates a vortex that orders that which has been separated and concentrates the forces of human nature. Like that of a spiralling tornado, there is, at the very centre, pure peace.

To explain my relationship with H, there is no better source than my recent diaries.

25th January

Brilliant, wintry sunset. Attack of migraine, downgraded to a class two headache by smoking a joint. Leon certainly is able to provide a very acceptable weed.

3rd February

Looked at the business pages as usual. Nice to see most stocks are soaring up. It's a pity the ones I have are bucking the trend. Nevertheless, I will sell, even at this price. It is a sensible cash investment in my ideas. After all, when the business takes off, a few thousand will look like small change.

Shame Susan doesn't have the same entrepreneurial spirit. You have to speculate to accumulate. But, I won't hold it against her. It will make her return even sweeter when I forgive her for not trusting in my business acumen.

15th February

Last night, I was just going to bed when I suddenly felt pain in my shoulder. And such pain! It passed over me in ceaseless waves, and it felt like someone had poked a red-hot wire from my neck all the way down my arm.

16th February

More intolerable pain.

17th February
Can't sleep. Not a wink.

18th February
Went to Accident and Emergency! Surely it will have to be renamed. Emergency! That's a complete joke. How come they kept a critically ill patient waiting for four hours before seeing him? I was told some nonsense about having a muscle spasm, but from the severity of the pain, I'm sure the problem is a lot more serious.

And what a God forsaken place, but such blessed relief in the end. A green bottle of goodness flowed into my veins, pure bliss.

Interestingly, five minutes after the injection, I was still able to distinguish the wave-like nature of the pain, but it was as if I was some third-party observer. The pain disappeared completely another five minutes later.

I also noted that I was mentally calm like I was sitting in dappled shade on an endless sunny Sunday. The incessant internal chatter had also ceased.

I was told it was morphine in the green bottle. How did someone discover that poppy-heads could produce such comfort? It must have been divine intervention. Whatever, the first man who extracted opium from the poppy-head was a true benefactor of mankind.

After the morphine, I slept soundly and well for the first time in days, months even, when I really think about it.

19th February

The shoulder pain came again this evening, but it was a mere shadow of the last time. But it is worrying. If only I had some of what was in that green bottle, just in case.

20th February

Had a chat with Leon in the Dog and Bottle. He said he could get me some H, which he informed me is a refined form of morphine. Just for emergencies. For one-off instances of pain relief there is absolutely no chance of becoming an addict.

22nd February

Smoked H for the first time - just to test it.

From the very first minute there was the sensation of being touched on my neck. The touch grew warmer and spread.

A gentle, happy stream flowed through my joints and, in its wash, all my senses gently bobbed about like pleasure boats on a placid lake. Were those church bells? No, just honking horns and the distant sounds of city life. Life was mild and safe.

All unpleasant sensations stopped completely.
Slept soundly. It was so beautiful.

24th February

Pain in shoulder returned. Smoked another H. The pain completely went away and left such clarity of mind. I'm surer than ever that my ideas are profound. When I see just how beautifully they fit together, I am quite tearful.

2nd March

Leon says injecting is better for me than smoking H. In fact, he said something like, 'Don't follow da false prophet. Turn towards da one and bow down for you will be mightily rewarded.'

I was wary, but he came and showed me how to do it. His massive frame made my front room seem decidedly pokey. At the pub, I hadn't noticed Leon's peculiar odour, but in my house, he smelt of old bed linen. Preparation of the drug is a rudimentary process, but, with the way Leon spoke, the process took on the aura of a small religious service. At the end, after I had taken my first injection, he even stood before me, his wide shoulders obliterating the weak light and laid his hands on my head; a blessing of sorts.

After Leon had left me alone, the feelings I experienced from smoking H reappeared, but they were more intense, more alive, more within me. There was a sudden surging feeling of cold in the pit of my stomach, after which I started to think more clearly and experienced a burst of mental energy.

White light flowed up my arms and legs and into the chest cavity and head. The same light as when I met Jesus. The Alpha and Omega.

I experienced transcendental clarity of mind, a tying together of the strands of my life, a lucidity so bright it dazzled. Oh, my singing blood, penetrate me more deeply, take me, I am yours.

I saw the happiness of mankind. I saw a cloudless eternity and the great light of the majestic intellect.

I could see the full scale of my ideas. How they connect into a glorious whole, an integrated system. Nothing less than absolute

19

brilliance. My inner powers are manifested at their absolute peak.

I think I'm going to do my best work after an injection.

I shall go to bed early and rest my head on the wings of angels.

3rd March
I'm sure some people would express caution, but this is an aid to my work. I am redoing the business plan, and it is so much better. Still have to completely nail who the customer is, and how they will benefit. But, what is wrong in saying everyone can benefit? It's a total system after all.

19th March
Two syringes today. You can quickly get used to H but surely mild habituation isn't the same thing as becoming an addict.

Fortunately, I am remarkable for having tremendous willpower.

20th May
Three syringes today. In the quiet, I am lucid. I have a sense of past and future all being integrated into the glorious now.

H has helped generate the most amazing insight. It's like I've just had my eyes opened to a whole new dimension. H allows you to enjoy observing the motion of time.

In reality, the lived-in-moment encompasses the past, present and future. Nothing is fixed; nothing is inevitable. Everything is in constant interaction.

Time is not linear as we experience it rather it surrounds us all and envelops us.

I didn't know I was capable of such profound thinking. I put this down to H helping me discover my true potential.

28th May

Today, for the first time, I discovered in myself a nasty tendency to lose my temper. Business must be getting on top of me more than I appreciated, as I haven't experienced such rage before.

Susan came around for some of her things. I tried to use the opportunity to explain my insights about time, but she wasn't interested. Instead, she had a go at me about the state of the flat. I admit it looks like a blizzard has just blown through. When she screwed up her nose and said it smelt of old bed sheets, I went completely berserk to the point of losing control of my actions. It's often said that a red mist descends, but I now know it is pink and comes with a screeching internal noise that blocks all thoughts.

For a minute, or perhaps less, I was without past or future, I was caught in the moment, in the grip of the purest emotion; rage. It's lucky I'm not a violent man or, in that condition, anything could have happened. It was bad enough that Susan left in a hurry, crying.

Susan left her handbag and I ran after her to return it, but not before I had looked inside and liberated two twenty-pound notes from her purse. She snatched her bag from me in a very ungrateful sort of way and shot off.

An hour later I was myself again and, naturally, I tried to phone Susan to allow her to forgive me for my abruptness, but she didn't take my call. I don't know what happened to me. I was always so polite before. It appears the path of an entrepreneur isn't always smooth.

A visit to Leon soothed me and now back at home I'm able to relax in H's embrace. Nothing concerns me. I need nothing and there is nowhere I need to go.

I want rest after my trials today and to forget my little temper tantrum.

And, there, I have forgotten it.

Susan, I'm sending you an S.O.S. The love you gave me. Nothing else can save me.

Where are those happy times? They seem so hard to find. I try to reach you now but it seems you've closed your mind. Whatever happened to our love? If only I understood. It used to be so fine, it used to be so good.

I'm getting quite poetical as well as sentimental.

I really didn't know I had such ability with the prose. I am pleased with my originality at these difficult times.

18th June
I woke feeling a great sense of shame. Why? I really had stolen money from my wife. That's not the way to win her back, but I will make it up to her somehow.

So, I am a thief. I must remember to tear that page out.

Interrogation

As you can see, my diaries weren't going to help me too much. In fact, I was no further forward in developing a coherent case for salvation when St. Peter returned.

He walked in, holding himself in an unnaturally upright position, and as he sat down beside me, I could see pain etched on his face. Desperate to start building some rapport, I asked him whether he was taking anything for his back. Like before, he looked at me with a stern expression on his face as if I were being too familiar, but I pressed on, 'I can recommend something for the pain. It worked for me.'

'You must be joking!' For a moment, St. Peter looked like one of those clowns at an amusement park with mouth agape waiting for the ball to be thrown in. I was thinking of paracetamol and codeine tablets, but it suddenly struck me that St. Peter had assumed that I meant H. Realising that St. Peter thinking that I was pushing drugs at him wasn't going to help my quest for salvation, I clammed up.

'I would prefer to concentrate on your meetings with Nicholas De'Ath but protocol demands we look at your case in detail.' St. Peter said and I furrowed my brow for it sounded a bit like he wasn't the all-powerful gatekeeper I had supposed him to be. Nevertheless, I breathed a sigh of relief, as I felt sure that a proper, close look at my life would show that I did actually deserve forgiveness.

I detected sounds of weariness in his voice. This was not surprising, given how long he had undertaken his role. However,

I worried that it might have resulted in a combination of boredom and cynicism that would prejudice his judgment of my case.

St. Peter retrieved some papers I recognised as my old school reports from one of the box files. After a lengthy perusal of the yellowing documents, he said 'If these reports from your junior school are anything to go by, there's not much to be said about your childhood years, apart from the fact that you were an annoying pupil. *Disturbing element* and *Must learn to engage brain before opening mouth* are typical comments made by your teachers.' Needless to say, I had to defend my reputation.

'Well yes, that was the sort of thing I had to take home for my father to tut-tut about. But I'm sure most of my classmates had this standard nonsense on their reports, so there's very little that sets me apart.'

St. Peter didn't respond and, after flicking through some later reports from my secondary school, added, 'These here are a little more barbed. *Arrogant; you can't teach Bill anything.* That was from your old maths teacher.'

'Too true in this case; with Mr. Davies' broad accent he might as well have been talking in his native Welsh, plus he was speaking the unintelligible language of mathematics.'

'Then there is *Obsessive personality – except when it comes to Physics.* That was written by Miss Chapman.'

'Is it my fault there's a lot of maths involved in her subject?'

24

'And what about this? *A little too clever for his own good.*'
I had to admit that my history teacher's comment was uncomfortably close to the truth.

St. Peter read out some more. 'Mrs. Manly writes, *Willie must learn to listen to others and be more modest.*'

'Modest! I am one of the most modest individuals you could ever wish to meet.' I was trying to be ironic, but I think this was lost on the grumpy gatekeeper, who continued with his perusal of my reports.

'Mr. Dobbin writes, *Wills can be socially inept and over-emphasises his achievements.*

'I don't think you can over-emphasise the importance of learning to swim well as a young person.'

'And what about this from Miss Taylor, *Willy's greatest pleasure comes from seeing the failure and humiliation of others. An unusual characteristic in one so young.*' The image came back to me of when she had come into the classroom with her skirt tucked into the back of her knickers. I'm sure I wasn't the only one who had laughed fit to drop.

'Here is a report from Mr. Duffield, *Billy must learn to reflect on and take responsibility for his actions.* And what about this? *Wills always has the last word.*'

'Well, I might have taken more heed if they'd got my name right.' Finally, for how long can such humiliation go on, St. Peter didn't quote any more from the school reports and put them back in the box file.

There was a long pause before St. Peter asked, 'So now, if your teachers were to write a report covering your life as a whole, what would they put?' I could almost hear Mr. Duffield's booming voice, 'I told you so.' I didn't voice this, and I had the presence of mind to point out all the sins I hadn't committed.

'I think they would praise me for not leaving in my slipstream nervous collapses, suicide bids, suffering, shattered careers and blighted marriages.'

'Suicide bids you say, suffering, shattered careers you say? Blighted marriages you say!'

'Well... only my own.'

St. Peter, looking older and more tired than when he came in, continued, 'So, to your adult life. The diary entry for June 1986 reads, *Asked Susan to marry me. I think this will be the best decision of my life.* Tell me a little about your marriage.'

'There is not much to say really. We loved each other and then fell out of love. It happens.'

I wasn't keen to go into too much detail with St. Peter, but I will provide you with a bit more background information.

Susan and I met at university. She started the psychology course two weeks after the rest of us, having originally enrolled on a degree in geography but finding it not to her liking. My first words to her, when I had the opportunity, were, 'At least you could find us.' She looked at me blankly. It's a look I came to know well.

Despite my obvious charms, we didn't start going out together until we were in the third year of the course. Many years later, Susan said she'd only agreed to a date as she felt sorry for me after my dad died, but I think she was just trying to hurt me at that point.

I like to think I was the first person to see that Susan was about to metamorphose from being a bit of an ugly duckling into a beautiful swan. Swans though, I have found to my cost, are quite competitive and can be aggressive. Don't get me wrong though, I like assertive women; at least until they try to boss me about. And before you take this as some sort of sexist comment, the same sentiment also applies to men. I'm not good at being given orders, or taking advice for that matter.

Honestly, in our early years together Susan and I were happy. Well, I certainly was and a joint income allowed us a comfortable life and a quick move up the housing ladder. Our last purchase was a second floor flat in a very desirable property in trendy Camden. We even got to the level of income where we could afford Brabantia slim-line waste bins and similar middle-class paraphernalia, so you can tell we were doing well for ourselves.

However, instead of supporting each other, we gradually began to compete, I say compete, but she was playing in a much higher league than me. However, I made up for this by saying that I was more tired than she was.

Susan poured her energy into her work. When I first met her, she had long blonde hair but over the years it became shorter – along with her temper. For my part, I possibly spent too long reading

27

philosophy books, often late into the night – hardly a crime, I would say.

St. Peter asked, 'Do you have children?' That was a bit below the belt, as he must have known the answer. I replied honestly but abruptly.

'No.'

'That is probably a good thing.' This rattled me, which was possibly his intention. That sort of comment was completely uncalled for. I would have made a good dad and would have been a model parent. With a mouth to feed, there was no way I would have got into the risky business of changing the world. No, Susan should have been in the dock, not me. I remembered her being adamant that she wasn't prepared to forego fifty percent of her IQ for the sake of being the mother of my child. I, for one, would have been happy living with someone whose intellect I matched-up to. I am, of course, referring to Susan and not the baby!

St. Peter didn't probe further about the marriage and its sad ending. Instead, he asked, 'What about your career?' This was another subject I wasn't keen to expand on, but I felt obliged to provide a basic outline.

'After graduating I studied for a Diploma in Personnel Management and Industrial Relations at The London School of Economics.'

'So, you are in Human Resources?

'Everyone makes a mistake once in their life.'

28

'Human Resources – the name says it all!' St. Peter clearly wasn't a fan.

Thinking that this might be an area where I could build some rapport, I quickly responded, 'Personnel, or HR as it has become, might not be your favourite department. Rest assured, I fully understand your sentiment.' For the first time, I registered a slight softening in St. Peter's features. It briefly crossed my mind that HR might not only be feeding him the wrong files, but they may be behind keeping him in his role for too long. After all, I had helped senior managers put together many succession plans and found that the people least likely to be chosen to rise up the management chain were those who were good at their job. This pattern was repeated so often that I used to say to my boss, 'Only shit rises to the top.'

As St. Peter continued, his attitude seemed to have softened a little and the intonation of his voice was less authoritative. He said, 'Well. I suppose, we'd better carry on and take a look at your career. It seems that yours was particularly undistinguished with the only highlight being a spell working abroad.' I just nodded.

I certainly didn't want to delve too deeply here. I had been working for a petroleum company, which had invested in a Kazakhstan oil field following the dissolution of the Soviet Union. I remember returning from my singleton overseas assignment in Kazakhstan a changed man. This was partly because of the very long winter and, in fact, there generally being nothing to do at any time of the year. I had developed an interest in oenology or is it onanism – anyway, one of the two, but I got quite a taste for it. Maybe that was why my marriage took a serious nosedive, and before St. Peter took the conversation in that direction I interrupted with, 'Do you want to

29

hear a funny story?' I thought I would try again with the bridge building.

'It has all been amusing to date.' I didn't appreciate the quip but carried on in any case.

'You will see from my file that I went to work in Kazakhstan. Well, I had a translator as only a few people spoke English. When I introduced myself as the Human Resources Director everyone took a step back and looked at me in an odd way. Initially, I put this down to a post-soviet mentality of being glum and reserved. However, after a number of these introductions I asked the translator, 'Am I being clear in what I say?''

''People have not heard of term human resources.' She replied in her unsmiling way. Fair enough, I thought, then she added, 'And in fact, we don't have direct translation of phrase.' Now I was the one to be puzzled.'

'If there's no direct translation for human resources then how are you getting this across? I asked her. The answer was quite perturbing.'

''Well,' the translator began, 'nearest word to resources is spare parts.' I quickly appreciated the audience's reaction and lack of interaction.'

I looked at St. Peter and waited for a reaction. As this wasn't immediately forthcoming I said, 'Human Spare Parts Director... Get it?' I then, felt my heart thump in my chest as I realised, just too late, that I was talking to the Head of Human Remorses.

The thought, *So much for trying to build bridges,* had just entered my mind when St. Peter sat back, crossed his arms and said, 'Certainly, those in our HR department are spare parts.' It wasn't the sort of thing you would expect to hear coming from God's right-hand man and I have to say that silently, I experienced a deep and meaningful laugh.

St. Peter started his interrogation again but with just the slightest perceptible softening apparent in the intonation of his voice. 'After you returned from your brief assignment abroad, a cushy job in Head Office allowed you time to develop some sort of framework. I can't make head nor tail of the thing. Can you explain?'

I couldn't have been more pleased to be asked to provide further details. I was accustomed to so few people being interested in my ideas that I reacted like an asthmatic after suddenly being given pure oxygen. I immediately perked up and launched into conversation with, 'This framework measures the complexity of the decision-making environment. It also measures work in terms of its output or, as I refer to it, its contribution. Then it links this to a person's capability to do the work and handle its complexity. Rather snazzily, I called this my *3C Taxonomy.*'

'Why?' I was disappointed that I had to point out the connection.

'Three Cs.' I exclaimed.

'What Cs?'

'Complexity, contribution and capability. Three Cs.'

'Oh. That's interesting.' This was said with more than a hint of brain-numbed boredom. I ignored the fact that St. Peter's complete indifference chilled the room. As he had asked me about the framework, he was jolly well going to hear about it.

Jumping back in, I explained how the integrated system made a dynamic link between the three Cs. I ended with, 'It's the basis for a new approach to management.'

'Really!' This was obviously feigned interest as St. Peter looked at his buffed nails, but I needed to press the point home.

'Yes, it puts being human, and a natural decision maker, centre stage. You can use the classification to build healthy organisations with the absolute minimum number of management levels.'

'Now that could be useful in the Church!'

I was not sure if I detected sarcasm or real interest. It was probably the former, as when I was about to expand on how the classification could be used to at least cut out the Pope in the Catholic Church, St. Peter put up his hand to stop me. He then read out an entry from my diary dated 20th February 2003. 'Sacked, fired, let go, downsized, call it what you will; such a relief!' He shrugged slightly, 'Can you tell me about this?'

As a matter of fact, I could and was eager to do so. My sentiments on the matter continue to be strongly felt and I was very forthright, some might say brusque, in my reply. 'I ask you, what does my old boss know about building healthy and efficient organisations? Yes, precisely nothing. It was time to set up a new company. My mission statement, *Change the World*; well not in all its aspects, but certainly in the way institutions, companies and corporations are organised and managed.'

'Change the world.' He repeated my phrase and added, 'Eh! I know of another man who did just that. Fortunately, you are not the messiah.' St. Peter didn't follow-up on his original question about being fired, so I didn't offer him any reflections on my sad end in the world of employment. But, I can tell you.

In my last few months of employment I realised that every day I went to work was irredeemably wasted. On one occasion, I was called into some airless conference room (offices had long gone) to have my boss share anonymous team-member feedback with me. I was told I was arrogant and distant – that would be by Paedo Phil, as I called him, and terrible at spreadsheets; that I accepted. Subsequently, in a performance review I was told I was in the lower decile and needed to pull my socks up. All I asked was, 'How high?' My manager, straight out of kindergarten and totally lacking a sense of humour, said, 'That is just the sort of thing I am referring to.' She added, 'If you are the sort of person who needs guidance, you aren't cut out to work here.' I was let go soon afterwards in another round of 'right sizing'.

Being 'let go' was just what I felt I needed. Unyoked, I planned to develop my framework into a whole new management system.

Anyhow, back to the interview with St. Peter. He continued with, 'And pray, may I ask, how were you going to change the world?' He added an ironic little laugh. By this point, I could see that his eyes had begun to glaze over, so by way of a final flurry, I just said, 'The system automatically matches people to appropriate jobs, so you cut out the middlemen.'

'Like who?'

'The fat intermediaries.' I finished with a dismissive exhalation.

'I don't like the idea of cutting out the intermediaries. I think Jesus might have something to say about that.'

I was taken aback and wondered, *Am I going to be charged with blasphemy or something like that?* I certainly hadn't intended to subvert the role of Christ as the intermediary between mere mortals and God. I have to say the system is clever, and has many uses, but it doesn't extend its remit quite as far as that.

I was looking for a way to spin the conversation back to my advantage when St. Peter continued, 'Why was it not taken up?'

'God knows.'

'He does.'

'Well, I might have over-complicated the proposal.'

Even now, I can all too easily shed a little tear thinking about the combination of the profundity of my ideas with the fact that no one understood a word of what I was talking about. This included Susan, who was not shy in telling me that these ideas would lead me to a career dead-end.

St. Peter asked rather wearily, 'In a nutshell, tell me what happened then?' I struggled to sum up all that had happened. Years after being fired, what had I actually achieved? My wife, sorry ex-wife, Susan, had gone to live with her parents. Due to an obsessive focus on developing my ideas and building the 3C Taxonomy, most of my acquaintances had long abandoned me and, as you know, I had acquired an expensive habit.

I was not able to sum up my recent life and so, by way of an answer, I ignored St. Peter's question and continued with my pitch, 'I am convinced that it is only a question of time before these ideas have the massive impact they deserve.'

St. Peter ran a hand through the curly locks at the back of his head, sighed and asked, 'What did you do to get your ideas to market?' Again, I wasn't keen on being totally honest with him, as I'd wasted a considerable amount of time in the Dog and Bottle. I knew it wasn't in my best interests to wax lyrical about its charms to St. Peter, so I simply shrugged my shoulders.

St. Peter thankfully moved on and asked. 'Where did you get the notion that you could change the world?'

'I went on a course.'

'Oh, I am keen to hear about that.' St. Peter said, but I can honestly say that his tone sounded completely at odds with the words he had spoken. Warily, I looked at him to see if there was any sign that his attitude towards me had softened. Unfortunately, his dour features were as smooth and unresponsive as alabaster.

St. Peter rather curtly said, 'It seems you took on a new religion. This demands we look in detail at what happened.' He opened the laptop, tapped on a few keys and turned the screen towards me. Then, he sat back and, if I wasn't mistaken, he puffed out his chest a bit, as if he were proud of his efforts with the I.T..

I had no chance to ask what he meant by new religion as I was suddenly observing myself in the public library finding out about the very course I had just referred to.

'What is this?' I asked.

'It's a recording of your life on the day of the course.'

'I didn't know it was filmed.'

'It wasn't filmed as such. I can't tell you too much about how we operate, but we have detailed records. Anyway, as an HR practitioner, you will appreciate one of the features; we have access to your inner dialogue.' He tapped the side of his nose with an index finger in a manner I could only assume meant, *we've got you banged to rights sonny.*

'Really! Shit!' That was all the comment I could muster as I was enveloped by a deep sense of foreboding.

With regards to the inner dialogue feature, as we progressed I was grateful that this did not seem to be working correctly. All I could hear was a strange voice uttering half-finished sentences liberally scattered with swear words. To give you an impression, it sounded something like, 'What the hell, something else... where did I put those frigging... no, surely not. How was I supposed to...? Never mind, calm down, wait until I... What the hell. Do I know her? If not, why is she looking at me like that? What the... where have I

36

put my… Frigging mobile phones.' It was completely incoherent and St. Peter will have to make drastic improvements before it deserves to be called a feature.

The New Religion

I had become convinced that the applications derived from the integrated system needed to be Internet based, thus avoiding, once and for all, unnecessary face-to-face interactions. However, I knew even less about getting a business idea online than I did about sales and marketing so I understood I needed help in this area.

One day, I was in the library reading the local paper when a flyer dropped out advertising 'The Success Secret'. The strapline ran, 'You Can Do Anything, the secret of success for entrepreneurs'. I speed read the leaflet and at the bottom was printed, 'Find out about how to get your business online. Enquire at the Library.'

The librarian who normally manned the reception desk reminded me of one of my favourite singers, Gloria Gaynor with her big hairdo and chiffon scarves set at jaunty angles. However, I had begun to dislike her because she seemed to look at me with disapproval whenever she saw me. She even used to turn her nose up when I borrowed books. However, I went to the desk and showed her the leaflet and enquired, 'Who is running the course?' She pointed to a line on the leaflet, and employing her usual annoying habit of emphasising the last syllable of her sentence, as if holding a musical note at the end of a verse, said 'World famous self-help guru, Biella Zebuv and her husband Stannn.'

I laughed because, whilst reading it to myself I thought that Stan's name had been misprinted as Satan. 'Never heard of them.' I replied and Gloria looked at me as if I'd just said I'd never heard of The Three Degrees. 'Where and when is the course being held?' I asked.

'It's on now, here in the Council's main conference roommmm.'

'Excellent. Can I go in?'

'Yes, but you need to pay two-hundred and fifty poundsss.'

'Two hundred and fifty pounds!!'

'Yesss.'

'Any discounts?'

'Nohhh.'

'Students?'

'Nohhh.'

'Unemployed?'

'Nohhh.'

'Pensionersss?' I held the 's' for a while and hissed at her. I'm not a pensioner but two hundred and fifty pounds, really!

'Nohhh.'

I was downcast. Here was this potentially life-changing event, but I was going to be denied entry because I had reached my credit limit. What's more, I didn't care for the way Gloria was looking at me. It was if I were some low life who didn't have the wherewithal to pay a measly two-hundred and fifty-pounds entry fee.

Thinking I would at least make a show of paying for the course, I gave her my credit card. I had expected her to use a new-fangled card reader and for the payment to be declined but, surprisingly, she filled in an old-fashioned payment slip. I added my name, and she ran it though an imprinter. 'Have a nice dayyy.' Her face told me she had no such wish.

'You tooooo.' I replied between gritted teeth and hurried off to find the course.

I should have asked if there was a discount for latecomers as the course was well under way when I pushed open the conference room doors. I was presented with an image that immediately reminded me of the occasion when I'd first met Jesus in Central Hall, Westminster. The room was packed with what appeared to be an audience of worshippers, all standing. Powerful spotlights drew my attention to a couple, both wearing white suits, on a dais facing the audience. The woman was clearly in a demonstrative, preaching mode. Every time she said the word 'believe', the audience raised their hands and said, 'I believe.' My first impulse was to shout, 'Crackerjack,' instead of 'I believe,' but I restrained myself. If you don't understand why I wanted to shout such an odd word, you clearly have the misfortune of being too young to have seen children's TV in the 1960s.

I walked to a free seat at the end of a row towards the back of the hall and positioned myself next to a man wearing a hairy suit of the thickest tweed that you could possibly imagine. From there, I studied the two performers.

The man, who I took to be Stan, was slim and handsome. He had the darkest skin I'd ever seen, which contrasted not only with his suit, but also with white afro-style hair and pointed beard. The woman, presumably Biella, wore a ruffle of white feathers around her neck enhancing the effect of the white suit and her very pale complexion.

Turning the usual stereotype on its head, Biella was the main presenter with Stan taking the part of her glamorous assistant.

Biella's theme was the importance of taking time out of a busy day to de-stress. She asked everyone to turn to their left and administer a massage to the person now in front of them. My tweed-wrapped neighbour immediately, turned me around, slapped me on the back and began to knead my shoulders. Actually, he was quite good at massage, and I was disappointed when the exercise came to an end.

I have to hand it to them; Biella and her sidekick were really funny and entertaining. As their performance progressed, the more I was reminded of my conversion experience. Biella had the same imploring style as the preacher who had introduced me to Jesus. Even the content was similar, 'There are mysterious forces in the cosmos that can unleash unimaginable wealth, happiness and success. Take these unto thyself. You can have the new car, the super job, the smart house, the good health and exceptional fitness, because God wants to prosper you.' I was not sure about the God bit, or her use of grammar, but I was happy to go along with the success formula. I thought to myself, *if I am now invited to accept the Internet into my life, I shall go to the front of the room.*

The similarity with the occasion when I saw the light was uncanny, especially when Biella asked us to say the 'Entrepreneurs' Prayer';

> 'Our fortune, which art in the cosmos,
> hallowed be thy name.
> Let my kingdom come,
> my will be done,
> tax deductible as it is in the City.
> Provide us this day our daily cappuccino,
> and extend to us credit,
> as we also squeeze our debtors.
> Lead us not into trepidation,
> but deliver us from audit-induced anxiety.
> For mine is the kingdom,
> the power and the glory.
> For ever and ever.'

After we had all recited this, Tweedy even said, 'Amen,' although he might have just coughed.

The course revolved around two things, firstly, expanding on the success secret and secondly, creating a sense of excitement about the finale of the show, the fire walk.

With regard to the secret, Biella was adamant, 'The first step is to develop as clear a picture of your destination as possible. Once you have pictured the size of house, bank balance, or business you want, you are ready to realise this through passion and commitment.'

As part of this 'visualisation experience', we had to tell our neighbour about our vision and were encouraged to be specific. so, turning to Tweedy, I listed the trappings that would define my

43

success: a red Jaguar XKR 4.2 litres with grey leather seats, an Industry Award and a Georgian Villa in St John's Wood. Tweedy suggested that I should aim for a blue plaque once I shuffled off the mortal coil, to demonstrate my significance to the world. I agreed that this was a good idea and would be appropriate considering the massive impact on society my ideas would have.

Tweedy told me about his intention of investing in a gin distillery and I immediately gave him my advice, which was to leave well alone. Gin was far too old-fashioned. He needed something that would appeal to a young market – especially women.

Biella moved on from the vision to the process of realising it. She said that the answer is to network, network, network; that old chestnut. She even talked about developing an elevator pitch.

If you are not in the know, 'elevator pitch' is business speak for what you would say to a potential investor, if you just happened to bump into one in a lift and had forty seconds to pique their interest. It is just one of the silly ideas that seem to have overtaken us these days. Even the poor sod going for an interview has to behave like some spivvy entrepreneur and sell himself in the opening pitch.

Honestly, I thought, *I have paid good money to listen to stuff I already know*. I was becoming a little annoyed but went along with an exercise involving forming small groups and practising inspiring others with our business ideas. I found myself in a group of five comprising a young white man wearing a tight fitting T-shirt that emphasised his pumped up pecs; an Asian guy with swept back hair kept in place with a hairband (David Beckham has a lot to answer for); a plump, red-faced lady who wore flat shoes, a tartan skirt, white blouse and a choker that looked like a dog's collar; and a bald headed man with tattoos up his neck (David Beckham really does have a lot to answer for).

Everyone, including me, turned to the toned body and asked what he did. He replied, 'Hello, my name's Peter, I'm a vegan body builder, and I help people reach peak physical performance without having to ingest the animal protein so often perceived as a prerequisite for the perfect physique.' I considered this for a short time, and thought, *Peter picked a peck of pickled peppers.* If this exercise was to be of any use, I considered it necessary to give him some feedback.

'Plenty of pees to practise in your perfect pitch.' I said.

The plump woman obviously didn't understand my witty remark and retorted, 'You can never have too many peas, especially in a vegan diet.' It became clear that she just wanted to flirt with the young man, as she continued, 'How wonderful and it obviously works. Can I feel?' She lent in and squeezed a bicep. 'Oh my.' For this woman, that alone was probably worth the two hundred and fifty pounds she had paid for the course.

'And you, what do you do?' The bodybuilder graciously asked her.

'I'm the inventor of Doggy Doo. This is a self-inverting silicone cup that captures and seals your dog mess without all that horrible feeling about with your hand in a plastic bag for warm faeces.'

'Yuk.' Is all I could utter, but the David Beckham lookalike must have been impressed as he immediately asked where he could buy one.

I was just about to tell the small group about myself, when the plump lady looked at the bald guy and asked, 'And what do you do?'

'I am the owner of a body art studio that I want to expand.' *Really! Body Art*! I thought, and was about to add, *don't you mean self-mutilation,* when he rolled up his sleeve and showed us a wall of tattoos covering his whole arm. The rest of the group all seemed to be impressed, but if I hadn't known they were tattoos, I would have assumed he had caught his arm in an industrial press, and that this was the resulting multiple bruising. I didn't comment on his work but did give him the benefit of my advice, which was to get out of the business whilst he could. Tattooing was a passing fad and would never catch on for the masses.

I thought it was a bit off, but the bald guy abruptly turned away from me and asked David Beckham's hairband to explain his business.

'I own a web development company.' He answered. 'We help realise people's online ambitions.' *This*, I thought, *is the moment when the planets align in my favour; this was why I had come on this course.* I almost cried out 'hallelujah'. I planned to catch the man at the end of the presentation and talk to him, one to one, about how he could work with me to build my company into a global brand. Maybe I should have asked him more about his business, but I was keen to pique his interest and I launched in. 'I provide a complete management system that makes a dynamic link between contribution and capability.'

46

'Oh!' David Beckham exclaimed, clearly impressed.

'I know I'm paddling upstream against a heavy management 'current' (I used my fingers to indicate the apostrophes) that focuses on information systems and processes, but I aim to put individual choice, decision-making and human agency at the centre of a new approach to managing people.'

There was a lengthy silence whilst the others formulated questions to ask me, but Stan, by telling us to move on to another person if we hadn't already done so, unwittingly ruined the moment. The plump lady immediately turned her attention back to the body builder. No doubt, she was angling for an opportunity to touch another part of his body.

I wasn't able to bring the conversation around to me again as Mrs. Doggy Doo started a conversation with Peter by asking about his vegan diet. As the exercise was wrapping up, they handed out business cards. As I had yet to have any of mine printed, I wasn't able to reciprocate but I put theirs in my wallet.

I must have missed the stuff about taking a business on-line because of joining the course after it started, and I can't say I really learnt much that was of practical use as the course progressed. However, I was struck by Biella's insistence that we should all write a book. She specifically said, 'If you want to be seen as a subject expert this is something you have to do.' Otherwise, the course continued using a range of quotes and jokes to make memorable Biella's points about the power of positive thinking. She asked us to practise a mantra, 'Think big, take massive and irreversible action, strive and if you fail, start again.' There were plenty of other slogans such as, 'You were born to win. Fulfil your potential by planning to win, preparing to win and expecting to win.' This was the call to arms for us to try the fire walk.

Biella and Stan asked the delegates to move their chairs to the sides of the room and in the vacated space they laid down what looked like fire blankets. On top of this, they placed a long, shallow, rusty metal tray. Up to this point there had been no music but with a final flourish, extolling us to believe, Stan cued the sound of Mariah Carey singing, *Hero*. Immediately, four firemen strode into the room carrying large buckets of hot coals in both hands, which they scattered onto the metal tray. The coals gleamed red hot and there was plenty of smoke. I expected the fire alarm to sound at any moment and sprinklers to spurt into action. My misreading of the marketing flyer came back to mind and I thought, *this is Satan's home turf.*

Biella told us that there was no danger of walking over the hot coals, if we simply believed we could. She then asked for a volunteer to go first. Tweedy shot two fingers into my ribs and my hand went up involuntarily. This was greeted by Biella saying, 'Way to go. Come and show the rest how you believe.' I could have refused, but Biella's preaching must have had its desired effect, as I really did believe I was capable of anything. Also, it had been some time since I had been hailed a hero and I basked in the attention of the audience.

After sitting down to remove my shoes and socks, I was then marshalled by Stan to one end of the line of fiery coals. At the other end, Biella stood, adopting an exaggerated welcoming pose with her arms stretched out wide. Dressed in white with pale skin and wearing a white feathery scarf, she looked like a celestial cloud of protons or whatever light is made from.

48

A disembodied voice instructed me to walk quickly towards her, not to run, while repeating the mantra, 'I am a winner, I will succeed, I can do anything'. To the sound of Heather Small singing, *What have you done today to make you feel proud? I can feel my soul ascending. I am on my way. Can't stop me now* and the clapping of the assembled audience, I set off.

I am a winner, I will succeed... I only got that far before I smelt burning flesh and, immediately afterwards, felt searing pains emanating from the soles of my feet. I picked up my feet as if I was dancing on a hot tin roof and did a little jig before running as fast as I could towards the end of the line of coals. In my haste I slipped and sat down heavily in the tray scattering the coals all over the conference room floor. Like a jack-in-a-box, I shot back up and jumped out of the tray and started hopping around, patting my backside, whilst some kind gent poured his gently bubbling Malvern Water over my singed feet. After the hubbub had died down, and the attending firemen had extinguished the small fires caused by the scattered coals, Biella implored the rest of the audience to have a go. There were no takers.

The holes in the back of my trousers were testament to the fact I was the only person brave enough to have a go on the fire walk, but Stan was quite rude to me at the end of the show.

Whilst I was putting my shoes and socks back on, Tweedy came up to me to say goodbye and in an attempt, I think, to lift my spirits, he told me how much he had enjoyed meeting me. I replied 'I might change my career. Two hundred and fifty pounds a ticket! It's money for old rope.' His eyes opened wide.

'Two hundred and fifty pounds? He sniggered, 'I filled in

49

the coupon at the back of the local paper and got in for free.' I can tell you that this revelation put the cap on my day.

I went straight back to the library and found Gloria still sitting at the reception desk. Believe me, I looked into the eye of the tiger and gave her a piece of my mind. But, I might just as well have walked on by, for all the good it did. In the end she said, 'I never said it was a good buy, no, no nnnno.' With that she got up and rang the bell.

That night, as I was getting into bed, I used a mirror to inspect the damage to my feet. I expected to see blisters at least, but there was nothing. I was amazed at my recuperative powers and then felt miffed about Stan's reaction.

Lying in bed, I reviewed the day's events and took comfort from the fact that whilst I was two hundred and fifty pounds and a pair of trousers down, I had now set myself some very specific goals and adopted the idea that one day I would be a famous author.

I decided to put both Biella and Stan out of my mind, and to the sounds in my head of, *What have you done today to make you feel proud?* I drifted off to sleep.

Diary

20th January 2006

This is the most creative time of my life, but how wearying it is. I am in a permanent state of unease; constantly finding loose threads and missing detail and all the time - spending, spending, spending. Money just slips through my fingers and disappears, like I was carrying water in my hands. There is no help for the true entrepreneur in this country. Oh, if I were a single mum, it would be a different story; can we give you a flat, can we provide this, can we provide that? But there are no handouts for me. Do I care? At the end, when the money rolls in, I can take satisfaction in declaring that I am a self-made man.

The night-time is the worst. How tedious they are: these troubled, part-formed thoughts that continually writhe and wriggle and wrestle sleep from my grasp. In the dead of night, beginnings of new thoughts fasten onto others prematurely before my mind has finished assimilating them. I make too many associations and cannot form them into concrete ideas and actions.

I must stop this unguided thinking and start doing instead.

What should I actually do, who should I talk to? It's a good job I have a pad and paper to hand. The nights are long indeed, but, at least, I can write.

12th February

Despite a complete lack of commercial success so far, I still haven't lost faith in my integrated system. I only have to think back to the inventor of the ballpoint pen to be inspired. I can't remember his name – was it Bic or Biro? Anyhow, it took a hundred years for his idea to really take off. At least nowadays, things have speeded up a bit when it comes to turning good ideas into profits. Surely, I'll soon see the rewards. Maybe then, when I'm rich and famous, my wife will believe in me and return home. That will cure my moody behaviour and insomnia.

14th February
Susan is a swan. Even if she is a bit bossy, I am looking forward to having her back in the marital home.

21st February
The business plan is pure genius, even if I say so myself.

Now, all it really needs is a punchy opening statement that quickly sums up what the business actually offers. If I can just get the, so-called, elevator pitch right, customers will soon be banging the door down.

4th March
In my dingy study, inside my dim house I have moments of doubt. I often softly call Susan's name, half expecting a response. It feels like all this effort and sacrifice could easily come to nothing. I sometimes think I'm walking over the thin gauze of existence and could easily slip through and disappear completely. But, when I take H, it is like it comes to life somewhere inside me. My thoughts take flight and I believe in myself. I am present. I am here. I will succeed.

10th March
Never before have I had such vivid dreams at dawn. There is a recurring one, in which I'm in a state of anxiety, continually retaking my degree and weighed down by the thought, 'will I ever

finish this?'. Then, I am letting these thoughts drift away as I find myself in the pure light of a Caribbean summer's day, sailing along in a transparent yacht. I am looking into the water and watching all the sea creatures following me. The wind is in the sails and the whole world, in some glorious way, is aligned to me. Interestingly, and slightly out of place, a large raven is flying behind the yacht and occasionally swoops down towards me.

Is there any harm in these dreams? Who knows, but when they are over, I am left wide-awake and cheerful in the early morning light.

11th March
Asked Leon about the dream. He sees himself as a latter-day Freud and is often telling me about his dreams and what they mean. He said something like. 'You, my son, have passed life's test and da dream heralds a new phase, a new beginnin'. Seize da day.' I asked him what the raven signified, and he said that I had simply mistaken an albatross for a raven. Apparently, all mariners are followed by an albatross, but I'm sure in my case the bird was a raven.

30th March
Got it. Dynamic Link will be the name of the company. Even if I say it myself, this is a great brand name.

1st April
Heard about my application to appear on Angels. It seems ITM, Independent Tele-Media, likes my profile and written presentation.

It's a pity I have to go on such a dreadful show. It's a bit like putting pearls before swine; will they really appreciate the jewels

I have to offer? But, needs must. Even if these clowns don't want to invest, other people who hear about Dynamic Link will be impressed. I will prepare my pitch so that it knocks 'em dead.

20th April

I have such clarity when I take my beloved H, but it's not always easy to capture the essence of my deliberations when I'm at the computer. When Einstein came up with his theory of relativity, did he have to make a pitch and say, if you use this you are going to do something better, faster or cheaper? No! So, why do I have to bow down to these stupid capitalist pretenders? Anyone with half a brain can see how my ideas can be easily and effectively applied. Do I need to spoon-feed them?

21st April

I've paid a small fortune for a list of contacts. Tomorrow, I will start to telephone them. But, I hate this job most of all. What should I say? It will be much easier to sell them something if I know what their problems are. But will they confide in a stranger? Unlikely. I will have to get the elevator pitch really slick, so they won't be able to resist wanting to know more.

22nd April

Tried to telephone people on the stupid sales list I bought. Result; three calls to phones where number not recognised; five calls that went straight to answer machine (didn't leave a message; no one gets back to you from just a message); one person answered. He had a strong, foreign accent and I couldn't get across that I was calling on behalf of Dynamic Link. He kept saying Dynamo Blink. No one here by that name. Sorreee.

Won't try again until after Angels. One of these investors is bound to have an army of sales people ready to make outbound calls.

After a frustrating couple of hours, I felt I needed the welcome embrace of H.

For me, there is one pleasure that H gives me above all – the ability to spend time in reflective solitude. This means deep, significant thought, calm contemplation and wisdom.

I recall a quote from a French guy: 'All men's miseries stem from not being able to stay quietly in their own room.' Surely, I will reap the rewards this profound happiness augurs.

6th May

It is a long time since I wrote anything in my diary. This is a pity because, in fact, this is not a diary but a chronicle of how a great business was born and became a household name.

I overcame my aversion to numbers today and did a few calculations in support of the business plan. Wow. My integrated system can save corporations millions. Even if I get 1% of the market, that is a lot of money. Unfortunately, I can't work out exactly how rich I will be, because I'm not sure how many noughts there are in a billion.

The Call to Nicholas De'Ath

I liked living in London mainly because of the weather. However, a hot spell had made life rather unbearable and I was relieved when this was ended with an impressive thunderstorm. After this the air freshened and, after a quick uplifter, I decided to set off for a walk by the canal.

The after effects of the storm were very evident. I watched, with satisfaction, every gutter and drainpipe gushing murky water as the deluge tried to wash London clean. Water visibly gurgled into the canal and I mentally traced its onward journey from canal to river to sea to continue the hydrological cycle. That was the power of H; she made everything mean something and I was in a joyous mood until I got to Camden Lock Market.

I used to enjoy the mad bustle of the place, the vast range of food for sale and the ethnic clothes. Of late though, I had become annoyed with the noise and the smells of cooking, which turned my stomach. I wouldn't have ventured into the market, but a strange looking man, with a face straight out of a Dickens novel, collared me.

This peculiar chap had florid features, a bulbous nose and ginger sideburns. He carried a walking stick with a bird's head handle and his Prince of Wales check suit, with an old-fashioned fob watch and chain hanging from a pocket of the waistcoat, emphasised his short, fat figure. I assumed he was going to speak like some cockney spiv. Instead, his diction was that of an educated man with the well-modulated accent of an early BBC newsreader, 'Splendid weather we are having, don't you agree?' His voice was so old fashioned I almost expected to see him in black and white.

I tried to move away from this strange character, but he somehow clung fast and guided me into the market. Not far from the entrance was a small marquee emblazoned with the name Nicholas De'Ath and Partners. My immediate reaction was that I was going to be sold a pension, PEP or bond of some kind, and I again tried to extricate myself from the annoying man. Then, I caught a glimpse of his umbrella's handle, and I could have sworn that the bird actually winked at me. This distracted me, and against my better judgement, I allowed myself to be guided into the marquee.

Inside, I was surprised to see huge chandeliers hanging from the roof and Persian rugs covering the floor. I assumed that these were special effects were created using some holographic trickery. I also thought I saw two semi-naked woman wearing feather boas disappearing behind a sheet at the far end of the marquee, but I put this down to being temporarily blinded by the bright light.

I was sure I was about to get caught by some sharp suited salesman offering me guaranteed returns on some dodgy investment or a time-share opportunity I couldn't afford to miss. Before I was given the sales patter, I asked, 'What is it you actually do?'

'We provide solutions.'

'Solutions to what?'

'Solutions to problems.'

'What is your job?' I pointed to him to make sure he knew he couldn't fob me off with more corporate speak. If he'd said, 'salesman' or 'advisor', I was out of there. Instead, his reply surprised me.

'I'm a Time Manager.'

I expected him to say that he was some sort of PA or he managed Nicholas De'Ath's diary but his explanation stunned me. 'I am responsible for creating kinks in time.'

'Kinks in time?' I repeated to highlight my confusion.

'Yes – the time when effect does not follow the cause, when B does not follow A.'

'When B does not follow A?'

'Yes, the time when the apple doesn't fall to the ground, the time when your toast is golden before you put it in the toaster, the time when you open the fridge to get the butter that was already on the table. Only little disruptions, glitches, if you like, in the programme of life. But, these little kinks in time create opportunities.'

'Opportunities?'

'Yes, what do you think life would be like without them? We would be headed for some specific future, carried on the twin track of cause and effect. There would be no place for free will as everything would have been determined by the first shove of life. There'd be no way of getting off. But, with a few well-placed kinks, the future can be what is imagined.'

This seemed to chime with my own late-night musings about the nature of time but I didn't like the idea of getting into a conversation with this strange man, as it was clearly part of a clever sales pitch. *One minute it is apples falling from trees and the next, it is please sign away your life savings for an unspecified return.*

I insisted that I couldn't stay, but before I managed to prise myself away from his surprisingly tight grip, the funny looking man gave me a business card and said, 'Give us a call old-boy. If you need any help; personal, financial, business or moral, you know where we are.' He then picked something off my shoulder. I asked him what he was doing and the man gave a strange answer, 'Nicholas likes to collect people's eyelashes.' He then took out a kind of little pillbox from his waistcoat and placed my eyelash inside it. I didn't like his familiarity, nor the sound of his boss and made a hurried exit.

When I was back outside on the street, and far enough away that I would not to be pestered by any more hawkers or vagabonds, I looked closely at the business card. Printed on it was the name of Nicholas De'Ath, but there were no contact numbers, website details or business address. I decided to go back to give them a lecture on how to design business cards that are actually useful, but when I returned to where I thought the marquee was it had disappeared. I reasoned that I had probably returned to the site through the wrong entrance. By then I was bored with the whole thing. *Anyway,* I surmised, *is it any of my business to give Nicholas De'Ath some free advice on how to properly promote himself?*

At the time, I took it as good news that some people were even worse at sales and marketing than I was. I thought, *Nicholas De'Ath must be doing quite nicely, so there is hope for me yet.*

Later that day, I recalled stealing from Susan but it no longer felt like theft. I thought, *Have I not given everything to her? And how does she repay me when I need her? Yes, by running off.*

That evening I went to the Dog and Bottle and sat down next to Leon on the badly stained, velvet bench seat. Susan was still very much on my mind and I found myself asking him, 'Am I being unfair to Susan?' Then I answered my own question by adding, 'Maybe I have neglected her in my obsessive efforts to start Dynamic Link.' I also confessed, 'I think it's because I am putting so much emphasis on being a success on this stupid Angels programme. But getting an investor would make such a difference to everything. At the moment, I am all over the place, I can't focus and it's affecting my ability to finish the presentation I'm writing for the show.' Leon was clear in his reply.

'I can recommen' to ya da cocaine. It brings to mind even greater clarity of tinking dan H.' He went on to suggest that I tried the Rolls Royce variety, the direct injection model and who was I to argue?

Leon provided the necessary phial, and when I got back home, I wasted no time in taking Leon's advice.

Here is the diary entry I made at the time:

'Lying on a piece of gauze beside a phial is the syringe full of cocaine. I pick it up and, after giving my puncture-riddled arm a cursory smear of iodine, I dig the needle into my skin.

Immediately after injecting that first syringe I am experiencing a foretaste of the euphoria, which I anticipate will soon overtake me.

61

And here it comes. I'm aware of its onset. The TV, which is on in the background although I did not notice it until now, is playing the most wonderful music. The announcers have angelic voices and the hoots and toots from the street below ring out like a celestial choir. I feel a state of calm and, yes, it is growing quickly into a delightful euphoria.

This euphoria lasted for a minute or two. I was riding a wave of pleasure that could have only been matched by a reunion with Susan. Then this happy state vanished without trace as though it had never been. What a let down, cocaine isn't what it's cracked up to be.'

So, cocaine had been a big disappointment but this was not the end of the experience. From my diary the next day, it was clear that it had a nasty side.

'I, the unfortunate William Taylor Findler, who started taking H in February, warn anyone not to attempt to replace H with cocaine. What was Leon thinking of to give me this foul and insidious poison? To any future reader of this sorry tale, accept my apologies for the scratchy handwriting.

The devil is in the phial. Cocaine – the devil is in the phial!

Beautiful H is a gentle joy, making her disciples happy by providing the keys to paradise. But cocaine is a red, rending beast, which creates a wild, wretched, even wicked world, a dystopian, distorted damnation.

By some mysterious process that isn't explained in any textbook on pharmacology, after the briefest of highs came a moment when,

62

the cocaine inside me transformed into something very different. I know what it is; my blood mutated into that of the devil.

Everything I looked at, the array of empty bottles, dust-covered table, old papers stacked on the over-burdened coffee table and quivering curtains in front of the open window, seemed to bristle with a wordless, but intense and vital message, the meaning of which was just beyond grasp. Then, I heard the whisper of, 'loser'.

The sound of the music faltered and I found that I hated the TV, hated the announcers and the bloody noise from outside. I mumbled, *Why can't people just leave me alone?* Inside my chest, I felt a tremendous pressure, as though I was about to explode. My heart began to beat so hard that I could feel it thumping when I put my hands to my temples... then my whole body sank into an abyss of fear, of flashing blades and flowing blood. These feelings washed over me several times in the course of the evening. I realised I had poisoned myself and there were moments over two nights when I wondered whether I would ever come back to life.

In the horror and pain, I cursed God and asked the devil to take me. Little did I know I would, in the very near future, meet him personally.

The Devil

When I awoke from the deep oblivion that had stood in for sleep, my reaction was absolutely clear, never, ever again! What was Leon thinking giving me that dreadful stuff?

My enfeebled body was reluctant to get off the couch that had been my bed for the last two days, even though the cushions had shifted creating a raised crease that dug uncomfortably into my hip. Somehow, I managed to stand, though my head felt disconnected from my body. It seemed that my commands to move were only relayed after a delay and were then only partially received by my limbs.

In the kitchen, I scraped together the last spoonful of instant coffee, most of which had adhered itself to the jar. But, when I tipped-up the milk carton out fell a large glob of soured milk, which immediately curdled. Nevertheless, I swallowed the coffee and something started to stir in my brain; my hands were not shaking quite so badly, my stomach was working, just. Even so, my resolution held firm, never again!

Still feeling wobbly and feeble, I ventured downstairs to the communal hallway and picked up the day's post that lay scattered on the mat in front of the entrance door. After sifting out the letters addressed to me, I dropped the remainder back onto the mat. I then noticed an envelope addressed to me, propped up against an ornament on the table by the door. Inside it, I found a handwritten note, which read, 'Dear Bill, would you please stop pacing around at 3.00am. If you do have to, could you not walk so heavily or wear cushioned slippers. I am also fed up of hearing ABBA blasting out at all hours. Best wishes, Bruce.' I was rather taken aback. Did I pace around at such a Godforsaken hour? Anyway, what if I did? Was it any of his business? *Best wishes Bruce, you can get lost* I thought, *and by the way it's William.* Disdainfully, I flung the letter down onto the mat with the rest of the communal post.

Back in my kitchen, I carefully divided the post into junk mail, bills and personal letters. I threw the junk mail and bills straight into the bin and opened the first of two personal letters. I was disappointed to find that this was from a local double-glazing company that I had used some years before. They were offering me, a valued customer, a discount on a range of bifold doors designed to give wide access onto a patio or rear garden. I briefly wondered what bifold garden doors would look like on a second floor flat before screwing up the letter. I laughed, because here was evidence of another company being even worse at sales and marketing than I was. I hadn't as yet actually carried-out any sales and marketing for my new company, but at least I hadn't wasted time and money on it.

I took another swig of coffee. The mixture of caffeine and self-congratulation marginally lifted my spirits and the world around me seemed to become less jittery.

The other letter also proved to be a marketing communication. However, it interested me as it was from Nicholas De'Ath and Partners, the company whose Camden Lock marquee I had briefly entered.

This letter, with the company name printed in bold, gold embossed letters, struck me as odd. It referred to my recent visit and thanked me for my interest, but I was sure I hadn't given them any personal details, not even my name. The letter informed me that Nicholas De'Ath was currently available at the company's Docklands offices for private consultations. Unusually, as made clear by its slightly misaligned characters and corrections, the letter had been typed on an old-fashioned typewriter.

I was particularly intrigued by the assertion that Nicholas De'Ath, or the company bearing his name, specialised in coaching people who were due to appear on reality-TV. Despite my befuddled brain not wanting to tax itself, the letter piqued my interest. What an odd specialism! How big was his potential customer base? Unless he charged an exorbitant fee, how could he survive? I was amazed at the timing of the letter as I was soon to be filmed as an invited entrepreneur on Angels, ITM's imitation of BBC's Dragons' Den.

I'd applied to go on Angels, because I was desperate for funds. Dynamic Link, my creation and brainchild, had yet to find either customers or backers. However, given the oxygen of TV, I was sure that its time would come. Any fool would be able to see its vast potential. However, as is clearly evidenced in my diaries, I was finding it hard to focus on the sales pitch. My deliberations gravitated towards the underlying philosophy and the theoretical basis of the concepts. A succinct marketing-oriented summary of the benefits eluded me. Maybe the time was right to obtain and take heed of some much-needed independent business advice. It was true that, to date, I had ignored every piece of advice I had received, especially if it started with, 'You'll fail. These ideas will bring you down, they will bankrupt you.' In my mind, I always recalled these words being spoken in my wife's haranguing tones, but to be fair, they were not uttered from her mouth alone.

With the benefit of hindsight, what I should have done was to put the letter in the bin along with the bills and junk mail. But, in my defence, at that point in time, how could I have known about the cause and effect sequence that would inevitably be invoked if I replied? Despite my head and vocal chords still struggling to properly connect, I decided that no time was like the present. So, I picked up the phone and dialled the number on top of the letter. Seemingly without ringing out, my call was answered and I found myself conversing with a woman who spoke with a very silky voice in an exotic sounding accent that was difficult to place.

After introducing myself, the silky voice replied, 'Ah yes, Mr. Findler we have been expecting your call.'

'Have you?' I stammered.

'Indeed, Nicholas De'Ath is very much looking forward to meeting you.'

'He is?'

'Yes, we have you in the diary for this afternoon at two o'clock.'

'Do you?'

'Yes. We look forward to seeing you then.'

'Are you?'

'Two o'clock sharp.'

I was taken aback. So, there was such a man as Nicholas De'Ath!

Why were they expecting me to call and why was De'Ath looking forward to seeing me?

I desperately needed another coffee but had to make do with reusing a tea bag. Although I squeezed it hard, the tea remained resolutely weak. Nevertheless, it was hot and soothing and I tried not to fret about my minor physical needs.

I reflected on the meeting I had just arranged and, understanding that marketing was becoming more and more sophisticated, I was open to learning something from this Nicholas chappy about how to target customers. I decided I would definitely go and meet him and thought, *Where was the harm in that?*

As life gradually returned to my mind and body, I replayed my experience of taking cocaine and resolved, once again, not to repeat it. I was happy in the gentle arms of H and thought, *if I didn't spoil this relationship, there is no reason it can't go on forever in the same way.* H soothed me and helped relieve the stress-induced grumpiness and bad temper brought on by setting up and running, what I planned to be a household brand name. *Wait until I see Leon*, I thought, *I intend to give him a piece of my mind.*

Despite continuing jitters and shakes I took hold of my pen and scratchily added an entry in my diary. After capturing the horrors of the previous days in my diary, I decided that, to help me feel a little more human, I would make an effort to tidy up my appearance. I found a shirt that wasn't too creased, which went well with my dark blue, made in Italy, suit (bought in the days when a joint income allowed such luxuries). There was a stain on one of the lapels (God knows where that came from) but I decided that it could be tolerated. After dressing, I was pleasantly surprised to see someone in the mirror looking business-like, suave and even debonair. My face was much thinner than it had been for years and this actually seemed to make me look younger. If I ignored the dark circles under my eyes, I would say that I passed for someone in their mid-forties.

The offices of Nicholas De'Ath were located at Canary Wharf; a simple journey from Camden, with a single change at London Bridge, which I knew well. However, I decided to give myself plenty of time as sudden movements were still a problem.

I experienced a sense of déjà vu as I headed off towards the tube station as I had done on a daily basis years before. In fact, as I strolled in the sun, I began to feel almost normal; like an ordinary person going to work. How I had hated it at the time and complained bitterly about being some kind of automaton, but now it felt like complete freedom. It was such a simple pleasure. I resolved to get my old self back; pleasant, tolerant, good-natured and generous. As a down-payment on this intention, I even offered a cheery smile to a homeless beggar, who was selling the Big Issue by the tube station.

As I disappeared down the escalator at Camden tube station, my walking descent (I had also decided to increase my level of exercise) was blocked by a couple that could only be described as 'out-of-towners' – all locals know you have to stand on the right-hand side. After I had said, 'Excuse me,' and pushed past, I muttered, 'bloody foreigners' under my breath, but clearly too loudly as it engendered a response of, 'Up yours mate.' I wondered when exactly I'd turned into a grumpy old git.

70

Even the rush of hot air pushed ahead of the next train as it swooshed out of the tunnel, carrying with it the Tube's unique smell of brake dust and city living, didn't make me recoil as it would once have done. This day was going to be special indeed and nothing could spoil it. For once, I felt like a man on a mission, rather than a harassed entrepreneur constantly writing, revising and binning the latest version of his business plan. As the carriage rocked through Holborn I sat back, on a surprisingly comfortable seat, and reflected. Year one – Planning, Year two - Building, Year three – Launch, Year four - Success. I was only in year three and the Angels were about to hear my ideas. I was on-track and success was as assured as London Underground delivering me swiftly to Canary Wharf.

Unfortunately, I realised I was on the wrong branch of the Northern Line. Instead of changing at Bank Station I had to take a longer route via Waterloo. However, my optimism was unaffected and as I transferred to the Jubilee Line I shouted out, 'Wha Wha Whaterloo.' In the morning I had felt like the defeated Napoleon, crushed; later, walking along the echoing tunnels I felt ready to take on the world. 'I was down but I won the war.' I added in full voice and let the vibrations fade away. Even if I did get a few strange looks, it showed that I was in a positive upbeat mood.

I arrived at Canary Wharf and, emerging from the glass and steel station, felt a slight churning in the stomach. I think it was the unsavoury sight of ugly skyscrapers and the smell of money. Even the suits emerging from the bowels of the earth around me had a self-satisfied swagger. The whole of the City and this overspill were full of arrogant people, money-obsessed and short-term, so called masters of the universe, who had come to the self-deluded conclusion that they deserved vast wealth.

71

Despite the diversion, I had plenty of time to spare before my appointment. This was a good job as it took quite a time to find the address. 666 North Colonnade was not too far from the station, but there was no mention of Nicholas De'Ath and Partners on the plaque outside this prestigious office building. The receptionist told me that she had never heard of the company. I looked at the letter again and noticed that the address was actually 66b North Colonnade. As I headed further along this impressive street, its silver towers almost seemed to be leaning in to protect me from the glaring sun. Despite their efforts I was becoming hot and tired. With not going out much, I was finding that I had very little stamina these days, and this trip was becoming a gruelling ordeal. Should I even bother with it? But I decided this was the start of a new me, or at least a return to the old me, and I pressed on.

I eventually arrived at 66 North Colonnade, but I could not find 66b and enquires resulted in no one having heard of Nicholas De'Ath. When the receptionist asked, 'Which company does he work for?' I bared my teeth and growled as if it was her fault I had been duped. I left the building intent on finding a pub as I felt extraordinarily thirsty. However, as I passed a service road, I nearly bumped into a strange looking, eagle-beaked man with tufty hair. He wore a navy hazmat suit and held a placard. I expected it to say something like 'Jesus Saves', but instead it just had '66b' and an arrow pointing the way printed on it. The arrow was oriented down the service road and I immediately headed there. However, when I looked back the man had turned around. I chastised his sloppy approach, as clearly anyone else looking for the building would be sent in the wrong direction.

Surprised and a little relieved, I ventured down the service road and not too far along it I came to a shiny black door with a handwritten note attached to it. It read, '66b, Please ring.' There was no bell, but as the door was ajar I walked straight in and was surprised when the small, dark tunnel-like corridor leading from the door opened into a vast, brightly-lit and impressive foyer with a marble reception desk at one end.

After the darkness of the corridor, I blinked in response to the bright lights and I thought I saw a massive raven sitting behind the reception desk. I am embarrassed to admit that the bird turned out to be a black woman with a feathery boa around her neck. I approached The Raven's desk and soon saw that she was strikingly beautiful. Before I managed to say anything, the receptionist stood up and said, 'Mr. Findler, we are so pleased to see you.' I was shocked.

'How do you know my name?'

'It is nearly two o'clock. Time for your appointment.'

'Oh.' This seemed a logical answer, but didn't they have other visitors?

'I will let Mr. De'Ath know you are here. He is very much looking forward to meeting you.'

'He is?' I knew this whole set up was decidedly fishy.

The Contract

If the entrance to the office was strange, once fully inside, I could not help being impressed by the huge foyer in which fancy chandeliers hung over comfortable grey-leather sofas. I sank into one of these, pleased to have the opportunity to rest, and picked up a corporate brochure. This was titled, 'Nicholas De'Ath, Investments and Disposals', but there was nothing in it about coaching or reality-TV. Again, I was convinced I was being set up. *At the end of this*, I thought, *if I hadn't been sold a pension or a PEP, then my name isn't William Taylor Findler.*

The brochure was full of buzzwords such as 'social responsibility', 'ethics' and 'values' but there was no mention of what Nicholas De'Ath invested in or disposed of. On the back cover there was a strap line, 'No job too small.' I couldn't help chuckling, as this phrase, so typical of the small-time builder, seemed out of place. I was sure there were a few things I could teach this, so called, coach.

Once I had recovered myself a little, thinking that it would be a good idea to speak to the receptionist to glean some information about the mysterious Mr. De'Ath, I eased myself out of the sofa and went over to her desk. As I approached, I looked closely at her face and neck. She was unquestionably beautiful. One of the side effects of my condition was that I could really appreciate beauty but had no desire to possess it. So, I was able to look at her with an objective eye. Such hair, so black it had a midnight bluish tinge. Such skin, so smooth and silky it was like the finest, most luxurious, chocolate. And what startling eyes! Yes, her yellow eyes had the look of a raven's; clever and utterly ruthless.

The Raven enquired, 'May I help you?'

'I wonder if you can tell me what Nicholas De'Ath and Partners invests in?'

'Certainly; debts.'

'Oh, and what does he dispose of?'

'Debtors.'

'Yes, of course.' I decided she was probably employed more for her looks than her industry knowledge. I returned to my chair and sat down and waited for what seemed like an age. I'm sure I even had a brief doze. However, when The Raven announced that Mr. De'Ath was ready to see me I was shocked a little to see that the hands of my watch hadn't moved at all and were dead on two o' clock.

The Raven led the way and the only fault I could find with her physical features was an odd gait. She moved with a slight waddling motion, which exaggerated the swish of her black chiffon skirt. We turned left by the reception desk and walked along a corridor past a row of offices to the left with an open-plan working area to the right. The workstations were all unoccupied but had blinking screens, and it seemed to me that the keys on the keyboards were being spontaneously depressed and released. Office automation had clearly taken an alarming turn for the worse since I was last in such a place.

One of the office doors had a plaque that read, 'Investments'. I wasn't able to see inside but it sounded like a number of photocopiers, or other printing devices, were hard at work. At the end of the corridor we turned left again and passed a door with a plaque, which I read as, 'Human Remains'. I smiled at my obvious mistake and then caught the sound of a rather gruff voice saying, 'That was when we were trying to hire you. Now you are employed'. I wondered whether I also caught the sound of a muffled sob.

At the end of this corridor we turned left yet again and passed the 'Disposals' office. From behind the closed door I heard mechanical crunching noises that sounded like an industrial meat grinder in operation. I shuddered to think what was being disposed of.

We came to a corner of the building and turned left again. I was feeling light headed and disoriented by this point, but I was sure that four sharp lefts should have brought us back to the reception. I made a mental note to check how many right-angled turns it takes to go around a square. Anyhow, we carried on along the corridor until it ended at a set of grand double doors. The Raven asked me to wait in a small vestibule and then slipped through to the main office. She left the door slightly ajar so I could see partly in.

I could make out a green light emanating from a writing desk. After taking a second look, I realised that it was actually a complicated sort of bureau with dozens of small drawers, vertical compartments for letters and, bizarrely, a built-in ship's compass. Its drop-down lid supported a telephone with a blinking light, an old-fashioned typewriter and a Rolodex card index. Tucked-in by the side of the bureau, a strange red light emanated, seemingly infernally, from a large half-opened box, decorated with Chinese writing. I could hear snatches of an animated conversation, which included, 'Dongles bongles, it's all the same to me. Just sort it out.'

'Yes Sire. Sorry, leave it with me.'

Soon afterwards, The Raven returned and ushered me out of the vestibule and into Nicholas' imposing, but surprisingly dark, office. As I walked through the doorway, I just caught sight of the back of someone disappearing through a door at the other side of the office. I was alarmed to see he had a knot of snakes around one of his arms but then realised that they must be a set of computer leads and wires.

The Raven announced, 'Mr. Findler, this is Mr. De'Ath.' I immediately felt let down and cheated, as standing by the desk was the strange, Dickensian looking, fellow who had buttonholed me only the other day at Camden Market. I opened my mouth but could not immediately find the right words of complaint. Then, from behind a large pair of soles, which were resting on the desk next to the typewriter, a face appeared and announced, 'No need to look like a fish. I'm Nicholas De'Ath. Charmed to make your acquaintance.' Nicholas then took his feet off the desk and raised himself from a slumping position in an executive office chair. He had hair as dark as a moonless night and the most pointed of beards I had ever seen. He was wearing a grey suit with a dollar green pinstripe running through it.

Nicholas came around the desk to meet me and I saw that he was a tall, elegant man of indeterminate age. I noticed a few wrinkles around his eyes but the skin on his high cheekbones was completely unblemished. He gave my hand a squeeze of some considerable force and I found that his palm was unusually cold. Then, he introduced the man I had previously met at Camden

Market as Kairos and I thought, *that's a strange name for someone who reminds me of Captain Mainwaring's inebriate brother.*

Nicholas pointed to a red velvet sofa in a corner of the room and, as we walked towards it, I heard the sound of distant laughter. Nicholas signalled to Kairos to shut an open door at the far side of the room. In fact, he slipped through the door and closed it behind him, leaving us alone. I sat on the sofa and Nicholas lowered himself into an adjoining chair in such a graceful way that he appeared to hover and then glide down into it. He then rested his feet insouciantly on a marble coffee table placed in front of us.

I looked at Nicholas carefully. His most notable feature was that each of his slightly slanting eyes was a different colour. His right eye was the colour of olive oil and resembled that of a cat or perhaps a hyena. To my mind, it had more than a hint of cruelty in it. His left eye was the colour of pale grey-blue cinders and resembled that of a dog or horse or some other honest, faithful creature. As he looked at me the olive colour predominated and I said to myself, 'Nicholas De'Ath; cruel but fair.'

Nicholas addressed me in a hypnotic, singsong voice, 'Mr. Taylor, or may I call you Willy or Billy, which do you prefer?'

'My name is William.'

'William, I understand you are in dire need of personal, financial and moral help.' I was offended.

'I...' I started to give him a piece of my mind for wasting my time but then quickly decided it was better to stay calm. So, I shut-up and then lamely said, 'I could do with a little luck that's

79

all.' Nicholas laughed, revealing slightly pointed and incredibly white teeth behind fleshy and surprisingly red lips. But it was the audible rather than the visual aspect of his laugh that mainly gave it a demonic quality. It resembled none of the normal forms of laughter such as ha, ha, ha or hee, hee, hee. Nicholas's spine-chilling laugh was like a distant machine gun rattling over the killing fields of the Somme, ta, ta, ta.

'Yes, luck is very important,' he said when he had finished laughing, 'but good luck is in very short supply and mostly comes once you have earned it. Now, tell me why you are here?'

'Because you invited me.'

'Ta, ta, ta; no, don't you remember, you called me?'

I looked around for the support of Kairos, the Time Manager, but he hadn't returned. I didn't want to get into an argument, so let Nicholas' comment go.

'I am due to appear on Angels soon.'

'Angels?'

'Angels, the TV show. ITM's version of Dragons' Den.'

'Never heard of it.' I was sure that everyone had at least seen one episode but decided to explain in any case.

'It's where entrepreneurs pitch to a panel of celebrity investors. It's glitzier than the BBC's offering. The pitches are made in a swish boardroom in a Docklands skyscraper and the presenter and panel fly-in by helicopter. At the end of the show those who get a backer fly-off in the helicopter with the presenter and the panel. The celebrity entrepreneurs themselves are the same type as appear on BBC's offering, in a word, shits.'

'When is it being recorded?'

'31st August.'

'You could do with some coaching before then.' It was a statement rather than a question.

Nicholas almost levitated out of his chair, and once he was standing upright bent back slightly as if he was stretching a stiff muscle. 'Have you any questions?' He asked and sauntered over to his desk and rested his bottom on its edge.

'I certainly have. For a start, I'm wondering why you're interested in me. After all, you seem to be a man of considerable wealth and influence, how come you want to coach me?'

'Oh, I am wealthy. But, making money has no appeal. It is so easy.'

'Really! What do you invest in and dispose of?' I was not normally so direct with people.

'There is no secret in that; debt.'

'Debt?'

'Yes, debt.'

81

The Raven had been correct after all. It reminded me of all of the bills piling up at home and I commented, 'Debt has never sounded good to me'

'Ta, ta, ta. Debt is what makes the world go around, haven't you heard that expression? Spread thinly, it's like manure that ensures the health of next year's harvest. Without debt there is no profit and without profit there's no surplus to share out. Of course, spread too thickly it is a suffocating layer of, well let's not put too fine a point on it, shit. In either case, for me it's like printing money.' I wondered whether the photocopiers I had heard in the Investment office were doing just that, but dismissed the possibility.

'May I ask what exactly you do – with debt?'

'Do you know anything about the financial world?' I could not lie and had to answer truthfully.

'Nothing.'

Nicholas shook his head ruefully as if he couldn't quite believe he had heard such innocence before and launched in with a lecture on how bankers simply conjure money from thin air. However, I knew that their lending had to be backed by something tangible. Why else did they have huge safes stuffed full of gold or piles of fifty-pound notes? I was not going to let him get away with this tosh without any challenge. But, by way of a finely crafted interrogative question, I could only come up with, 'Are you sure?'

Nicholas laughed and, instead of making me smile, a cold feeling crept over me like an icy glove. 'Oh, delightful! How simply naïve you are.' He smirked and said, 'Gullible, just like the rest of the population. It brings joy to my heart. The banker of today lends you that which he does not have and commands you to pay it back from something you do have, namely your hard-earned cash. A truly treacherous sleight of hand wouldn't you agree?' I wasn't going to let him off so lightly.

'But if they lent me money, I could draw it out immediately, so they must have it?'

'The next time you ask for, say, forty thousand pounds see if you can draw it out.'

I was sure that I had just won that argument but nevertheless asked, 'And where does all this cash come from for the loans?'

'That's where I come in, or more accurately, Nicholas De'Ath and Partners. Poof! We supply the noughts.'

'The noughts!'

'Yes, where else do you think they come from?' He opened his palms and shrugged.

'I'd never really thought about it?'

'Few people do stop to think about it, especially those who are paid to keep the banks from getting too free and easy with their tap, tap, tapping.'

The image came to my mind of the computers in his offices with their self-depressing keys and I wondered if they were, at this moment, authorising the allocation of more noughts. 'Do you supply the noughts to everyone?' I asked.

'Yes, but I take no responsibility for how debt is used.' Nicholas stood a little straighter and looked at me. The pale ash colour of his left eye told me he was sincere. 'I can rest easy with a clear conscience, I'm only the supplier.'

The word supplier had come to have a specific meaning to me, but I didn't comment and Nicholas continued. 'However, unfortunately, it's so simple it holds no challenge at all. Oh, I almost forgot, you will have to sign a contract.' I stiffened and immediately became wary.

'I don't have money or assets, only debts and that, in my case, is the reverse of making money!'

'Ah, money, money; so much evil it causes in the world! We all think of nothing but money, but how many of us have ever given a thought to our soul?' Nicholas looked at me, sat back, licked his lips, and then drew one lip over another reminding me of how undertakers rub their hands on the news of new cadaver.

Before I was able to consider this question, Nicholas asked another, 'Tell me, what would you like me to help you achieve?'

'Success of course!'

'Success comes in all sorts of shapes and sizes. Can you be a bit more specific?

'I would like to be rich. Not that I'm in it for the money.'

84

'Really! We'll see about that.' Nicholas sounded competitive.

I was keen to explain my selfless motivation to Nicholas, 'If I quote vast profits, it's not because I'm interested in wealth, it's just that money is an indicator of how much the world values ideas. And my ideas are priceless.'

'Yes, of course, but how rich?'

'Rich enough to live in a Georgian villa in St Johns Wood and drive past my mother-in-law's in a red Jaguar 4.2 XKR.' I gave myself a metaphorical pat on the back for having already done the visualisation work following the 'Secret of Success' course. I could even see myself ostentatiously honking the horn and showing Susan, my wife, that she had been too quick to dismiss me and my ideas.

'Apart from houses and cars, what else would signify your success?'

'An industry award would be nice.'

'And...'

'Oh well, if it's not too much to ask, I would like a blue plaque at some point. Not for my own sake, oh no, but it would be nice if my grandchildren knew that society recognised the profound difference I made to it.'

'You have children?'

'No.'

The flow of conversation was interrupted by a bleep from the phone on the desk. He turned towards it, stared at a message on its display screen and pulled a face as if he had smelt something foul, before saying, 'Look at this, scientists have found the fat gene.' He took on a mocking tone, 'Oh no, don't criticise my fat legs and belly; it's not that I eat chocolate all day, it's my genes.' I didn't appreciate the interruption and became irritated.

'What's that got to do with me?'

'Quite a lot as it happens.' Nicholas didn't expand on this but carried on with his tirade. 'Highly talented people seem to find their greatest pleasure in magnifying every mechanism, every inevitability, everything where human freedom does not enter or does not appear to enter. A great shout of eureka goes up whenever anybody has found further evidence in physiology, psychology, sociology, economics or politics that people cannot help being what they are or doing what they do.'

'Quite so.' I decided it would shut him up if I agreed.

'Yes, a concentration on mechanisms, processes, genes, coding, environmental factors or whatever is a denial of freedom and as a consequence it is, of course, also a denial of responsibility. There are no acts only events; everything simply happens, no one is responsible.' Nicholas paused, shook himself gently and added, 'Now, where were we?'

At that precise moment, and without Nicholas summoning him in any visible way, Kairos returned holding a thick document. He

86

held this out towards me and announced, 'Your contract Sir.' I took it from him and started to scan the legal text. 'Should there be', 'in so far as', and 'here to forthwith,' occurred quite frequently and every point seemed to begin with, 'The client does not have the right...'

One point disrupted the uniformity of the document. *The client undertakes unconditionally and immediately to make best endeavours to introduce such changes, additions or cessations, as are required by the board of Nicholas De'Ath and Partners or individuals, institutions, organisations or corporations invested with the relevant authority.'* I decided 'best endeavours' could mean I didn't need to bother and so dismissed this clause as irrelevant. In fact, I considered the whole contract a worthless piece of paper offering 'coaching' services of dubious value.

I saw no mention of money or charges and asked, 'And how much do I have to pay?'

'Ta, ta, ta, I'm not interested in your money. Haven't I just explained I have more than enough? You will find no mention of money in the contract. Poor souls and debtors, now that's another matter.'

The last page was for signatures. Nicholas had somehow already signed his name. Kairos helpfully supplied me with a fountain pen, and I added my own signature (the red ink looked a little too much like blood for my liking). When I looked up, Nicholas had disappeared and Kairos was trying to shake my hand in a way that indicated the meeting was over. 'Is that it?' I asked.

'Mr. De'Ath is terribly busy, but he is a man of his word;

give him a call when you are ready for some coaching. Now, may I show you out?'

Kairos accompanied me to the foyer and, strangely, this required two more sharp left-hand turns. The Raven was no longer at her desk but, oddly, there were several black feathers scattered about.

Later, I couldn't remember a thing from the moment I shook the Time Manager's hand to when I found myself back on North Colonnade. I smiled to myself; if I spent more time with Kairos, he'd have me believe my memory lapse was actually a kink in time. Back on the main road, I was feeling tired, hungry and terribly thirsty. I badly needed some H, but decided I also needed alcohol, or perhaps both, by way of celebration. With Nicholas De'Ath on my side, surely my luck had changed.

Unfortunately, there was no cosy pub nearby, so I had to make do with a trendy wine bar full-to-bursting with sharks of all types, basking, hammerheads and great whites; all killers, all slapping each other on the back. After pushing my way to the bar, and ordering a glass of Riesling with a vodka chaser, I squeezed onto the vacant edge of a bench-seat and began to reflect on the strange meeting with Nicholas De'Ath. Even then, I wasn't sure why I had signed it, considering that I thought the whole business was a complete con trick. However, I put my doubts to one side and I thought about The Raven. I hoped that the promised coaching would involve more contact with this beautiful creature.

A Day in the Life

After my taxing day with Nicholas De'Ath, I let myself have a lie in and, in that lovely state between deep sleep and waking, I had vivid images of plucking The Raven's feathery boa. When fully awake, I had an intuitive sense that using Nicholas's services would lead to serious and unpleasant consequences, so I decided not to bother following up on his offer of coaching even if that meant not seeing his receptionist again. Despite this and maybe because I had actually got out the house for a change, I felt motivated and decided to start the day by making a 'To Do' list.

Of course, I needed the obligatory three coffees and a cigarette before the brain valves had sufficiently warmed for the task ahead. I also listened to Woman's Hour, which I always find enlightening.

I no longer watched Breakfast TV. This is partly due to the fact it had usually finished long before I had emerged from my pit, but I didn't miss it in the slightest; well apart from the toothsome figure of Carol Churchwood. The presenters sounded like they are fronting Blue Peter, or some similar programme for the four to eleven-year age range, with endless human-interest stories that always seem to involve some celebrity or other promoting their latest book. Afterwards, unless you liked snooker or darts, there was nothing on,

After listening to a rather unpleasant discussion on female genital mutilation, (I am sure that in the past Woman's Hour was a slightly easier listen) I switched the radio off and got down to work. The 'To Do' list was easier than I had imagined;

- Set up Internet account.

- Write elevator pitch.

- Sell.

- Sell out to Google.

I also added, 'Clean the Flat', as I knew, even then, that it was a biohazard. I sat back in the chair and had another cigarette whilst contemplating the size of the task. I noted that dust lay thickly on all the surfaces with the exception of the record player. I wondered how that could be as I rarely played any of my extensive vinyl collection. The only free place to put a coffee cup in the lounge was on the large pile of out of date copies of the Radio Times. Considering that I never actually watched the TV, I made a mental note to cancel the standing order for the magazine.

The list might have been easy to write but the first task was harder than I had imagined. I found the number for BT in Yellow Pages and gave them a ring. I was met with the customary, 'To help us direct your call, please choose one of the following eight options. Please listen to all, as these have recently changed.' After listening to the entire message, I couldn't remember whether 'new customer' was option two or three, so I pressed three and was put in a queue. 'Your call is important to us. You are number ninety-three.' By the time that I had reached position number eighty, the call was no longer important to me and I hung up.

Afterwards, I recalled the words of Biella about how entrepreneurs keep bouncing back and raised sufficient enthusiasm to have another attempt at talking to someone in BT. However, I wish I hadn't bothered.

Once I had endured the terrible rap music whilst on hold, and eventually managed to get to the front of the queue, the conversation went like this:

'Hello, I would like to open an Internet account.'

'Unintelligible response – but included the phrase pissword pliss.'

'Hello, Internet account. I… want…one.' I slowed my speech and emphasised each word.

'Unintelligible response but included the phrases, nim and data bith.'

'Can I speak to your supervisor?'

'Unintelligible response'

'Your supervisor.' I used the old trick of raising my voice to make sure I was understood.

'Unintelligible response'

'Bloody hell, why on earth would you locate a call centre in Glasgow.' I hung up.

Admittedly, falling at the first hurdle with the 'To Do' list was not a good omen, but technology was never my strong point. I then recalled that I had the business card of the I.T. guy in my wallet and, after a protracted search for that, I managed to pull it out. It read, 'Ramdeep Parkavakar. Solutions Provider.' I repeated the name a few times, smiled for some reason, and gave him a call. I was pleased to immediately get through and, after reminding him who I was (yes, the man with the holes in his trousers), we arranged to meet at his office later in the day. Luckily, the office was not far away.

Given that the meeting was set for four o'clock, I had some hours to kill and I decided to go to the library, as they would have a new copy of the local paper. I particularly enjoyed reading the 'Court Reports'. Mainly it was filled with names of people fined for minor misdemeanours such as not having a TV Licence. I was amused that the fine for this was typically the cost of the licence so it confirmed my decision not to pay the fee. I thought, *The BBC can take a running jump. Nobody just sends me a cheque!*

When I got to the library, there was no sign of Gloria. I was pleased it must have been her day off as I was still smarting from her ill treatment. However, I was disappointed that the *Camden and Kentish Town Gazette* was not in its normal position on the rack. I couldn't immediately see who had it, so I pulled up a chair at the reading table and sat down there. Rather like a cat at a fridge door, I was prepared to sit it out until the return of my treat.

As I sat back, I noticed a slim volume on the desk in front of me with the off-putting title of *The Mathematical Analysis of Logic* by George Boole. Despite having a deep aversion to numbers, I started looking through it. For the most part, it was like trying to read Egyptian hieroglyphics. I didn't understand a single formula.

When I read the introduction, I could not quite take it in. The mathematics Boole presents is that of the human intellect. His *Laws of Thought* provided the scientific basis for my taxonomy. OMG!

It felt like the top of my head had been opened and golden, illuminating light was being poured in, filling me. I was ecstatic. *Everything aligns. Two dimensions of time and laws of thought. These are the bedrock of the system.*

I even stood up, raised the small tome above my head and cried out, 'Hallelujah.' Gloria's replacement gave me a nasty, piercing look and put her finger up to her lips. I was so excited I wanted to celebrate and there is nowhere better for that in my part of town than the Dog and Bottle. I borrowed the book and scurried off.

If you were able to see the pub you would understand why I liked it so much. It's not a gastro-pub. It's not a sports-pub. It's not a themed-pub. It is an old-fashioned London pub; one of a dying breed. That is to say, the carpet is beer soaked, the velvet benches are worn, even sticky in places, and with regard to food, it sells nothing fancier than pickled eggs and its own speciality; yesterday's cheese, tomato and lettuce sandwich. The patrons are honest souls who need a little help to get through the tedium of a normal working day. They don't want to be disturbed by the ringing of mobile phones or even Radio Two's banal chat and pat nostalgia; far too nineteen-nineties for my liking. It's a haven from the ubiquitous gaming machines and TV monitors showing twenty-four hour rolling, and highly repetitive, news about the ever-rising FTSE index. I am getting quite tearful thinking about it.

I was hoping that I could share some of my new-found insight with

Leon but, most unusually, his velvet bench was unoccupied. I presumed that he had gone to see his suppliers.

I had three glasses of a rather splendid Riesling the pub provided in boxes and reread the introduction to Boole's little masterpiece. Then, in a really upbeat mood, I headed for the office of Ramdeep Parkavakar for my four o'clock meeting. The stars must have aligned in my favour as it was on my way home and I was looking forward to a celebration with H once back.

Ramdeep's business location, a converted Georgian Villa, was very impressive, if a little stark. If I had not known he was an I.T. guy, I would have thought it was the sort of place people came to for a boob job judging by the smoked glass table and clinical, white surfaces in the reception area. In fact, I wondered if this was the real purpose of the building as, whilst I waited, the receptionist seemed to be sizing me up.

Perhaps, because I had arrived fashionable late, I didn't have to wait long before I was shown through to Ramdeep's office. Ramdeep sat behind a large desk and was speaking into thin air when I was ushered in. He gestured for me to take a seat and, as I looked at him, I realised that the hairband I had seen him wearing at the conference was, in fact, a device for holding a small speaker to his ear. If he was so au-fait with techno-gadgets, I knew I was in the right place. He was also wearing a polo shirt rather than a suit so I knew he was one of the new-breed of Internet entrepreneurs.

Whilst Ramdeep was finishing his call, I decided not to immediately ask him how to get an Internet account as I thought that, without some dressing-up, this low-level request would

94

betray my lamentable ignorance.

Ramdeep must have clicked something because the call finished and he stood up to greet me. Instead of a normal welcome he said, 'That is quite brilliant. Snatch Chat. It is going to be soooo big.'

'Snatch Chat?' It sounded dodgy to me.

'It taps into the teenagers' obsession with sending pictures of body parts.' I couldn't help pulling a face.

'Sounds weird?' I mumbled.

'Oh, we would have to restrict it to under-sixteens only. Older than that, yes, that would attract all sorts of perverts. Now, how can I help you?'

'Well I would like my business to go global.' I thought I would start with the big picture.

'And what is your business?' I was a bit miffed as I had clearly explained to him, and the rest of the small group, what it was I did.

'I have a complete management system.'

'Really! What can it do?'

'Lots of things.'

'Such as?'

'For instance, it improves the recruitment process. When you write a job specification using my classification system and get people to complete a capability profile according to the same system you can easily match people to jobs.'

'Now that sounds interesting. And, if you did this online, you could get the computer to do the match.'

'Oh.' I didn't want to sound like I hadn't already thought of this.

'Yes, you could transform the market and cut out the middlemen. Presumably that's why you are here?' Ramdeep opened out his hands in some sort of symbolic offering.

'No... errr, yes. I guess so. Is that something you could help with?'

'That is exactly the sort of solution I supply.' He stuck his finger towards me to make the point.

'And you do this?'

'I will work on the technical architecture and strategy, and all the programming I subcontract to India. In today's world you don't need employees, or even your own office, you hire it when you need it. Like this one.'

I was impressed and wondered whether I should hire a similar office when dealing with investors, or the functionaries from Google who would be making an offer for the business. Bringing myself back to the present opportunity, I asked 'How much do you think this development will cost?'

'Well, I would have to see your system but from what you say, let me think. Well, we would need servers, software programming, AI Development.'

'Servers, software programming, AI Development?' I didn't really know what he was referring to, but repeating the terms seemed to spur Ramdeep on.

'Yes, and matching algorithms and security features. Ok, just a ballpark figure - about three million. That would prove the concept. It would cost more to scale it up to the size of Facebook.' I must say, my jaw went slack. *No one was going to give me three million for starters,* I was sure of that.

'Do you think it will pay back?' Ramdeep could probably tell by the tone of my voice I was doubtful. He, however, started to talk like some prophet of the God I.T.

'Oh, this is the way the world is going. If you are not online, you are nowhere.' He took out of his pocket a new smart phone and said, 'When I hold this in the palm of my hand, I'm holding the global brain. We are no longer simply humans, we are Homo Universalis. When you add high-tech capabilities such as artificial intelligence, nanotech, biotech, quantum computing and robotics to our social and spiritual evolution, you have a species with powers of our ancient Gods.'

'Ancient Gods!'

'Yes. We are approaching the quantum shift from

97

creature-human to high-tech human, the augmented human, who is the inheritor of god-like powers. Of course, the weak and useless, the non I.T. literate, must be eliminated from the social body.'

'Eliminated!' I couldn't take the sense of shock out of my voice.

'Entirely. What do you think we are going to do with all those doctors whose roles have been made obsolete? Once you move to an advanced analytical platform that accesses the best diagnostic techniques, the latest research and recommendations from the pharmaceutical industry, you will never have to sit in an unhealthy waiting room again. The world's best medical diagnostics and prognostics are an Internet call away.'

'Sounds a bit far-fetched to me.' I shouldn't have been so honest as it provided the opportunity for Ramdeep to start again.

'Far-fetched! It is around the corner. Just need everyone to have a digital I.D. and it is all in place.'

I don't think he had actually addressed my question, but Ramdeeps' ramblings confirmed to me that everyone in high-tech was not only completely mad but dangerous too.

To stop his futuristic nonsense, I decided to ask for something smaller as a first step. 'Can you start by getting me an Internet account?'

'Sure. Can I have your details?'

'How much do you charge?' I was too astute a businessman to give him any work before establishing his rate.

'Two hundred and fifty pounds an hour.' I gave him my details and then shot out of his office as quickly as I could, just in case the clock tipped into another half hour.

Later that evening, and whilst H began to surge within, I sat back in the armchair, put my feet up on the handily placed stack of Radio Times and reviewed the day. I was pleased with my achievements. Not only was I well on my way to ticking off the first task on the list, I had added a whole new dimension to my system.

I realised that Boole's laws of thought would allow me to identify the demand in a job for a certain level of logic. On the other side of the matching coin I could identify a person's capability to think in this way. As the demand for different types of logic varied according to the timescale over which decisions play out, this linked to my ideas about the nature of time. I stretched, puffed out my chest and mused, *Who would have thought that I could have come up with a system that is based on a philosophy! Wow. More than that. Based on the nature of time. More than that, based on mathematics.*

I also thought about Ramdeep's quote for making an online version of my matching process and realised that no one was going to give me three million smackers to test the concept. *No, I would sell the system for other uses first - like building healthy organisations with the minimum of hierarchy, before turning to the big opportunity. But even so*, I thought, *the potential is vast.*

Coaching

With my complete management system even more complete, I spent pretty much of the next week in front of a mirror perfecting my sales pitch to the Angels. After the usual introductions, it went something like this: 'We provide a 5D world that provides the necessary measures for creating efficient organisations. Understanding a five-dimensional world, three spatial and two time related, leads to the ability to measure and understand prime aspects of human behaviour that have, until now, been assumed to be non-measurable.' I knew this pitch wasn't for the common man: I was planning to attract the best and brightest – the change makers, rain-makers, thought leaders, thinkers outside the box.

If that didn't pique their interest nothing much would.

After that, my presentation put forward the argument for ditching pop psychology and building a new approach based on the insight that there are two dimensions of time. By way of a triumphant finish, I planned to end with, 'Make a dynamic link between human assets and profit.'

You see how clever all this was! Believe me, I felt pretty smug. However, I had a nagging doubt about how well I came over and realised that I needed to trial the presentation on someone before the big day. Despite my misgivings about the man, I decided to contact Nicholas De'Ath again to arrange a time to rehearse my presentation in front of him. After all, he called himself a coach to those appearing on reality TV, and I had signed a contract.

In my then upbeat mood, I considered that no time was like the present, changed out of my pyjamas, grabbed a bag, and left the flat. It was only when I was half way down the stairs that I realised I hadn't arranged an appointment. *Never mind*, I thought, *be positive*.

By the communal front door of the house, I picked up a letter addressed to Bruce, my complaining neighbour and popped it into my pocket.

During the journey, I noticed a postal-worker wearing shorts and a sleeveless jumper standing nearby the doors of the tube carriage. This reminded me of my postman who wore a similar outfit in all seasons. When did this crazy trend start? Getting up at three in the morning must be bad enough, why compound that with freezing your cods off? Sorry, I have gone off-piste and no, that is not one of the main existential questions I want your help to answer.

This train of thought reminded me that I'd picked up an item of Bruce's post. I took the letter out of my pocket and opened it. If I'd hoped to find some titbit that I could hold against him if he got shirty with me again about my early morning meanderings, I was sadly disappointed. The letter announced that Bruce had been especially chosen to receive eight thousand pounds of credit and it contained a mocked-up credit card designed to help the recipient visualise the offer. Then, I began to wonder, *what would I do if this were a real card. How could I use it if I didn't have the PIN?* Would I have used Bruce's card? Admittedly, I was low on funds but, really, who do you think I am!

I again arrived at Canary Wharf and emerged into one of the great powerhouses of free-enterprise. *These wealth creators,* I thought, *aren't that bad after all, especially as they were going to help me become rich.*

102

This time, I found my way to 66b North Colonnade in no time at all. I was beginning to feel jittery and nervous and increasingly annoyed with myself, because in my haste I had forgotten to take H before leaving home. However, when I entered and saw The Raven sitting at the reception desk, I was reassured and immediately felt calmer. Again, she looked amazing. The air was motionless in the foyer, but it seemed like a wind was slightly ruffling her lustrous hair. I noticed signs of a deep décolletage between the top button of her shimmering, black blouse and her feathery scarf. I hoped Nicholas only had appointments later in the day, so that I could spend time in her company.

The Raven recognised me and smiled. 'Ah Mr. Findler, two, o' clock, Mr. De'Ath is ready to see you.'

'Is he?' Obviously, that caught me off guard, since I had come on a whim, but I was also pleased that positive thinking had brought results.

'Oh, yes. Walk this way.' I found myself acting the fool by trying, unsuccessfully, to emulate her slight waddle as I walked in her wake. I breathed in her scent, it was definitely natural, not flowery and in fact like nothing I'd smelt before. I detected hints of moss and resinous pine. We followed the same route through the offices as before. There were no noises from the HR Department, but the photocopiers in Investments seemed, if anything, even louder than before.

This time, I didn't have to wait in the vestibule but was shown directly into Nicholas De'Ath's office. I found him looking at something Kairos, the Time Manager, was pointing to on a laptop computer. In the gloom of the office the glow from the screen uplit his face, accentuating the paleness of his complexion and the redness of his lips, so emphasising the diabolical aspects of his features. Nicholas looked up and addressed me. 'It's unbelievable what some people put on social medium.'

'Media.' Kairos corrected.

'That's what I said. This is the most amazing thing ever. If only I'd invented it. There is such opportunity for mischief. Now, welcome William, what can I do for you?' Before I was able to answer, he ushered me to the settee and ordered a cup of tea, which The Raven went off to fetch. Nicholas watched her retreat through the double doors.

'Have you noticed how shapely Corvid's legs are?' So that was her name. Of course I had, but felt that it was inappropriate to comment – such blatant sexism. I was about to point out that referring to how pretty or otherwise a woman is was actually illegal but Nicholas continued, 'How are the preparations going? Have you a presentation that'll knock the Angels dead?'

'Yes, as a matter of fact I do. I am hoping you could critique it for me.'

'Oh indeed. Pretend I'm an Angel; give me your pitch. Try it out on me.'

By this time I didn't feel like pitching at all. In fact, I was feeling increasingly sick, but I knew that I needed to practise. So, despite feeling light headed, I got up and went towards the desk and turned back to face him. Nicholas struck the pose of a hard-bitten Angel. Kairos had sat himself down next to him on the sofa and looked

104

like he was thinking about bacon sandwiches or something equally banal. *Role-play here we come,* I thought, trying to motivate myself.

Where to start? OK, let's begin with the money, I thought and then launched in. 'My name is William Taylor Findler and I am the Founder and CEO of Dynamic Link. I'm here to ask for an investment of one hundred thousand pounds in exchange for a twenty percent stake in my business.' I wasn't sure I sounded confident.

'Good. Go on.' I was heartened by Nicholas' encouragement.

'I started Dynamic Link over two years ago because there is a huge need in the market.'

'For?'

'For... an integrated system.'

'Yes...'

'Yes... An integrated system with an underlying philosophy.'

'And...'

'And... a philosophy that recognises two dimensions of time.'

I was heartened to see Kairos nodding his head but disappointed that Nicholas had started to fiddle with his mobile phone. I paused and it took some time before, drawn by the silence, he lifted his head slightly and announced, 'I hate these things, but they can be useful. How about this App? It allows you to find your mobile if you lose it.'

'Does it?' I said in as a bored voice as I could muster.

'But, there is a fatal flaw; you actually need to have your phone in your hand to use the App. I wonder if they could invent an App that helps locate glasses. That, I would pay for.'

Nicholas slid off his spectacles and put them on the coffee table. I felt annoyed. 'Didn't you listen to my pitch?'

'Oh, was that what it was?'

'Well, I hadn't got to the point of being specific.'

'Really, I'd never have guessed.' I was offended by the ironic tone.

'You have to understand what the proposal rests on. Without that, I will just sound like every other management consultant pushing the latest fad.'

'Possibly, but you don't need to tell me about time, I've experienced far too much of it.'

'Really?'

'Oh he certainly has.' Chipped in Kairos. Nicholas

ignored him.

'Really! But that's another story. I see I have a lot to teach you.'

'In what way?'

'You need to convey the benefits.'

'Yes, I know.'

I felt myself stiffen and the throb of blood in my temples; I had read all the books and didn't need to be told the difference between a feature and a benefit. In a monotonous, whiny voice, I continued, 'How do I speed up the process, improve productivity, reduce costs or increase quality.' I gave a yawn, 'Is that what you mean by a benefit?'

'No.'

'No!' My eyes widened.

'No. You have to appeal to what really motivates people. And what motivates these Angels is bound to be getting one over on their fellow investors, or showing the world how clever they are, or simply becoming the wealthiest of the wealthy.'

'And how do you do that?'

'Simple. It is brush.' In elongating the last word so that it sounded like berrrush, Nicholas had caused his face to produce a beaming smile and his white teeth sparkled as if they were starring in a toothpaste advert.

'Brush; is that an acronym?'

'Ta, ta, ta, no not at all. Try to say it.' I did and I have to say that with a little practise it had the effect of creating a beam of a smile, almost to order.

Nicholas got out of his seat and indicated that we should exchange places. Then, pretending to come in front of a camera, he mouthed an elongated 'Brush', revealed his sparkling teeth and, setting his mesmerising gaze directly at me, he said. 'My name is William and I'm the Chief Executive and Founder of Dynamic Link. Before telling you more about my company and myself, can I ask you a question? At the end of your allotted time, what would you like to be remembered for?'

Nicholas looked at me directly as if I was one of the Angels and said, 'Really look each of them in the eye.' I could not avert my gaze. 'Would you like to be so rich your family and their heirs will live in the utmost luxury?' He paused as if moving his attention to another Angel, 'Or would you like to establish a foundation that achieves the end of world-poverty?' I could imagine two of the Angels specifically drooling over such prospects. These were rhetorical questions and Nicholas continued in his seductive tone, 'Dynamic Link can make any of your dreams come true, but you need to be far braver and more imaginative than ever before.'

Nicholas again addressed me, 'Once you have piqued their interest, take them back to where they are now.' He returned to presenter mode, 'Of course, you will all be remembered as wise investors in small start-ups, but what if your legacy was more profound; in fact, much, much more important? Would you like your future to be transformed out of all recognition?' I wanted to say, 'Yes, transformed,' but managed to keep quiet. Nicholas continued. 'As an investor, you are a kind of time traveller; skilled at looking through your window into the future, you pull value into the present. But this time, instead of a clear window, I want you to look into the future through a semi-transparent membrane. Not everything will be as clear as you would like it to be, but put your hand through it in any case. What you take from the future and pull into the present will I guarantee be of huge value.'

Despite the fact that watching Angels always made me angry, I was hooked on the show and, as an avid viewer, I knew the celebrity investors invariably looked to trip-up entrepreneurs at the first opportunity. So, I interrupted Nicholas with a tricky, angel-type question, saying, 'What have time travellers got to do with it?' Nicholas looked at me with his cruel eye and I shuddered.

'As a time traveller, or for those without imagination, William, as an investor you are always asking, if I invest will this happen or won't it? These questions are sometimes easy to answer and sometimes difficult without further work and consideration. Indeed, sometimes they are impossible to answer in advance. You know that the more that is certain, the lower the element of risk and consequently the lower the reward. In contrast, I am offering huge potential. Just because you cannot know everything in advance, don't let that stop you coming on this marvellous journey. Are you ready? Are you brave enough?'

I couldn't help saying out loud, 'I'm brave enough.' I swear, that if I'd had the money to invest, I would have given it to him right there and then. Instead, I gave a short, appreciative clap. 'Thank you.' Nicholas said and bowed slightly, 'I'm humbled. Remember, don't give them too much detail in the pitch. Concentrate on selling the benefits that appeal to each investor's own nature, and, of course; Brush,' He repeated the last word in its exaggerated form and his face again lit up before he added, 'and don't go on about time.'

Talking of time, I considered that it was high time for the tea to arrive, but when I looked down, I saw that a tray with a teapot, milk jug and cups and saucers sat on top of the coffee table. I noticed that Kairos held a half-full cup in his hand and belatedly, I poured myself one.

Nicholas rested against his desk and looked over at me before asking, 'Let's cut to the chase, what is your unique selling point?' As, you will have gathered from the diary entries I've shared with you, I had struggled with identifying this. Certainly, the outputs were the same ones that any other HR consultant would be peddling, for example; better recruitment, job profiling and efficient design. I needed to find something that was really different and would set Dynamic Link apart from run-of-the-mill competitors.

Its uniqueness lay in the integrated nature of the methodology but this was difficult to encapsulate in a few words. I collected my thoughts and answered Nicholas' question with as much confidence as I could muster. 'It is an integrated management system based on a philosophy that appreciates time, uncertainty and the nature of being.'

'What did I just say about not going on about time?' Nicholas sounded quite sharp, but I wasn't going to be side-tracked.

'We look at the complexity of the decision-making environment, the contribution of the job and the level of an individual's logic that they apply to make sense of their situation.'

'What are you talking about? And when you talk of 'we', to whom do you refer?'

'Well it's just me... My integrated management system, I mean my 3C Taxonomy...'

'Taxonomy! Do you think that helps?' Nicholas sounded irritated but two could play at that game.

'Ok, for those with a less extensive lexicon, I have invented a ruler that makes important connections.'

'What has a ruler got to do with it?'

'Let me start again from a different angle. George Boole, the famous mathematician...'

'Never heard of him.'

'Well, he describes four logical types of proposition; 'or-or', 'and-and', 'if-then' and 'if and only if', depending on the hypothesised truth or falsity of their elementary statement.'

At this point Kairos, who had been sitting quietly, intervened. Actually, I thought he had gone to sleep, but he said, 'Brilliant, old boy. I love it. Very profound. May I take this one step further?'

'He is going to in any case.' Nicholas shrugged and Kairos continued.

'What if these four logical types are also demonstrable in the animal kingdom? This would mean that all living creatures use the same logic at different levels of abstraction, whether or not they are capable of expressing their thoughts in language.'

'I knew it!' Nicholas snorted, 'The only person who will understand what you're talking about will be Kairos. Do you want him to be your target market?'

'No.' I was adamant about that.

'Then go home and work out what you practically offer the customer.' Nicholas' tone was abrupt.

Our conversation was cut short by a bleep and Nicholas dug a mobile phone out of his pocket. He looked at it and then asked Kairos, 'Battery low, how do I change it?'

'You don't change it, you plug it into your computer with the USB cable.'

'USB?' Kairos got up, took the phone from Nicholas and attached it to a loose cable on the desk. I considered this to be rather strange, as even I knew how to recharge a mobile phone.

We didn't resume our conversation as, unannounced, Corvid entered the office and began clearing away the teacups, clearly signifying the end of the meeting. To emphasise this, Nicholas De'Ath added, 'Kairos will show you out.'

112

The long and winding walk back to the foyer provided an opportunity for a lengthy conversation with Kairos who started with, 'I really liked the presentation.' His opening words raised my spirits, 'So few people appreciate the importance of time. If they do, they simply equate it with money. In the space-time dimension, time is the most fundamental element. Time is like the landscape that rivers flow down, finding as they do the easiest path to eventual rest.'

'Eventual rest?' I responded. Kairos swung his fob watch around on its chain and, as he did so, it seemed to slow in its rotation.

'Time is the landscape that gravity flows down to its resting place and, as it flows, time itself slows down. Few people fully appreciate how important time is. It's about time, excuse the pun, for time to be brought into the realms of management science.' Even I hadn't considered the space-time dimension as relevant. Interesting it might be, but I had no intention of adding this to my 3C model. Even I knew this would be business suicide.

Back on the street I felt empty. In fact, I was both ravenous and thirsty. I looked at my watch and was surprised that it was just coming up to two o'clock. I thought, *If I'm quick I can grab a bite at the wine bar.* I hastened there and was disappointed to find it was again packed with powerful predators. The London Aquarium doesn't have as many big fish as were in there and most of them were showing nasty, pointed teeth. I had to sit closer than I wanted to a man whose spiky hair reminded me of a dangerously poisonous Puffer Fish. He shouted into his phone, 'Collateralised debt obligation, I don't know what it is, but buy.' I was heartened and thought, *People seem prepared to buy anything, sales might not be as hard as all that.*

I ordered a Prosecco with a vodka chaser and sat back to reflect on the strange meeting. In particular, I remembered Nicholas' advice to find something practical to present to the Angels, *Some Goddamn stupid App, no doubt*, I assumed.

I was becoming irritated by the Puffer regularly shouting into his phone. Luckily, he soon got up to leave and, as he picked up his jacket, a card slipped to the floor. He didn't notice and I deftly covered it with my right foot. A minute or two after he left I retrieved the card, which turned out to be a coveted Barclays Bank platinum debit card. I was once the proud owner of such a card and knew Fishy must have an income of more than sixty thousand pounds per annum to qualify for one. In which case, he might not miss a little money going to a good cause, namely myself. I returned to my earlier thought about how to use a debit or credit card without a PIN number and I realised I actually knew a man who would know about such things. As soon as I had quaffed my drinks I was off to see Leon at the Dog and Bottle.

Meeting the Angels

On the day of the filming I woke feeling jittery and nervous. Unusually for me, I had set my alarm for seven o'clock but ignored it when it rang and stayed hunkered down in bed contemplating the day ahead. Even the bedclothes seemed to be pressing down on me making it difficult to get going.

The big question was whether or not I should take any H. It was difficult to imagine making such an important presentation without her, my partner and supporter, but at the same time there were risks. H made me laid back and I knew I couldn't afford to be too spaced out. However, I also needed to control my nerves. Eventually, after gathering enough energy together to decant myself out of bed, I decided to take a small dose. So, I started the day with a coffee, a cigarette and half a syringe.

I didn't draw back the blinds in the kitchen or the heavy, bedroom curtains as the bright early morning light had become offensive to me. However, I knew what I wanted to wear and I picked my dark blue suit out of the wardrobe and laid it on the bed. Finding clean underwear and an ironed shirt proved more difficult.

In the end, I scraped together clean socks and underpants after rooting through my chest of drawers, but I had to make do with a crumpled shirt. I stood in front of the mirror in my bedroom and realised that the shirt really was unacceptably creased. Despite the weather forecast predicting a scorching day ahead, I pulled on a cardigan to cover the shirt's rumpled appearance. I considered I looked rather 'arty' but wondered if it made me look too much like the host of the programme, David Evans. To differentiate our styles, I added a rather snazzy cravat, also found in my chest of drawers.

Suited and booted, I looked again at the letter from ITM that provided instructions for the day. I found I was due to be at their studio in the City at twelve o'clock, which was surprising as the last time I read the letter I was sure it said two o'clock. *How can I start a global brand*, I thought, *and manage such details?* A PA would be the first investment I made after winning backing from one of the Angels. I even considered offering Corvid a job.

The earlier start meant that I only had a short while to review my presentation. Nevertheless, I needed to wait for the post as I had ordered some promotional material to hand out. Delivery was promised for that morning and I decided to postpone my departure until the last minute.

Strangely, the filming was going to be done at 666 North Colonnade, near to Nicholas De'Ath's offices. I wondered whether the man himself could just stroll in but then understood this was unlikely, as he would have needed a pass or something. Not that I considered I actually needed any coaching. *In any case, I thought, I've probably seen the last of the strange character now that he knows I'm broke.*

I ran through the figures in the business plan. I didn't know how the Angels calculated the value of companies, but they never put that much of their own money in for the large percentage of business shares they demanded. Therefore, I decided that the top-of-my-head request I'd made to Nicholas De'Ath should stand. I was sure I could easily justify asking for a lot more once they understood the transformatory nature of my ideas.

116

I practised in front of the mirror. Remembering what Nicholas De'Ath had told me, I ran through the ideas about time travellers looking through windows and pulling value from the future. 'Brush,' I mouthed and was pleased with the effect, as I too could produce a winning smile on demand. 'I am William, I'm here to take you on a fabulous journey. Normally, as sound investors, you want to have all the details laid out in front of you, but I'm asking you to take a risk, to be a real entrepreneur and I guarantee that you will reap a great reward.' I was very happy with this opening. It sounded like a winning offer and I was confident and in control.

Next, I double-checked that I'd put my overhead presentation slides into the bag I was taking with me to the filming session. I'd given a lot of thought to what method I should use to present my ideas and had decided a low-tech approach was probably best. I'd had problems in the past with incompatibilities between floppy disks or those new-fangled memory sticks and unfamiliar computers. It was comforting to know I could get out the acetate slides without any fear that technology would scupper the presentation.

At ten-thirty the parcel still hadn't arrived and I was beginning to get nervous. I didn't want to rush and get all hot and bothered before the filming even started. Therefore, I decided to leave without the promotional material and made my way to the front door. I noticed another letter addressed to me in Bruce's handwriting propped up on the hall table and stuffed this in my pocket before leaving the house. As I did so a glum-looking man appeared and, wordlessly, thrust a box into my hand together with a delivery note on a clipboard for my signature. He accepted my illegible scrawl without comment and turned and walked away. I spoke to the courier's departing back in an American drawl, 'Have a nice day now.' At least my sarcasm elicited a grunted reply and, clutching the newly arrived box together with my briefcase, I headed off towards the station. Spitefully, I wished I had just signed for something expensive bought by Bruce but was nevertheless happy that my promotional material had actually arrived.

The heat of the day hit me as I walked to the station and it seemed like there was no air to breathe. I wondered whether I should go back and take off my cardigan but realised that there was not enough time and pressed on. As I hurried on my way, I passed a house being renovated and heard a workman's radio blaring out the prattle of some DJ. 'Eighty-one degrees downtown today.' Downtown! From where the hell was he broadcasting? I had come to detest the faux bonhomie of all presenters and this reaffirmed my resolve to boycott both TV and radio whenever possible.

While sitting on an almost unbearably stuffy tube train, I read the note from Bruce. This time he threatened me with the police if I didn't stop walking around and playing ABBA records in the early hours. I pondered on whether there is a law against walking about in your own house? In any case, I didn't believe what he said about music. He must be hallucinating as I rarely played my records. However, I resolved to buy him a set of earplugs once I had secured the backing of one of the Angels, and he would have to put up with any extraneous noise until I was able to jump in the Jag and head-off to my Georgian villa in St John's Wood.

A broken-down train at Euston and the resulting delay meant I arrived at Canary Wharf at twelve-fifteen. It was lucky that I knew where the filming was taking place. I set off as fast as I could. The sun was so fierce that its violence bruised the pavements but despite the heat, I hurried on.

When I reported at the reception desk for 666 North Colonnade, I was met with a curt, 'You're late,' from a young lady carrying a clipboard. She escorted me into the lift and pressed the button for the 18th floor. I thought that, given the appropriateness of the location, I would take the opportunity to try out my elevator pitch. She had two disks of silver, the size of ten pence pieces, embedded in elongated earlobes, so I broke the ice by commenting, 'Funny place to keep your small change.' She didn't respond to my quip, and in any case, we arrived at the 18th floor before I had a chance to introduce Dynamic Link. Proof, if it was ever needed, that the elevator pitch is just a figment of a marketeer's imagination.

She ushered me into a conference room to join a group of people sitting in a semi-circle around a woman I took to be a Production Assistant of some kind, power dressed in Chanel-style jacket and pencil thin trousers. She had the same ferociously cut hairdo as that sported by Susan and I immediately assumed she would have a similarly short fuse in the temper department. In confirmation of this, she broke off in mid-sentence, tapped her watch and pointedly said that good timekeeping was critical to the successful completion of the shoot.

I quickly sat down with the rest of the audience and she restarted her interrupted monologue. If timekeeping was so critical, I wondered why she waffled on so much as she welcomed us and generally introduced the programme. She could easily and quickly have told us that they would start with filming us individually as part of some staged arrival of the entrepreneurs, and then we would just hang around in a 'Green Room' until called to make our presentation. That would have taken only a minute. Instead, she went on about who the Angels were and their particular interests, as if we had been randomly swept in off the street and none of us had ever seen the programme.

I let my mind wander and looked out of the window past the silver phalluses, erected to show the world the power of bankers, towards the ordinary London beyond. The heat made the scene shimmer. I found myself thinking back to when I was in Nicholas De'Ath's offices watching the computer keyboards, seemingly, automatically depressing themselves. It was as if I could hear his voice saying, 'We supply the noughts and the bankers keep on tap, tap, tapping.' Then, in my mind's eye, the buildings opposite began to expand as if they had middle age spread. As they grew fatter and fatter, I could hear Nicholas singing, 'Debt, glorious debt.' It was so real I actually thought that it was happening, and I could only dispel the image by vigorously shaking my head.

I was brought back to reality by the power suit asking, 'You disagree?' She looked in my direction and my face flushed with embarrassment as if I had been caught napping in class.

'Apologies, I didn't quite catch what you said.' I mumbled.

'Let me repeat myself; if the Angels decline to invest, you, the entrepreneurs, must not argue. You must say, thanks for the opportunity to pitch.' I didn't want to start thinking about the possibility of such a negative outcome. Instead, I visualised shaking their hands, after they decided, all four of them, to invest in my business.

At the end of the welcome and introduction session, the woman said, 'Guys, I will soon be bringing in the Angels. Feel free to ask them any questions.' Instead of formulating any questions, I was about to correct her appalling sexist attitude. Didn't she know there were women in the room?' Guys! However, I restrained myself and thought, *It's probably a collective noun commonly used in the gender bending media.*

We were kept hanging around for five minutes or so, before the Angels were ushered into the room, led by the host of the show, David Evans - strange, as I hadn't heard a helicopter arriving. Do I need to describe these people to you? No. I don't think so; you have undoubtedly seen them on TV. I must say, though, John Lewis looked taller than I had expected, Delores Headon was shorter and stouter and Jimmy Bannaman more ill-tempered looking. On reflection, that was how he always looked on TV, like he wanted to pick a fight with anyone who spoke to him. There was also a new guy, of Chinese extraction, small but thick set, wearing a linen suit. David Evans's campness was more pronounced in the flesh than I remembered from his TV appearances. I noticed that he was wearing a cravat and wondered whether or not to take mine off, as I didn't want to look like I was imitating him. In the end, I decided that my cravat was actually much classier and left it on.

The celebrities introduced themselves and I obviously misheard the name of the new Angel as I thought he said, 'So Sue Me'. I smiled because it seemed to sum up the spirit of the new-age entrepreneur. All of the Angels made a point of reassuring us that they would listen carefully to our proposals and, as long as we had done our homework, especially on the numbers, they would be kind and helpful. I, for one, was put at ease and relaxed back in my chair, hands behind my head.

A trolley of hot drinks and biscuits was wheeled into the room, but before I could help myself to a welcome cup of tea, I was accosted by a young man, wearing tight jeans and a V-neck T-shirt. He introduced himself as the Stage Manager and said, 'Bill, the first shooting…' I had to interrupt him. Today was about becoming famous, and I wanted to make sure of being known by my proper name.

'It's William.'

'Will, the first shooting will be you arriving at the offices by bike.'

'By bike!'

'Yes, by bike.'

'Whatever for?'

'Didn't you listen to the briefing?'

'I must have missed that bit.'

'OK. It's to create dramatic, rags to riches, aspect to your story. Let's hope you will be leaving in the helicopter.'

The Stage Manager then told me to collect my things and showed me back down to the ground floor and then out into the street. It was odd to see large lights set up, even in the bright sunshine, and cameras ready for action. A dodgy old racing bike was wheeled over to me, and I secured my parcel and case to the rusty rack above the rear wheel using a bungee cord. The Stage Manager then told me to simply get on the bike, ride down the road a short way, then turn and ride back, parking the bike against a lamp post, which was clearly a stage prop as it had no lamp on the top.

Despite it being such an obvious put up stunt, and incredibly hot out on the street to boot, I would normally have welcomed the activity as I had had a similar bike in my teens. Now though, I felt uneasy. H was good and kind, but she had affected my sense of balance. Therefore, I tried to dissuade the Stage Manager from the idea and suggested that I just push it along the street and then lock it to the lamppost. But, he was intent on his mission, so I reluctantly mounted the trusty steed and, with a few violent wobbles, set off down the road, narrowly avoiding being run over by a black taxi. Actually, once underway, I did enjoy the experience. The agitated air cooled me down and I was transported back to my teenage years when I used to spend days tootling off into the countryside on my bike.

I hadn't intended to go far, but when I turned around I could hardly make out the Stage Manager in the distance. However, I realised that he was beckoning me back, and I resolved to show them I was a dynamic entrepreneur, full of vim and vigour. I managed to put on quite a spurt and was travelling at a fair lick of speed when I hit the brakes. Belying the bicycle's shabby appearance, its brakes were far more responsive than those on my old bike. The back wheel slewed across the road whilst I put one foot down to the ground like a motorcycle speedway champion. Pretending that I had meant this to happen, I calmly parked and secured the bike against the lamp post and walked away, very much satisfied with my spectacular entrance. After basking in glory for a moment, I remembered I had left my parcel and case tied to the rack and had to rush back to get it. I heard the Stage Manager say, 'Priceless.'

He must have been impressed too.

TV Humiliation

All in all, I felt that the build-up to the presentation had gone well enough. However, the same cannot be said for the pitch itself.

The downside of exerting myself outside in the heat was that back in the office, I started to perspire profusely. I asked a bored looking adolescent, carrying the ubiquitous clipboard, if he could arrange for the air-conditioning to be turned on or set lower and he scurried off, never to be seen again. That is the youth of today. All have a nice day to your face, but putting two fingers up behind your back.

The Green Room, which I found out is TV-speak for nothing more than a waiting room, was a converted conference room furnished with a few comfortable chairs and two large TV monitors. One of the monitors showed the Angels sitting behind a huge desk in the boardroom. Presumably, the other was to focus on an entrepreneur pitching his or her idea. The running order for the show was posted on a large board on a tripod stand near the monitors. I was disappointed that I was scheduled to appear in the middle of the programme as I would have liked to have been first on then, basking in the knowledge of my future being secure, I could have sat back and enjoyed watching the others give their presentations on the TV monitor.

Pre-presentation nerves seemed to get the better of me, and I found myself walking around the room excitedly introducing myself to the other entrepreneurs.

The first person I talked to was a lady called Harriet who, whilst tall and slim, benefitted from an ample bosom with plenty of cleavage on show. I immediately looked down into the softness of

125

her womanly curves and was reminded of H's gentle caress, but I must have looked too obviously and for too long as she pointedly pulled her blouse together.

It turned out that Harriet was the owner of King Tee Shirts. She told me that she had started her business on a market stall, had expanded into department store concessions and was now looking to go global. Who wasn't? She was accompanied by a number of attractive young women who would presumably model the T-shirts. It was inevitable that John Lewis would flirt with them, but I didn't see him investing in T-shirts.

There was another woman who was rather large and went by the name of Chlamydia (well, it sounded something like that). She was looking for investment in her handmade soap business, the unique selling point of which was that it was made from charcoal. Surprisingly, she had arrived looking less than perfectly groomed, and when she showed me one of her sample soaps I was less than impressed with the state of her fingers. Her nails were cracked and dirt was ingrained under them. Soaper Woman, as I decided to nickname her, was, it seemed, going to present on her own.

There were a few other no-hopers pretending that their business idea was the next big thing. Reggie, a big-cheeked man with a beaming smile, wearing dreadlocks, had brought along a sauce made from his grandmother's old recipe. What a joke! If, for some bizarre reason, the Angels didn't invest in Dynamic Link, I consoled myself with the idea that I'd bring a jar of Gran's chutney next time to make my fortune. Some people!

The daftest idea was for an egg boiler. The dunderhead inventor thought people would spend money on his contraption, which cooked the eggs in steam generated from a small amount of added water and made a loud noise once the water had boiled away. Clearly, he was targeting people who didn't own a saucepan and couldn't boil a kettle.

After a while, the chitchat about the products switched to being about the Angels. Reggie asked me which Angel I wanted as an investor and, as I didn't like Delores Headon or Jimmy Bannaman, I said I wanted John Lewis. Although, in reality, I wasn't keen on him either.

The discussion was interrupted when the Stage Manager came in carrying a large pink crash helmet. He ushered Egg Man away, and I guessed that the helmet was a prop for the arrival of the presenter - presumably on a motorcycle. The directors were obviously trying to make the poor sod look like a giant egg. I was pleased, as it would make my arrival at the venue look sensible in comparison.

Shortly afterwards, I sat down, to rest for a while, on one of the few comfortable chairs available in the Green Room. I hadn't really appreciated that shooting an episode of Angels involved so much hanging around. It was quite tiring. I quickly slipped into a micro-sleep but was disturbed by the arrival of a loud German who declared, 'Zat was fun!' He was wearing a Bavarian style jacket, emphasising his origins. I made the mistake of asking him, 'Vot Vos,' and he latched on to me. The man introduced himself as Otto and said that he had just been filmed getting out of a classic Mercedes in front of the office. I immediately wondered why I had been forced to arrive by pushbike but kept this piece of information to myself.

Otto explained that he was the owner of Ze Bierkeller in Camden and I smiled, as I knew the place. This was a recent addition to the crowded restaurant/pub/wine bar market in my area. I had considered going in, but only because it offered a potential refuge away from the madding crowd. Whenever I passed the place, it was completely deserted. Otto didn't ask me anything about my business and the conversation soon petered out. At this point, he wandered off but not before cheerily saying, 'Today Camden, tomorrow ze vorld.' *You don't need an investor*, I thought, *you need your head examined.*

Eventually the presentations started and the first into the boardroom was Harriet, trailed by the, admittedly, good-looking girls wearing hot pants with their T-shirts covered by silk shawls. Harriet, who had developed a husky and theatrical voice since I had spoken with her, proved to be a confident presenter, and she told the story of her rise from market stallholder to niche retailer in an interesting way.

John Lewis was the first to introduce himself - he always is when there are pretty girls and cleavage on show – and asked Harriet what she put her success down to. I thought that Harriet had started to ramble when she talked about how the French Connection, a struggling fashion label, had found global fame and fortune when it changed its brand to FCUK. She said that there was money in sexual referencing. This was the prompt for the girls to slip off their silk shawls to reveal that words were emblazoned across the fronts of their T-shirts. On each of them the word King' had three spaces before it, as in ---King, with a word after it. Clearly, Jimmy Bannaman thought the slogans were amusing as a rare smile suddenly cracked his normally aggressive looking mug and he said, 'King Ada, I love it! And King 'ell. Very funny.' John Lewis chipped in with, 'King Brill, and King Marvellous. What about a T-shirt with King Naff on it?' Delores Headon, who had clearly missed the point, asked, 'What about King Kong?' John Lewis put her right by telling her she was effing thick.

New Guy quizzed the entrepreneur on the costs of the product, the selling price and margins. Harriet gave confident replies and when Jimmy Bannaman asked her about the growth projections she gave an equally clear answer. Unexpectedly, both New Guy and John Lewis made investment offers and, after a little bit of negotiation, they settled on an amicable joint venture. Typically, the miserly Angels beat poor Harriet down and, in the end, she received a pittance for giving away sixty percent of her business. Nevertheless, I considered this all augured well. The Angels were in a good mood, and if they were soft enough to back T-shirts they were bound to go with my proposal.

When Harriet and her models reappeared in the Green Room, they were clearly over the moon and generally milled about, getting in the way of the monitor so that I had difficulty following Soaper Woman's presentation. She was very nervous and large patches of sweat had appeared under her armpits, which even I understood was not a good look for someone selling soap. In fact, it was soon clear that she wasn't going to get any backing when the Angels were encouraged to wash their hands with the charcoal soap but were left with a nasty black residue all over their hands.

As the time approached for my own presentation, I felt both jittery and sleepy at the same time. My small dose of H had worn off and, increasingly, I was feeling I couldn't go on without a top up. However, I was strong willed and resisted the urge. Also, it helped that I hadn't actually brought any supplies with me.

129

The next candidate to face the Angels was the owner of Ze Bierkeller. As if he wasn't already obviously German, he had at some point swapped his trousers for a pair of lederhosen. I expected him to be treated with scorn, or even thrown out, as soon as he was asked to provide details of current revenues for his restaurant. To give him his due though, Otto made a confident presentation. The main gist of this was that in Germany alone four out of ten people regularly went to a bierkeller. As Germany was the powerhouse of Europe, he argued, it was only a matter of time before the Brits would follow suit. Confident he might have been, but I was looking forward to the Angels reminding him that German cuisine was the most boring of any nation in the world, which might explain why Ze Bierkeller remained virtually empty every night.

I stopped looking at the monitor when the Green Room became true to its name, being suddenly suffused with a chlorophyll hue. Then I saw Nicholas De'Ath. He was wearing his familiar suit and the strange light seemed to be emanating from the dollar green pinstripes. Nicholas was in deep conversation with the Stage Manager who said, 'For the last time, you are not down to present.' With a serene look on his face, Nicholas walked over to the schedule posted on the board.

'Look here, I am the last to go on.' Nicholas pointed to the board. The Stage Manager squinted at the notice then at his clipboard, made a grunting noise and walked off.

I stood up and Nicholas came over to talk to me as if he was greeting an old friend. 'William, I hope you are ready and have practised saying berrushhh. It's the key to success.' I felt confident but surprised that Nicholas was also presenting.

130

'What's this show got to do with debt?' I asked.

'Are you worried I am diversifying my business too much? Don't worry, this is just for fun. Dealing with noughts all day is as much fun as a cat has playing with a dead mouse and I need a different challenge sometimes. Now, back to you. What are you going to ask for?'

'Hundred thousand.'

'Ask for more. You know you're worth it.'

My conversation was cut short by the return of Otto to the Green Room, fist-pumping the air.

The Stage Manager returned to the room. After looking very oddly at Nicholas, he came over and curtly told me it was my turn to present and led the way to a smart reception area that adjoined the boardroom. I had hardly sat down when the phone rang and the receptionist who answered it advised me that the Angels were now ready to see me. I turned to her and, as I think I had been instructed, said, 'Thank you for the opportunity.'

My heart pounded as I pulled one of the boardroom's double doors open to go inside, but it had a very fierce closing mechanism that trapped my trailing arm, leaving the box and briefcase I was carrying on the wrong side of the doors. New Guy kindly got up to help me through and I immediately warmed to him.

The bright lights hit me as soon as I entered the boardroom. I was expecting the brightness but not the intense heat. I put my box and case down and loosened my cravat, which was already soggy with sweat. I wished I hadn't worn the cardigan, but it was too late to do anything about it. I had expected the place to be stuffed with cameramen and technicians, but the recording equipment must have somehow been hidden from view and remotely operated. To all intents and purposes, the Angels were on their own.

Annoyingly, Delores Headon was already tapping her immaculately glossed thumbnail against her little finger. I had identified this habit when watching previous series and found it thoroughly detestable.

Jimmy Bannaman sat behind the desk but leant forward resembling a Rottweiler being held on a tight leash.

I knew the format and stood on a marker facing the Angels' sullen faces. However, this was totally different from standing in front of the mirror at home and for a moment I was lost for words. Luckily, before the pregnant pause become too excruciating, I remembered what Nicholas had told me. However, my nerves caused 'Berrush' to come out aloud as 'Terrash.' This caused the Angels' expressions to turn quizzical. I thought it best to press on quickly and without explanation. 'Hello, I am William Taylor Findler and I am the flounder and Chief Executive Occifer of Dynamo Blink.' I sounded incredibly nervous and luckily something I had once read about controlling nerves in the presence of powerful people came to mind. Unfortunately, I looked at Delores Headon and, in imagining her without her clothes on, I felt sick as well as nervous.

The pregnant pause was back and this time it was broken by John Lewis saying, 'Bill, could you say a little more?'

'It's William.' I thought, *Let's start by getting the facts right*. The nerves lessened as I recollected the presentation Nicholas had given me, and my own rehearsal that morning. My mouth started again, and this time, at least, the words coming out sounded stronger and more confident, even if I was not quite in control of the content. 'I am going to take you space cadets on a long road. Let's pretend we're on a bus together. Instead of nice clean windows to look out of, ours will be semi-permeable membranes and you have to put your hands through them.'

I, for one, was now looking out of an opaque window. It was like a windscreen in front of me had suddenly fogged. 'Why?' A disembodied voice asked.

'Why?' I repeated the question but was no longer sure why I wanted them to put their hands out of the window.

'Yes, why?'

'Why, because you will be looking at the future.'

'And?'

'And?' I tried to remember what Nicholas had said to me.

'Yes, and...'

'Yes, and you will be looking out onto fields of debt,' I thought of adding, *that smell of shit*, but stopped myself. I had really lost the thread.

There was a terribly long pause. I wanted to say something but sweat had run into my eyes and was making it impossible for me to concentrate at all. Through a veil of tears, I heard New Guy's voice say, 'Ok, calm down, it can be difficult under the lights,' Then he asked, 'how much are you asking for and in return for what?' I heard Nicholas' voice in my head giving me his last piece of advice and confidently replied.

'I'm asking for one million pounds for a five percent stake in the company.' The tears cleared from my eyes, and I looked at what can only be described as an array of shocked faces. I nevertheless stood my ground.

'Well, we've never been asked for so much before for so little.' New Guy said and added, 'You must be very confident in your products. Can we have a look at them?'

'There aren't any products as such.'

'Really!'

'No, it's an integrated system. With this you can do many things?'

'Such as?'

'Improve things'

'Tell us more about the integrated system.'

This was my opportunity to knock 'em dead with the presentation, which I took out of my bag. However, I was disappointed to find there was no overhead projector and screen immediately to hand. Holding an acetate sheet in my hand, I told them I wanted to make

134

a presentation and John Lewis actually gave a deep belly laugh.

A voice sounded from a speaker, 'Cut', and the Production Assistant who had given the briefing walked in. John Lewis put up his hand as if at school and said in an ingratiating tone, 'Please Director, Billy needs a flipchart.' I was miffed that he made me sound like I needed to be excused so that I could have a wee. Over and above that, I was surprised by the revelation that the assistant was, in fact, the Director.

Turning to me, the Director rather curtly said, 'Didn't I ask you if you had any specific requirements?' I knew then I had been right about the bobbed haircut.

In the brief interlude, instead of thinking about how to get my presentation back on track I contemplated the effects of a few more senior executives in the media. I was uplifted by the idea that daytime fare on TV would no longer be a constant diet of snooker and darts. Then I beat myself up for losing focus.

The Director soon brought back a flip chart and pen, which I considered was better than nothing. The short break had, at least, helped me calm down and I was able to start again. On the chart I wrote in big, black letters, 'complexity', 'capability' and 'contribution' and then connected them with a circle. To summarise, I told them I had developed an integrated system that connects these three elements. I ended with, 'We make the dynamic link between human assets and profit.' Unfortunately, as my mouth had become extremely dry, the word assets came out as asses.

The Angels sat unblinking and I was about to ask whether they had any questions when New Guy broke the silence, 'Tell us more about what is behind this?' I was beginning to warm to him and wished I could remember his name as I was switching my allegiance from John Lewis to him. I heard the voice of Nicholas De'Ath in my head saying, 'Don't go on about time,' but ignored it.

I knew I wasn't following my script but this felt more natural. I was on home turf; I knew my stuff. My voice was strong and confident, 'Physicists locate their events within one dimension of time. Where time is concerned they only need to know how long an event actually takes. This is the axis of occurrence. The Greeks have a word for it – Chronos and its measurement is called chronometry. Chronometers measure the duration of events that have already taken place and have been recorded. However, (I deepened my voice as this was the crunch point) Chronos isn't how we ourselves experience time.' I spoke expansively. 'Within Chronos there is no present moment as the big hand of time continuously sweeps around the clock face of life. But, (I paused for effect) there is another axis of time – one that isn't moving anywhere. It surrounds us all. It envelops us.'

'Your time might be up right now, fella.' John Lewis interrupted.

'No, no, let me explain. In the living present expectations of the future greatly influence present reconstructions of the past whilst reconstructions are affecting expectations. The living present isn't linear; rather it is a circular interaction between the future and the past in the present. Understanding and appreciating a person's living present is key to identifying their capability and potential.'

136

'It certainly is circular. I feel I've been here for days.' I really had begun to despise John Lewis.

'No wait, one minute.' I retorted, but I had lost the discipline to bring my focus back to my business ideas and launched into what I remembered Kairos saying. 'No, this is important. This is where there's a disconnect between cause and effect. B does not follow A; the apple does not fall from the tree. This is where opportunities are. The future is what you imagine it to be.' I was just about to touch on the space-time dimension when Delores Headon, thankfully, intervened.

'I think the apple has fallen on your head… Tell us about the valuation, we have never had a start-up being valued at such a high amount.'

'Oh, that's easy. The market is worth twenty billion pounds and I only need one percent of the market for the company to be valued way above what I am asking for.' I might even have given her a wry smile to go along with the winning proposition.

Delores looked directly at me and her eyes narrowed as she said, 'If I'd been given a pound every time I've read this in a business plan or, we only need one percent of the Chinese market to be millionaires, I would be rich - I mean richer than I already am.'

'Delores, I'm not talking about going into China.' I countered.

'I know, I'm just saying…'

Clearly, Delores Headon had been going in the wrong direction and switched tack. 'So, how much revenue have you achieved so far?' She asked.

'I'm talking about potential revenue.'

'And real revenues?'

'You mean pounds, shillings and pence?' I asked.

'Britain went decimal in 1971.' It was that smart ass, John Lewis, again.

'In actual pounds and pence then... Nothing.' I had to be honest.

'How many customers have you got?' Jimmy Bannaman chipped in. With his Glaswegian accent he might as well have said, 'Ye snivelling Sassenach, how'd yooze like a kidney removed.' I felt weak at the knees.

'None.' I muttered.

I felt like a bloodied piece of meat just dropped into shark-infested waters. Delores Headon circled around menacingly. 'Do you own the Intellectual Property? She asked.

'Yes.' I replied without a great deal of confidence.

'Where's the paper to prove it?' I took hold of the pen and drew a copyright symbol on the chart.

'That is it. I'm told with that,' I said, pointing to the ©,

138

'people can't copy my work.' I am not sure if it was a collective moan or whether Delores was just a loud moaner.

I had nothing else to present to the Angels in terms of the business plan, but I remembered the promotional material I had brought with me. I managed to slice my finger opening the box but was pleased to be able to hand out the Dynamic Link baseball caps. John Lewis looked at the label, which he read out as, 'Child 6-11,' and placed the small cap on top of his head. The other Angels burst out laughing. If I hadn't felt so utterly mortified, I would have laughed too because it looked like a purple pimple on his big, fat bonce. Instead, I just wanted the lights to finally melt me into a sweaty puddle, which the cleaner could mop up.

Once the laughter had died down, John Lewis addressed me and said, 'I think you are barking up the wrong tree here, but you're clearly a man of style. With such sartorial elegance, you should start a fashion chain.' I stood upright, making myself visibly taller, but this only served to expose my solar plexus and John Lewis took aim. 'Yes, with those odd socks, you would make a killing.' I looked down at my feet and cursed myself for dressing in the dark.

Given my thorough humiliation, Delores Headon could have been kinder to me. Instead, she said, 'You are a financial and business imbecile. And for this reason, I'm out.'

'Up yours Delores.' I also gave her the finger knowing this would be cut.

Nicholas De'Ath Presents

The post-presentation debrief with David Evans was a complete blur and I returned to the Green Room in a haze. I went over to similarly humiliated Soaper Woman who was slumped dejectedly in an uncomfortable looking office chair. I noticed she smelt slightly like Leon but along with the odour of old bed sheets there was a sharper tang. I decided to sit further away.

Withdrawing into a sort of dream, still and calm with a sunken life force, I hardly noticed the excited chatter around me. Nor did I bother to look at the monitors. Even the failures of Reggie and Egg Man would have provided no succour.

Startled out of my lethargy by someone saying my name, I opened my eyes to see Nicholas De'Ath addressing me. 'What happened? Why didn't you say brush?' I was in no mood for banter.

'Call yourself a coach. I signed a contract and you promised success. Now look at me. Ruined!'

'Don't blame me, I told you to look confident and flatter the Angels.'

'You told me to ask for more.'

'Indeed, but you needed to offer more as well. And I did tell you not to bang on about time, did I not?' I couldn't argue with that.

My voice sounded distant, almost with an echo, when I asked, 'What am I going to do?'

'You are going to give people what they understand.' I couldn't imagine starting anything else and just felt weak.

'You promised success...' I felt a sob welling and suppressed it.

'To achieve success, you need to be on the right path. You have veered off and are now trying to clear a jungle single-handedly with a kitchen knife.' I was heartened by the fact Nicholas seemed to understand how hard my life had become. He then, rather enigmatically, added, 'Out of the darkness comes light. The future is imagined.'

'That's a bit cryptic.' I was getting fed up and snapped, 'Haven't you any specific advice?'

'Never trust a Chinaman.' I was stunned. Was anyone allowed to even think that, let alone verbalise it? Good job he didn't work for my old firm, as he would have been re-educated on a diversity, equality and gender awareness course. As I had gone on this course myself (twice) I was about to correct him, but I couldn't quite remember the acceptable nomenclature.

'What's that got to do with anything?' I simply asked but a man holding a clipboard interrupted Nicholas and told him he was on in two minutes.

'Look and learn.' Nicholas remarked just before he was ushered out of the room.

I was left thinking how anachronistic Nicholas had sounded making such a casually xenophobic utterance. For a moment, I

142

dwelt on the collapse of respect in society. I tried to comfort myself with the thought that Prime Ministers and Presidents in the free world still upheld certain standards and would never make such derogatory remarks about our friends from the Far East. By high mindedness didn't last for long, as I simply wanted to collapse back into despair. Nevertheless, I couldn't help looking at the monitors to see how Nicholas faired.

When Nicholas and his entourage appeared in the boardroom it was as if a jolt of electricity had passed through the Angels. They sat up and their eyes opened wide; perhaps they hadn't seen a group quite like this before. Nicholas stood in front of Kairos, Corvid and Sign Man. I hadn't seen them in the Green room and wondered how they had all suddenly appeared. Kairos wore the same suit I had first seen him in, but Corvid had changed her outfit. Under the lights, her black, close fitting trouser-suit seemed to shimmer as if covered in millions of tiny raindrops. She carried a large, red cardboard box with Chinese characters scrawled on the side of it, underneath the words, 'Odd Socks'. I have no idea where she got such a box, but it felt like she was deliberately rubbing salt into my wounds. Sign Man, as usual, was dressed in overalls but now carried one of those Stop/Go signs used by road workers.

Nicholas's prominent gaze, at least from this camera angle, epitomised honesty and charm. He lost no time in starting to hold forth in his distinctive sing-a-long voice, 'My name is Nicholas De'Ath and I'm here to talk to you about my company, Gorgo Industries. We design and produce individuated products.' There wasn't a peep from the panel of investors. It was as if they had heard the word, 'individuated' before. Nicholas carried on almost without pause. 'Individuated products are designed to be unique to the wearer. They bring out the best of the individual and

143

enhance their natural qualities. It is difficult to fully appreciate this until you have tried out a product. Let's start with perfume.'

Corvid took out of the box an ornate bottle filled with clear liquid out of the box. She removed the stopper and handed it over to John Lewis. He very obviously looked at Corvid's dark chocolaty skin and full lips before smiling at her, but he shuddered slightly as he looked into her yellow eyes. He sniffed the top of the bottle and handed it on without comment. Once all the Angels had smelt the contents, Sign Man turned his sign to Go and they all started to talk about the bottle. Delores Headon said, 'It looks like water and smells of nothing. I'm not impressed at all.' Jimmy Bannaman asked, 'Are you going to turn water into wine?'

'Ta, ta, ta.' Nicholas burst into his characteristic laugh. 'That's not my signature trick but there is a revelation on its way for you. Now, put a little on your skin.'

New Guy tipped the bottle up with his finger covering the end and, after using this finger to dab the perfume on his wrist, passed the bottle along to the other Angels. Even before it got back to John Lewis, New Guy commented, 'Wow, it smells of lemongrass and ginseng. It takes me back to my home in the fields of Sishuan Province. It's delightful.' Jimmy Bannaman said, 'Mine smells of leather and whisky, my favourite scents.' Delores Headon said, 'Mine is musky and seductive.' I'm pleased she didn't add, 'Just like me,' or I would have felt sick. John Lewis said, 'Mine smells citrusy. It's young and fresh, just like me.' I gagged.

The Angels exchanged glances with each other, obviously weighing up who would come out as a potential investor and thinking about what tactics to use. John Lewis kicked off with, 'I

144

am amazed. How does that actually work?'

'The liquid simply responds to your inner being.' Nicholas said in his persuasive, singsong voice. Delores Headon then asked her favourite question.

'Have you a patent?'

I was hoping that Nicholas didn't have a patent and that Delores would tear into him, but he responded, 'There is no need to file a patent. The secret is safe with me.' This seemed to satisfy John Lewis as he chipped back in.

'How can I help? How much investment are you looking for?'

'I'm not looking for investment.' Nicholas' reply elicited a small exhalation of breath from Delores Headon.

'No!' John Lewis exclaimed.

'No.'

'No. Then what do you need us for?'

'To sell and market the product. I'm the inventor and producer. I need you to get it to the customer.'

'I can get it to the customer.' John Lewis was the first to register his interest and Delores Headon immediately retorted.

'You! Sorry,' she addressed Nicholas, 'you need someone

with a great track record in retail.'

'Like me.' Jimmy Bannaman chipped in.

'Or someone who can help you go global, like me.' New Guy said.

Sign Man turned his sign to 'Stop' and the Angels shut up. Nicholas smiled and said, 'You haven't seen half of it yet.' Without any instruction, Corvid took a lovely silk-covered jewellery case out of the cardboard box. She opened the case and then passed it to New Guy, instructing him to take a piece of jewellery and pass the case on. The men took out rings and Delores Headon a large necklace. Once they were all holding an item, Nicholas said, 'Take a look, what do you see?'

'Plain glass.' John Lewis said.

'Simple paste.' Added Delores Headon.

'Now, try them on.' Nicholas urged, 'They'll change to reflect the colour of your soul.'

John Lewis slipped on his ring and immediately the glass stone turned emerald green. Likewise, the stone on New Guy's ring turned aquamarine as he slipped it on. Then Jimmy Bannaman put on his and it became sapphire-blue. Delores fastened the clasp of her necklace and the jewels radiated ruby red, the colour of sexual desire. They didn't need to express their feelings; their faces said it all.

Sign Man turned his sign to Go and Jimmy Bannaman, rather

146

greedily, asked, 'What else have you got?'

'Is that not enough?' Nicholas responded in a mocking tone but carried on, 'In fact I do have more. Who is into lingerie?' Jimmy made the faintest of moves to put his hand up and then stopped himself.

'I like lingerie.' Delores answered instead.

'Good,' Nicholas smiled and his kind eye twinkled, 'please can you try this on to demonstrate its effect.'

Corvid pulled a huge corset out of the box and the rest of the Angels smirked until Delores cut them dead with a withering look. Nicholas reassured her that it would flatter her and requested she try it on. Delores unhesitatingly, took the garment and left the room. Whilst she was gone the other Angels didn't talk to each other. Rather, they sat smelling their own scent and staring at the colour of their soul with pride. They were clearly calculating how they could become Nicholas's exclusive partner. Nicholas said something to Kairos and almost instantly afterwards Delores was back in the room. The other Angels were surprised to see her return so soon and were amazed with her transformation.

Somehow, Delores appeared to have lost about four stones and her hips flared seductively outwards from her slim waist. Above her flattened midriff, large, round and firm looking breasts beckoned, seductively straining the seams of her dress. Her scent was heady and intoxicating and the ruby necklace flashed like a warning sign. John Lewis leered over towards her and then hurriedly placed his notebook over his crotch.

Sign Man turned his sign to Go and immediately the Angels shouted in unison, 'Make me your partner.' Then, they turned to each other and started to squabble venomously with each other. The volume and intensity of the arguments increased. Just as Sign Man started to turn the sign around again, New Guy said, 'Why don't we all become partners?'

'Excellent, excellent.' Nicholas commented. They hadn't asked him anything about ownership of intellectual property or about quantities, guarantees or quality control. *What sort of business people are they?* I thought.

Instead of the Angels quizzing him, Nicholas asked them what they could contribute to his business. John Lewis was the first to reply, 'The products fit well with my portfolio. I already have a perfume range for men and women called The Sweet Smell of Success.' Delores sniffed.

'You mean the Sweat Smell of Excess.' She said, 'You need me to help brand the products.' Jimmy then laughed his unkind laugh.

'You couldn't brand a calf. You need someone who is known to be a guru in the lifestyle and fitness market. Like me.'

'All so yesterday.' New Guy's voice imposed itself insistently. 'You need me to help you sell through the Internet. Selling online cuts out the middlemen.'

'It's all about you, isn't it?' John Lewis glanced meanly at New Guy and they all started to squabble again. *This,* I thought, *is a prelude to an almighty failure.*

Sign Man then restored order by turning the sign around to 'Stop' and the squabbling ceased. Then, Nicholas invited them all to be his business partners and the Angels raced to be first to shake his hand. However, when Delores leaned in towards him for a kiss, this was clearly a step too far as he hurriedly withdrew.

Soon afterwards, Nicholas appeared in the Green Room and the Angels milled around him carrying on with their excited chatter. However, Delores was far more interested in her new figure than in the conversation. She kept looking at her reflection in the windows and was clearly pleased with the result. I looked for Corvid and Sign Man but they must have left after the presentation.

The appearance of the Angels reinvigorated Harriet and her models and John Lewis went over to talk to them. Once he had his fill of flirting with them, he sauntered over to me and handed me a T-shirt with '…King Priceless' on it. If I could have mustered enough energy to jump up, I would have done so and planted a bunch of fives on his miserable kisser. Instead, I sank further into the chair with the hope of being left alone. Unfortunately, that was not to be the case as New Guy came over to talk to me.

Unlike John Lewis, New Guy's tone was sympathetic, 'Don't take it too hard. It's difficult in there in front of the cameras. You aren't the first and won't be the last to…'

'Screw up.' I filled the pause.

'Well yes, but you are an entrepreneur, you will bounce back.'

'I'm not so sure. The real shame is I've created something that is really valuable but no one seems to want it.'

'Ok, I know you can do a lot of things, but if you had to put it on a T-shirt, how would you describe Dynamic Link?'

'I already have it.' I showed him the T-shirt given to me by John Lewis.

'No. In a few words, what's the best thing it can provide.'

'Well…one of the things… it matches people and jobs.'

'What's all this stuff about time got to do with it?'

'Understanding how people experience and make sense of time enables us to match a person's decision-making capability to the required contribution of the job.'

'Without talking too much about time, what are the benefits?'

'People best fit the demands of the job. But what's revolutionary is this; if you use my classification system, the matching can be done by a computer, cutting out recruiters and other middlemen. I can save companies a fortune in recruitment costs.'

New Guy's eyes opened wide and he asked, 'Why didn't you say that in your presentation?'

'Well, that requires a minimum investment of three

million and there are lots of other things the system can do.'

'Focus, Will, focus, that's what needed.'

'Well, I can't focus on anything now.'

'Why not?'

'I've run out of energy and money.'

'And if you had money, what would you do with it?'

'I'd buy a domain name called *All About You* and create an online system where individuals can create and update their profile and companies can post jobs. An algorithm would then do the matching using my 3C Taxonomy – sorry classifications.'

'Tell you what. Here is my business card. Send me your business plan and classifications. I'll take a look and let you know what I can do.' I looked at the name on the business card, So Su Mi, and decided to still call him New Guy.

New Guy then went off to talk to Soaper Woman, and I felt heartened. But I also had an urgent craving for the embrace of H. I wondered whether they would make me unlock the bike and ride off on it, thus capping the humiliation. I resolved to slip away unnoticed before that could happen.

These plans were thwarted by Nicholas walking over to me and saying, 'William, this is where the payback starts. Come with me.' I was intrigued enough to haul myself up and follow him over to David Evans who was chatting with the smiling Stage Manager.

David Evans turned to Nicholas and said, 'Well done, but you know there's a great deal of due diligence to be done before the Angels actually invest.'

'I'm not asking them to invest.'

'No... but they won't partner you until they see your production and warehousing facilities. They'll need to be sure you can do what you have promised before they put their names to this. And you don't seem to have much in the way of back up. Was that your team with you? And who, might I ask are you?' He addressed Kairos, and then a strange thing happened. Kairos touched his fob watch and, immediately after, David Evans repeated himself completely, word for word, with the exception of addressing the Time Manager. He finished off by saying, 'No, I don't think you'll find these seasoned business people are so easily taken in. What they say in the boardroom is one thing, that's for TV, what they actually do is quite another. There'll be a full due diligence on your products and capability to supply the Angels. There's still a great deal that needs to be looked into. They're not fools who will simply pay out to any old charlatan.'

I wondered how Nicholas would react to this aggressive assertion, but he remained calm in his response, 'Oh they are fools. I had expected you to have investors of some character and insight, not simpletons who are lucky to have a shirt on their back.' Evans then lost his amiable interrogator persona and squared up for a good old-fashioned argument.

'These are self-made men, oh, and women of course. They aren't simply lucky. They have developed well thought through strategies and execute them perfectly.' Evans said angrily.

152

'I beg your pardon,' retorted Nicholas quickly, 'strategy, don't make me laugh.' Then he did, 'Ta, ta, ta.'

'Why else do you think they are all successful millionaires?'

'I told you, luck! A strategy implies man has some sort of control of his own affairs, not impacted by the wishes, intentions and, yes, strategies of the myriad of other people around him. These people, including you, cannot even predict what is going to happen tomorrow.'

Nicholas turned to the Stage Manager who still hovered close to Evans, 'Imagine what would happen if you, for instance, were to start organising others...'

'I do, Lovey.' Interrupted the Stage Manager.

'And found you were good at it and wanted to develop a business from it,' Nicholas didn't miss a beat, 'then you suddenly had... Ta, ta, ta... a heart attack...' At this Nicholas flashed his teeth in a broad smile as if the thought of the heart attack gave him pleasure. '...yes, a heart attack.' He then grinned like a cat, 'and that's the end of you as an organiser. No one's fate, except your own, interests you any longer. You rush to a specialist and even perhaps a fortune-teller. Each of them is useless and it all ends in tragedy. You, who thought you were in charge, are reduced to lying prone and motionless in a wooden box and your fellow men, realising that there is no more sense to be had from you, incinerate you.'

Evans and the Stage Manager stood with mouths slightly open in shock. Nicholas continued. 'Sometimes it can be even worse; a man decides to fly off to, say, the City Airport.' Here Nicholas stared at Evans before continuing, 'A trivial matter you may think, but he cannot because, for no good reason, he completely loses his head! You are not going to tell me he arranged to do that himself? Wouldn't it be nearer the truth to say someone quite different was directing his fate?' Nicholas gave an eerie peal of laughter, 'Ta, ta, ta.'

The Stage Manager was pulling at Evan's sleeve to take him away from Nicholas. But Evans, used to winning arguments, replied, 'I really don't think your logic is sound at all; man is mortal, no one will argue with that...' He wasn't able to go further before Nicholas interrupted.

'Of course, man is mortal, but that is only half the problem. The trouble is he is suddenly mortal; death comes to him in an instant! He cannot even say that he will survive this evening.'

'Of course, he can.' Evans sounded exasperated. 'I know more or less, exactly what I'm going to do this evening, provided the proverbial bus doesn't run me over in the street.'

'A bus, what's that got to do with it?' Nicholas interrupted again. 'You in particular, I assure you are in no danger from buses. Your death will be different.'

'Perhaps you know exactly how I'm going to die?' enquired Evans with understandable sarcasm at the ridiculous turn the conversation seemed to be taking.

Nicholas looked Evans up and down as though measuring him for a coffin and then announced loudly and cheerfully, 'Indeed, your head will be cut off.'

'Hm,' grunted Evans, clearly upset by the little joke. 'That is, if you don't mind me saying so, complete bollocks. Now, if you would excuse me, I have a helicopter to catch.'

'I beg your pardon,' replied Nicholas, 'but it is so. Oh yes, I was going to ask you – what are you doing this evening, if it's not a secret.'

'It's not a secret. From here I'm off to the City Airport, and then I'm being taken by car to host News Day.'

'No, that's absolutely impossible,' said Nicholas firmly.

'Why?'

'Because Jason, the apprentice, forgot to replace the pin on the over-locking mechanism. So that meeting will not take place.' Nicholas smiled the sort of smile a spider would wear after detecting the twitch on his web signifying dinner.

With this, as one can imagine, there was shocked silence for a while. 'Excuse me,' said Evans frowning and pulling up his lower lip to create a sneer, 'but what on earth has Jason got to do with it?'

'I'll tell you what Jason's got to do with it,' said the Stage Manager, having obviously decided to declare war on the strange guest, 'have you ever had to spend any time in a mental hospital?' Nicholas was not in the least offended.

155

'Yes, I have, and more than once!' He exclaimed and gave a cheerful laugh, though the stare from his cruel eye stopped the Stage Manager in his tracks, 'Where haven't I been! My only regret is I didn't stay long enough to ask the doctors what schizophrenia was. But you are going to find out from them yourself.'

Our conversation was cut short by one of the assistants announcing that the helicopter was on its way to whisk the successful entrepreneurs away to a bright and prosperous future, so we needed to make our way to the top of the building.

Cameramen were positioned close to the helipad to capture the arrival of the helicopter and then the departure of the Angels together with their new partners. I guessed that Soaper Woman and I were needed on the roof so that we could be shot looking dejected as the helicopter took off and flew away.

I heard the distinctive tuck, tuck of the approaching helicopter before it appeared from behind us, huge and loud. For its bulk, it was surprisingly agile as it hovered over the large H painted on the top of the skyscraper and turned its nose to face its passengers now marshalled in a group to one end of the helipad.

As the host of the show, David Evans was the first in the line that headed out towards the helicopter, which was now parked, thundering and vibrating with the disc of the rotor blades slicing through the Docklands' air. As he neared the purple, noisy beast, I saw what appeared to be a flash at its tail. The aircraft quickly slewed around and the nose dipped, causing the angle of the scything disc to slope down just enough to slice David Evans's head clean off. Chop. Gone. It rolled unceremoniously towards the feet of the Stage Manager who picked it up and, clutching it to his breast, gibbered, 'David, oh, David.'

Ze Bierkeller

5th August

Bastards. Bastards. Bastards. All of them, even that David Evans, although he got his just deserts. The papers today are full of the helicopter incident. But there is not a word about Nicholas De'Ath being present or his prediction of Evans's early demise. It just says an investigation has begun as to why the Agusta 109 uncontrollably tilted forward.

An expert crash investigator suggests the over-locking mechanism of the rear rotor must have failed causing the helicopter to rotate on the ground. Then this shearing motion made the nose wheel collapse causing the rotating rotor blades to come dangerously close to the ground. There is no mention of Jason, but somehow, I expect him to take the blame.

6th August

Humiliation has really settled in. I just want to implode like some Death Star so that everything is obliterated. I know I wouldn't be missed. Probably all that'd happen is at the end of the Angels there would be an announcement saying, 'Since the making of this programme William Taylor Findler has sadly passed away'. No blue plaque, nothing. Nada, zip, I'm not going to disappear that easily.

7th August

I have H to thank for making me brave. After all, what should a man fear, certainly not humiliation meted out by some spivvy, celebrity investors, when he uses the divine, wonder working powder?

8th August

Had a visit from the police today. I assumed they were investigating David Evans's death, but this was not the reason for their visit. Apparently, there is a law against walking about your own bedroom late at night!

9th August

Spent time thinking about Nicholas De'Ath. What is he trying to prove with these individuated products? How was he able to predict the foreshortening of David Evans's life? I don't trust that man. I'm sure he's trying to con me in some way I have yet to understand. Did he say, 'Out of the darkness comes light. The future is imagined.' What sort of coaching is that?

10th August

Sent an email to New Guy reminding him of our conversation at the Angels recording session and suggesting that we meet up if he wanted to hear more. Then, what the hell, I actually attached the file containing my classifications and matching formulae. I know it's dangerous to give away intellectual property, but it isn't doing me any good gathering space-dust tucked, forgotten and unused at the back of my computer.

12th August

Had a weird dream. What I remembered of it involved the Sign Man. He had the same spiky hair, eagle-beaked nose, wore the same overalls and carried a sign, but this time there was only an arrow painted on it. He beckoned me over and I followed as he turned and walked on ahead. Eventually, I was standing in front of a theatre, looking up and seeing, emblazoned on a hoarding *Everything You Need to Know About Socks (but were afraid to ask).*

13th August

I told Leon about the dream and asked him to interpret it for me. He said it was a sign; I was being directed to write a play or film script. I replied that I didn't understand how to write a script, it was too technical. Then Leon boomed. 'In that case, thou art commanded to write a book. A work of great merit. It'll be yo legacy.' I am amazed at how insightful he is at times.

That is it then, I will lick my wounds by writing a bestseller. The egg will be well and truly on the Angels' faces by the time my episode is shown. They will be seen as the kind of idiots who turned down J.K. Rowling or the Beatles or Monsieur Bic (or Biro, one of the two).

14th August
Ideas for a book.

None.

15th August
Phoned a number from an advert from Ezee Equity Release. Arranged to see their man.

16th August
Found out another thing about time. It doesn't half drag when you have very little to do. Thank God for H, or I don't think I could cope with the slowness of each second ticking by.

19th August
The equity release man visited this afternoon. At first, I thought it was Kairos as he was short and fat with whiskery sideburns. However, this guy was much younger and had the most annoying

of accents; the new London one full of 'innits' and 'wha'evers'. 'So you finkin' of taking some money owt da value of your 'ouse,' he asked. 'I is.' I replied, having fun mimicking his way of speaking.

After asking me my occupation – entrepreneur – and the value of the property, he did some calculations and dangled what appeared to be a huge sum of money in front of me. I was all for signing a contract there and then but I realised that I needed Susan's agreement as she was a joint owner of the flat. I had the feeling that she would rather see me rot in hell than help me out in this way. I said to the representative, 'I'll have to fink about it.' He shut his case with what sounded like an annoyed bang and I'm sure he said, 'anchor,' as he left the house.

Note to self; check with Leon as to what anchor means in the new London argot.

1st September
Is a life of crime out of the question? Stealing that credit card wasn't difficult. But, I have decided it's not for me. Too scared of being caught I suppose and, anyway, the return on the last card was miserly. Leon took it off me in return for a few wraps.

2nd September
Met up with Leon. Wait until I speak to Sleezy Equity Release. That's no way to address customers.

10th September
Savings gone and shares sold. Why is it the shares I had languished at the bottom of the index whilst the financial market is in the grip of an almighty bull run? Took out an interest free loan on a credit

162

card. After six months the rate goes up to thirty-two percent per annum, but I'm planning on being a best-selling author by then.

If there is one thing I learnt from the Angels, it is to focus. I was being too broad. In future I am going to do one thing well. I will be a best-selling author. Then, as well as counting the royalties, I can work to my heart's content into the middle of the night without anyone thinking I am some sort of weird recluse.

12th September
Haven't heard a word back from New Guy about my methodology and classifications for matching people and jobs. *All About You* is such a brilliant idea, I don't understand why anyone wouldn't see its purpose and understand the benefits that should flow from it. I bet he didn't even look at my email. His loss.

13th September
Have been advised that the Angels programme I was in will be televised on 1st October. I had hoped it would take much longer to appear, but I am told this is to be shown as a special tribute to David Evans. They will not be televising the ending. Shame, that's the best bit, and it would take the spotlight off my miserable presentation.

15th September
Idea for a book.

Fiction.

Two young people meet, fall in love and then get separated, but are reunited and, as the country is run by a brutal dictator, they decide to escape.

The man will be my character; intelligent, handsome and very sensitive. Not sure about the woman. Either, she will be foreign or the story will be set in earlier times. English women are a lost cause these days.

18th September
Idea for a book.

I think it will have to be a business book but, unlike the usual offerings, one that doesn't pretend to give easy answers. I'll call it *Ten Commandments*.

Given that the female boss in my old firm started the trend of 'thou shall have no fun at work' and introduced the no smoking policy, then curtailed the customary trip to the pub on Friday lunchtime, I think the first commandment will have to be, 'Thou shall not have female managers.'

Given that men don't read books these days and my sentiment might offend the vast majority of the potential readership, I'd better think again.

As I can't immediately bring to mind the other nine commandments, I might have to change the title.

25th September
Every day, I get a bit more edgy about the showing of my Angels episode. Will I ever be able to look anyone in the eye ever again? Maybe it won't be a problem as I always avoid eye contact now anyway. My pupils are a complete give-away.

26th September

Notes for a book.

An autobiography.

The first few lines:

The golden nuggets in this book have been panned from the turbulent river of experience.

Looking back, I see that my career foundered on Technology. I hate it. Surveyed and under constant surveillance. Monitored and measured. Tracked and traced. You can't even pick your nose in an open-plan, hot-desk environment.

What is more, our working environment is continuing to get worse. It won't be long before we are simply digits in a huge networked world, controlled through digitalised, enforced adherence to some good citizen charter.

1st October
Tonight is the night. I can't stand it. I'm not going to watch the bloody thing. I just want to be out.

I didn't add any more entries in the diary about the evening but this is what transpired.

I gulped down a sixth cup of tepid coffee and sat mulling over the fact that David Evans would soon be appearing on the TV announcing the names of another batch of poor lambs, including myself, to be sent off to slaughter. I realised I should never have agreed to go on the programme. I knew then it was simply a way to satisfy the desire of bored viewers to watch other people being publicly humiliated. Really, the world hasn't progressed from the Roman amphitheatre or Victorian public hangings. My only consolation was that David Evans's head would be rolling around the helipad at the end of the show while mine, at least, was still on my shoulders.

My stomach refused to keep down the strong coffee, and as cold sweats came over me, my whole body began to shake. 'I'm going to die', I muttered but was not sure if this was from shame or a caffeine overdose.

At the last minute, I knew I could not go out alone and injected H for the evening ahead. A deep, holy peace immediately flowed into my joints and life.

Grabbing my jacket, I headed out to the Ze Bierkeller, the only place I knew would be quiet on a Saturday night. Also, I didn't want to diminish the effects of H by walking too far.

I sat on a nicely padded bench seat in Ze Bierkeller under a jutting ledge with fake snow on it. I looked around what purported to be the inside of some Alpine lodge. Old wooden skis hung from the ceiling and an aluminium milk churn stood by the doorway creating a potential trip hazard. Despite there being very few customers, the waitress was dilatory and took her time over bringing me the menu. She was an unsmiling middle-aged woman who wore a Bavarian-style top, which, contrary to German regulations, did not reveal any cleavage. Wistfully I thought back to when I had started work, to an age when you could actually advertise jobs with descriptions such as, 'must have good customer service skills and a double D bust'. Now it seems that good customer service is as rare as the plunge neckline. I nearly said to her, *Ve haff vays of making you smile*, but thought better of it.

I had a quick look at the menu without any intention of ordering. On the top it read, 'What's the würst that could happen?' It would have been funny if its crassness wasn't accentuated by the fact that the Angels had backed this stupid venture. I looked at the drinks menu – Make Mine a Stein!!! – and ordered a bottle of Tokaji Aszú, my favourite. I'm really not sure what people have got against semi-sweet wine.

After pouring out the first glass, I lifted it to my mouth, inhaled and thought, *Can I not delight in the aroma of wine, as I delight in the girls walking bare legged along the High Street, even though I no longer desire them?* Then, I checked no one was looking and emptied the glass into the wine bucket. The alcohol would fight with H and my only wish was to extend her effects for as long as possible.

The early evening passed quietly. The very slow in and out flows of customers satisfied me, and in my drugged state, I envisaged them as happy vineyard workers picking the grapes that became my wine, which now lay diluted in the bucket.

In the arms of my lover, I even felt happy. It was a good feeling to know Ze Bierkeller would soon go down the pan along with John Lewis's investment. I was sure that Bierkellers, good in their day, were a lost byway in history, which, like tank tops, platform shoes and beards, would never come back in fashion.

I dwelt on the fact that the Angels had investing in this business and so confirmed my opinion that they had no business sense whatsoever. I was more certain than ever that my bestseller would vindicate me and make the Angels look even more foolish.

My reverie was disturbed by the arrival of Otto. Unfortunately, he immediately recognised me and bowled up to my table. 'Vills, how gütt it is to see you again. And vot a coincidence, I have just vatched our episode of Angels.'

'My name ist Villiam,' I have no idea why I slipped into a cod German accent, 'and I didn't know it voz on.' Despite my grim countenance and expression of total boredom, Otto decided to give me the full briefing. Afterwards, he looked pitifully at me.

'And you, you ver so brave. Fancy giving Delores ze finger.'

'I thought zey'd cut zat.' Was all I could think to reply but something cold and metallic dropped heavily into the pit of my stomach.

Unfortunately, Otto decided to regale me with full details of his business plan. He went on about how the timing was perfect, because Britain had apparently fallen in love with all things European, and he even took a copy of some marketing literature out of his small, rather effeminate, European man-bag. On the top it said, 'Introducing Germany's other great export – the Kurrywürst!' God Forbid.

Otto asked, 'Haff you seen anything of zat strange presenter, Nicholas De'Ath?'

'Nein.' I definitely wasn't going to tell Otto about the

arrival of Sign Man or Corvid in my dreams.

'He must have been a complete hoaxer.'

'Probably.' I didn't encourage him to dwell on the subject of Nicholas De'Ath and he moved the conversation on by telling me that John Lewis was helping him roll out a chain of Ze Bierkeller in the New Year. I congratulated him but my inner dialogue was all about feeling pleased the Angel's money would be wasted.

Otto had ruined my evening and all I wanted to do was walk out of his fake bierkeller into fake snow, curl up and die.

As soon as I could, I went to the till and paid up. I was disappointed to notice the place had become quite full. On the way out, I'm sure the young manageress looked at me in a sad, despising sort of way. I assumed she must have seen Angels before she started her shift.

The next day, I decided to go to the library and read the local paper. A persistent late autumn rain had set in, and at least, it was warm and dry there.

Unfortunately, a man who looked like he had a lifetime's experience of placing high wagers on lame dogs had collared both the local paper and the Sporting Life. Reluctantly, I took the Daily Telegraph from the rack in the library's reading room and skimmed the headlines. As the national papers were continually full of the war and strife in the Middle East I rarely bothered to read them. I was taught as a kid to never stick anything into a hornets' nest, so what did they all expect? However, I wanted to distract myself from thinking of the Angels and my humiliation and started to read the paper although I deliberately avoided looking at the TV page. However, after confirming that there really was nothing of interest going on in the world, I picked up a copy of the Daily Mail and inadvertently opened it on a page containing a prominent review of the show. My first instinct was to screw the paper up and hurl it at Gloria. It was annoying that she wouldn't take her eyes off me. However, I controlled this impulse and reluctantly read the review. It was hard. For a start, the letters on the page seemed to take on a life of their own. Sometimes they rearranged themselves or spontaneously jumped out at me or simply vibrated.

The reviewer had found this episode of Angels greatly entertaining even though the accident with the helicopter had been cut. He referred to the gibbering entrepreneur who had confused the Angels and asked for a huge amount of financial backing for a worthless company with no products, customers or ideas. I wondered who he was talking about and then felt queasy.

The reviewer reported that the biggest razzmatazz arose from the appearance of Nicholas De'Ath and his 'individuated products' (he referred to the term as if he knew exactly what it meant). He suggested the Angels had invested wisely as ITM's help lines had been immediately swamped with people phoning to find out where they could buy the perfume, jewellery and lingerie.

If Nicholas is a hoaxer, I surmised, he certainly had the gift of the gab. I consoled myself with the idea that he was just a poor businessman. My thinking was that if he really had these individuated products available, they would have already hit the market. Obviously, the due diligence, which David Evans referred to, had shown that Gorgo Industries was a sham.

Leaving the paper open on the table, I got up and shot past Gloria, who was now openly smirking, and out of the building. She must have seen the episode of Angels and, annoyingly, judging by the way they stared at me, so had all the passers-by in the street.

The following day, a letter from Gorgo Industries awaited me on the mat. It was written in a similar style to the one I had received from Nicholas De'Ath and Partners with a gold embossed title and bearing the same address. It too looked like it had been typed on an old typewriter with misaligned characters and obvious corrections.

The letter was an invitation to join Gorgo Industries at the launch of 'Individuated Socks'. Socks! I could only assume that Nicholas De'Ath was having a laugh at my expense. If he was serious, then this revealed the real reason why he had approached me. I surmised that his was some sort of pyramid business, where poor suckers like me made untold fortunes for dishonest purveyors of trinkets and gimmicks.

That night I had a really unusual dream.

I rested my head on the pillow, and even before I had unthinkingly tiptoed into the world of z, I saw Corvid approaching me. Her eyes were blazing and she wore a scarf made from real feathers. I was all swaddled up, head to toe, in a sort of cloth bandage.

I tried to open my eyes but my eyelids felt like they were covered in boulders. Then, without a word, Corvid's nose became a sharp beak, and she pulled at a loose end of the swaddling cloth. I began to spin like a top as she pulled and pulled. The more she tugged, the faster I whirled. It felt like I was on a waltzer, and the more I shouted for her to stop, the harder she pulled.

Eventually, I stopped turning but was aware of the room seemingly continuing to spin around me. Corvid stood above me looking down at my, all but, naked body. All I wore was a pair of socks. Not any old socks, but the odd pair I had worn on Angels.

'Now, take the opportunity before you.' She said and I, looking down past my small and flaccid penis, assumed she must have been referring to my socks. With these words ringing in my ears, there was a huge flutter of wings and then all was black and silent. She had departed.

The Red Jaguar

Over the course of the three months, following my unsettling dream about Corvid, I was too busy to bother with the diary. What a time I had. I have seen enough Reality TV to be quite sure 'rollercoaster' explains it exactly.

On the evening after the dream, I went to see Leon in the Dog and Bottle for his interpretation. I wasn't keen on going out at all, especially as I feared I'd be the butt of many Angel-related jokes. To deflect them, or at least play along with them, I wore a pair of odd socks.

At the Dog and Bottle, the barman with the union jack tattoos took one look at me and then burst out laughing. My worst fears seemed to have been confirmed. I was about to slink away like some cowed cur when he raised his middle finger and said, 'Up yours Delores. Priceless!' I was completely shocked when he then gave me a drink on the house, an unheard of treat in the Dog and Bottle.

I found Leon, sitting on his usual bench seat dressed in his favourite bottle-green smoking jacket. He smiled in a warm and generous way and raised his middle finger before saying, 'Up yours.' Then he burst into a rich, deep laughter that sounded like rolling thunder. 'I love da odd socks. Man, you is a fashion prophet,' he added. It seemed my disastrous presentation had only been remembered for my obscenity and the odd socks. Not that I was complaining.

Keen to get Leon's interpretation, I quickly recounted my dream to him. He sat back and adopted a thoughtful pose.

'Hark, your full potential has bin revealed.'

'Only my odd socks.' I informed him, thinking of the rather small, snail like, appendage that Corvid had seen.

'I like your odd socks. Selling odd socks is da chosen path for you.'

'Hmm, that is a coincidence! I also had a letter inviting me to sell socks for this Nicholas De'Ath chappy who was on Angels.'

'You'll never get rich by workin' for someone else.' Leon passed me his empty pint glass suggesting that his interpretation of dreams and further consultation deserved payment.

As I returned from the bar carrying Leon's foaming brew and a Blue Nun for me, Leon looked down at my socks and said, 'Bogoff.'

'There's no need for that.' I replied.

'No, buy one get de udder one free.'

'That old marketing line!'

'Yes, if you do it so people buy the opposite sock in da second pack dey can recombine them if dey don't actually want to wear odd socks and, if you do it cheap enough, dey get a bargain to boot.'

'Leon, man, you is a genius.'

174

'And you can use 'As Seen On TV' when you advertise!' I didn't want to think about being on TV but realised that there really is no such thing as bad publicity. 'I might be able to pull a few strings an' get you in da paper for free.' Leon added.

'Can I borrow two hundred pounds?' I enquired, thinking I needed to get on and buy some stock.

'No.'

The next day I came up with a commandment I would put in my, soon to be started, new book, titled, *My Life as a Serial Entrepreneur*. This would encapsulate its main theme; if you don't succeed at first, try, try and try again.

I also reflected on Harriet's story. She had successfully grown King Tee Shirts very quickly moving from a market stall to department store concessions. I saw no reason why I couldn't follow the same path and Leon was right, why work for someone else when I could reap all the rewards myself. Nicholas De'Ath and his Gorgo industries could go to hell.

I obtained two hundred and eighty pounds in cash by pawning my wedding ring and gold cufflinks and used this to purchase stock. However, I knew nothing about retail and went to see Leon. Even though it was only five o' clock, I found him in his usual place talking to a respectable looking middle-aged man; an unusual feature for the Dog and Bottle. The visitor was sitting, shoulders hunched on the bench with his hands cupped together like a poor supplicant waiting to be offered the host. I thought, just to see the reaction, I would say, 'You're nicked.' I didn't but my mere presence was enough for him to shoot up, grab his briefcase and

175

beat a hasty retreat.

Settling in near to Leon, I told him that I had listened to his advice and was going to buy stock and set up an odd socks market stall. His first words were a warning, 'Billy man, listen unto me, markets start early in da morning. Will you be able to get up to run da market stall?'

'No problem. Anyway, once we are up and running, I'll employ a manager and my job will be to design and buy and set the strategy.'

'Wadja mean by we. I is not getting involved. Each to their own. I knows my strengths.'

'Ok, but do you know anywhere I can buy socks at wholesale prices?'

As I had hoped, Leon did have a contact in the wholesale business and he wrote out his name and address. The next day I awoke at nearly the crack of dawn and set off about eleven o' clock to China Town to visit Leon's contact. By the time I arrived the lunchtime rush had started, and the street was thronged with tourists and office workers seeking out their sweet and sour fix. In all this crush of people it was difficult to locate the premises of Lee Wong's Import and Export Emporium.

The search reminded me of the day when I had struggled to find Nicholas De'Ath and Partners' offices. I was heartened when I saw a man holding a large sign with an arrow on it. I hoped it might be Sign Man giving me a useful steer, but it turned out to say, 'Wang's' and an arrow pointed to an establishment advertising best crispy duck. Being a bit peckish, and partial to the odd Chinese takeaway, I decided to investigate in any case.

I pushed through the lunchtime crowd and noticed that beside the restaurant was a door with a nameplate reading Lee Wang – Import and Export. I just assumed that Leon had made a spelling error and that this was the location of his contact. As I rang the bell, I couldn't help laughing at a silly joke that had come to mind. This included the punch line, 'I wang the wong number.' I knew that this would now be considered to be politically incorrect, but it was the sort of humour I had grown up with. I wondered in which year exactly it had been banned.

The lock clicked and the door opened automatically. I then made my way inside and up a twisting flight of narrow stairs. On the second landing there was a decrepit and chipped door with a plaque displaying Lee Wang's company name and details. I pushed this door open and entered a room, which was in darkness save for a dim arc of light provided by a lantern with an ancient yellowing shade, veined like an old face. In the gloom I could make out a kind of bureau virtually submerged in paperwork. For some reason there was a ship's compass attached to its lowered writing slope. I wish now that I had remembered that I had seen a similar looking bureau in Nicholas De'Ath's office also sporting a ship's compass.

Most of the room was filled with piles of huge cardboard transit boxes. On the one closest to me I read, 'Sixty Inch Large Screen TV'. I wondered how anybody could fetch and carry such large boxes up and down the extremely narrow stairs. Then, a very thin man wearing a Chairman Mao style boiler suit appeared from behind the stacked boxes. He bowed gracefully like a reed in a strong wind and announced his name. He had to repeat himself a few times before I understood that this was Lee Wang's brother strangely also called Lee.

I carefully explained what I wanted but was already sure that socks were not part of the emporium's business dealings. However, I was pleasantly surprised when Lee disappeared behind his stock and soon came back carrying a large, red box with some Chinese writing on it. Underneath the Chinese characters was scrawled in large letters, 'Odd Socks.' I was shocked because the box looked exactly like the one Corvid had carried when Nicholas De'Ath gave his presentation to the Angels. I put it down as a coincidence that the boxes looked so similar, but I asked, 'Where did you get this box?' Lee bowed.

'I not know. My brother, he bring it here yesterday.' He bowed again, then added, 'They not in packs, just mess. You sort.'

I looked inside the box and saw a multitude of good quality socks, a jumble of plain ones in rich red, yellow and gold and many others in a range of different patterns. I told Lee that they were just what I wanted and, after a little negotiation, I handed over forty pounds for what looked to be about two thousand socks. I struggled to get the box down the stairs but eventually did so and headed home feeling like a real entrepreneur. Tired and happy, I treated myself to an extra syringe and spent a serene evening in complete solitude.

My good luck continued the next day when I visited Camden Market. I spoke to the Manager there and told me that, as a company had unexpectedly upped sticks and left, a small pitch was immediately available. In a way, I wasn't surprised when I later learnt that a marquee owned by Nicholas De'Ath and Partners had recently occupied my allotted space. I told the Manager I wanted the pitch for a week on approval to see how it went with the option to extend the agreement. He agreed and I paid one hundred and fifty pounds up front. For that I negotiated the use of a table and an awning in case of bad weather. I actually surprised myself with my attention to detail and innate negotiating ability.

The rest of the cash from the pawned goods was spent on labels and a machine to put socks into pairs using plastic fasteners. I designed the label, which bore the legend 'Odd Socks, as seen on Angels', and had a batch of them printed by a local printer. By the start of business on my first trading day, I had everything I needed and the socks had been put into odd pairs (if that makes sense) together with their opposite numbers for Leon's Bogoff deal to work. Then, I was able to rest for a short time in the arms of H.

I expected that trading would be light on my first day, but although the shoppers were relatively thin on the ground, they all seemed to come to my stall. I soon got used to people giving me the finger and saying, 'Up yours Delores', and I really didn't mind as most of them bought the Bogoff deal. In fact, by lunchtime on the first day I had sold out all of the two hundred and fifty pairs I had brought to the stall. I went home as happy as I could ever remember. Even the chore of getting up early had not seemed too arduous.

The next day, I took five hundred pairs to the market and sold them by two o' clock. Just before I packed up, a man with a camera slung around his neck approached me and introduced himself, 'Good day, I'm a reporter from the Evenin' Stan'ard.' I knew he wasn't a normal customer because he didn't give me the finger.

'Evening Standard.' I replied. I only wanted to confirm I'd understood him correctly, but he gave me a sideways look as if I was being snooty with him.

'That's what I said.' I was wise enough not to argue about his pronunciation, and he continued, 'I'd like to write an article on you. Possibly the title could be, *The Resurrection of the Fallen Entrepreneur.*' This sounded like a suggested title from Leon, but I had no objections, and he took a few notes and photographs. Before departing his last question was, 'What do you think the key to success is?'

'It's when preparation and opportunity coincide.' I have to say, it felt good passing on words of entrepreneurial wisdom.

The following day I sold the rest of my socks in next to no time and had to tell the Market Manager that I wouldn't be in again until I had sourced more stock. I could hardly believe that within three days I had made a thousand pounds or more. *Making money was easy after all*, I thought and, full of confidence, I decided to talk to Leon about how to expand the business.

After I had bought a pint for Leon and a Liebfraumilch for myself, I settled on the bench seat next to him intent on talking about my sensational success. However, before I started he pushed a folded copy of the Evening Standard my way with the words, 'Hail, the King of Socks.' The front page had a picture of me holding a pair of odd socks with a headline reading, 'Put a Sock in it Delores.'

Under my smiling face, the text ran, 'Only three months after leaving Angels with nothing and giving Delores Headon the finger, this serial entrepreneur has risen from the ashes and in his

180

first week of trading has broken all records.' I had to put the record straight for Leon and informed him, 'It was actually within the first three days!' Then, after quaffing the German nectar I added, 'This is just the beginning! There is so much more we can do'

'Do you really need to?' He replied, rather negatively.

'Of course, why not get as big as we can? I can become the Mr. Big in the sock world. I'm a born entrepreneur, it's in my blood. Today Camden, tomorrow the world!'

'Man! Be true unto dye self.'

I had no idea what Leon meant and, in any case, what did he know about business? I decided no time was like the present and, making the excuse that I was going to get more supplies, I shot off to make an appointment with my Bank Manager. After queuing for what felt like eternity at the counter, I was disappointed to find that the bank no longer had a manager. However, I was advised that an appointment could be made for me to see a representative on the following day. On the way home, I practised my spiel. This was; I needed to invest in stock to leverage (a sound financial word) my position by selling through concessions and other retail outlets before going global.

By the next day, I had decided I wouldn't ask for a business loan. I had yet to register Dynamic Link as a business and, even if I had, I doubted whether the losses would have inspired a bank to make such a loan. When I met the representative I simply asked for a personal loan to buy a car. I was not sure how much I could borrow, so I wasn't too specific about how much I wanted to spend on one.

The representative, who I'm sure was on some sort of work experience from school, tapped something into the computer and said, 'You have been preselected for a loan of forty thousand pounds repayable over forty-eight months.' I nearly fell off my chair; I had expected to be able to borrow something like a tenth of that amount. However, when he told me the monthly repayment, and after I had done a quick calculation of how many Bogoffs were needed to cover it, I decided to take the full amount. After the youth had conjured up a few more noughts on his computer, I was informed, hey presto, the money was already in my account.

Childishly, I had always wanted to take a suitcase full of cash out of a bank and asked the representative if I could withdraw the amount of the loan from my account in crisp new five-pound notes. The spotty brat laughed in my face and informed me that was impossible, but he gave no reasons. I wish I had remembered Nicholas telling me how banks conjured up money they did not have simply by tapping on a keyboard, as it might have made me suspicious enough that I refused the loan. I might have also brought his words to mind, 'When you next ask for a loan of forty thousand pounds...' but at the time these memories escaped me.

Instead, I walked out of the bank forty thousand smackers richer and only then did a picture of Nicholas De'Ath's office with the self-depressing keys come to mind. I speculated as to whether Nicholas himself had signed these noughts off. Then I realised I was being stupid; Nicholas would not have bothered himself with an inconsequential row of just four noughts.

After the meeting at the bank, I needed to go home for a quick snooze before heading off to see Lee Wang about more socks. I knew that, even if he wasn't able to supply me such cheap stock again, there was sufficient margin to make the business profitable if I could agree a reasonable price per pair. I congratulated myself on my financial understanding and decided to work out the gross profit - once I had checked out how to do this calculation.

On the way back, I passed a second-hand car lot that had opened that very day. It didn't look particularly professional, as the office appeared to be an old caravan with one wheel hanging off at an acute and untowable angle. However, parked on the forecourt, gleaming and almost shouting at me, was a red 4.2 litre Jaguar XKR. I immediately remembered Biella's secrets of success and how I had specified that I wanted to be rich enough to drive past my mother-in-law's house in a red Jag.

I took a closer look and was pleased to see it had a grey leather interior. *Here is a sign that I'm on the right path*, I concluded. Even before I had finished taking a turn around the car, a tall but obese man wearing a shiny suit with a red tie was standing in front of me. He was very striking. He sported a kind of blonde bouffant hairdo, which could only have been a wig, and an orange coloured spray tan.

The one thing I know about fat men is that they never buy trousers that fit, and he was no exception. The salesman's belt fastened over tightly just above the groin, leaving his protruding belly covered only by a straining shirt. 'Impressive eh?' I assumed he was referring to his girth and was going to comment negatively, but he carried on, 'She's a mighty fine motor hey mister!' He addressed me in an American drawl and I thought, *Oh no, a pushy salesman, I'd better put some distance between us.*

'Splendid indeed.' I responded.

183

'She's just in. Haven't even had no time to put the price on her pretty ol' nose. Not that I need t' because these shoot away as quickly as a golf ball struck sweetly by my ol' niblick.'

'How many miles are on the clock?'

'Forty-five. She's just run in. Hasn't even lifted her skirt an' got goin' yet.'

'What is the price, if I may enquire?' I tried to sound aloof.

'Why don't you step right over into my little ol' office here? I'm sure we can cut you a great deal.'

'Yes siree.' 'I was disappointed in myself for so quickly copying someone else's accent.

We ventured into the office. With its pink chintz curtains hanging over a chintz sofa with chintz cushions, it was quite homely in fact. In the corner there was a set of golf clubs and nearby was an old style red phone perched on a shelf. Next to that was a baseball type hat with the words, half hidden, which I think read, 'Make Golf Great Again'. An odd feature was the presence of a typewriter on the small table top. *What is it with typewriters*, I thought but didn't give it any more consideration.

The salesman didn't need to be that good. I knew I wanted the car and could afford it. Wasn't it Nicholas who said, 'debt makes the world go around? However, I haggled hard, paid a deposit of twenty-five thousand pounds and took out a hire purchase agreement for the balance of forty thousand, nine-hundred and fifty pounds. That still left me plenty of money to buy the stock.

and I now had the wheels to impress – especially Susan.

Oh, what joy it is to drive a Jaguar, especially a red XKR with its long hood as the Americans call it. Bonnet sounds so effete. I had never felt so powerful and in control as when I drove the car off the forecourt, through Kentish town to the Archway Road and onwards to Muswell Hill. I noted that the horn was loud and commanding as I passed Susan's parents' Edwardian semi. A couple of drive passes were enough for that day. Even if Susan wasn't at home, her retired parents would pass on the message that her husband had gone up in the world.

When I eventually got home, I was tired but happy and decided it was too late to go and see Lee Wang.

When I picked up the post the next day, I found that I had received a letter with 'Entrepreneur of the Year', printed on the reverse of the envelope. It was an invitation from someone called Miriam, who was identified as a PR Executive, to a 'celebration of the entrepreneurial spirit in the UK' at the Mansion House. She informed me that I was a late addition due to my recent high-profile media coverage. I immediately gave her a call (young sounding and posh) and accepted the invitation. I couldn't believe how chatty I was on the phone, saying to Miriam how terribly excited I was and how I was so looking forward to making her acquaintance at the awards ceremony. I might have even called her, 'darling'. However, she soon became a little distant and ended the call quite abruptly.

I set off to Lee Wang's Emporium a happy man. Even a note from Bruce wouldn't have spoilt my joyous feelings that were further heightened as I passed my gleaming Jag, parked a little way down the road. It seemed to shimmer to attention as I passed it and when I looked back, it loured at me, annoyed that I wasn't talking it out for a run. As I walked to the tube to take the Northern Line to Leicester Square, I thought, *This is my moment, I have to go big. Per ardua ad astra.*

This time I had no trouble finding the building housing Lee Wang's Import and Export Emporium and quickly made my way up the stairs. When I pushed open the door, I saw that the room was even more crammed with merchandise. In addition, it now contained a pile of suitcases and I couldn't resist asking Lee, who was standing by the bureau, 'Going somewhere?'

'Yes, er no. Not me, my brother.' He replied and bowed.

'Oh. Good, I've come to see you about a huge order. Twenty-five thousand pairs of socks, but I need the very best price.' Lee Wang rifled haphazardly through his papers.

'Pound per pair. Top quality. Twenty percent cotton.' He quoted then bowed.

'Sixty pence for the same quality as before.' I was going to be tough on him.

'Ninety-eight.' Lee bowed in a submissive way.

'Sixty-five.'

'Ninety-seven.' He bowed again.

'Seventy.'

186

'Ninety-six.'

'Deal.' I bowed. I knew I didn't need to haggle so hard to get a good margin. '

'Deal, but for such an order we need half payment up front.'

'Who do I make the cheque out to?'

'Mr. L Wang.'

'OK, but can I have a receipt?'

'Of course, but today I run out of letterhead paper. My secretary, she send you copy tomorrow.'

'Well, you are not leaving the country, are you?'

'Er, no.' I wrote out the cheque and left him my address.

The next few days passed in a glorious haze. The weather was just right for taking the Jag out for a spin and testing the horn at Muswell Hill. The only sour note was the arrival at the flat of the policeman who had previously warned me about making noise at night. Apparently, there is a law against tooting your car horn outside your parents-in-law's. Apart from this minor irritant, after a few days I became concerned that I hadn't heard or received anything from Lee Wang.

Looking back, I can see that I was too trusting and naïve. That is my trouble. The socks never arrived, and when I went back to Lee

Wang's shop I found that Lee's brother (Lee) had indeed left the country. With no receipt, I knew I could whistle for my money.

The evening after finding that Lee Wang had absconded with my hard earned dinero and left no forwarding address, I tipped all my paperwork from a filing cabinet on to the floor and rifled through it. Surely there was a premium bond with an unclaimed million-pound prize hidden between old bills or a long-forgotten share certificate.

The search proved useless and so I put my mind to work, for surely there was some treasure to be found and exploited in my experience, expertise and know-how? However, even a late night can of sardines was ineffective in firing up the grey matter and, despite digging away all night, turning over every sod, the barren wastelands of my career revealed nothing more than a few low-quality trinkets and baubles, which even the farthest flung Amazonian tribesman would have rejected as mere tat.

As soon as the bank's doors were unlocked the next day, I was straight in and managed to see the spotty youth I had seen before. As nonchalantly as I could, I asked, 'Can I take a personal loan for a larger amount - the car I want is more expensive than I first thought.'

'I am sorry sir, but you have borrowed up to the maximum amount we can advance you.'

'Just for argument's sake, what happens if I cannot pay the money back? Theoretically speaking of course.'

'Well, you can always return the amount loaned or, if you

have bought a car, sell it to fund the repayments. If not, you are still liable for the loan, and the bank is entitled to recover assets to the value of the loan.'

'Assets you say. Such as?

'Do you own a house?'

'Yes.'

'Well, you could always sell that.' The youth of today! Insensitive. Wait until they need help from a bank.

On the way home, I called into the second-hand car sales lot. There was a string-thin salesman standing around, digging dirt out from under his fingernails. I asked him, 'Theoretically, how much would you be interested in paying for a two-year-old, 4.2 Jaguar XKR?' He disappeared into the caravan and I could just make out a whispered conversation. When he came back he announced, 'Jags aren't really in demand at the moment but if it's in fantastic condition with less than ten thousand miles on the clock, then about eighteen thousand pounds.' Have you ever heard someone's soul whither? It's like the sound of cellophane being crushed.

My only consolation was H. She stopped my fall that night and even a bosom to rest my head on would have been less comforting. Luckily, in her presence I needed no one, only solitude. Silence and solitude are the indispensable conditions for the profoundest of reveries.

Industry Award

Sitting in the gloom of my flat and staring into the nothingness that enveloped me, I began beating myself up for squandering an opportunity to become rich. Now, with no money, only debts I couldn't repay, the future looked bleak indeed. I recollected what Nicholas had said about debt. For me, it had turned from manure into something a lot smellier.

I reread the letter about the celebration of entrepreneurs and wondered if this could be a lifeline. *Maybe*, I said to myself, *I could cash in on my celebrity status. Who knows, if I bump into Beetle and Dick, or their TV producer, maybe I could be on Jungle Fever.* The event was taking place that evening and I decided to give it one more roll of the dice. I thought, *Was there anything to lose?*

I headed off to the Oxfam shop on the High Street with the small amount of money I had left and found a fabulous dinner suit for next to nothing. I was concerned the trousers were slightly too short, but on reflection, I decided this would suit my purpose well, as they would reveal my best pair of odd socks. I was Mr. Odd Socks after all, so I decided that this would help the branding. I also purchased a very old, but unopened, Bri-Nylon dinner shirt, which saved the bother of washing and ironing one.

By the time I had driven in the Jag to the Mansion House, I was feeling a little calmer. I parked in a free space just around the corner and hopped out of the car. As I walked back to the venue, I made myself think positively, *After all, this could be a great networking opportunity.*

Even in the grandeur of the Mansion House, I didn't look out of place. This was my first visit and it was impossible not to be impressed. Inside the banqueting hall the light bounced about and shimmered off the gleaming cutlery, glasses and the gold-framed portraits of old men hanging on the walls. The only disappointment was that I was allocated a table at the back of the hall. Once most of the throng had finally taken their seats, I found I was sitting on the same table as Reggie and Egg Man. We nodded to each other in recognition.

I smiled at a rather attractive lady who, after checking her name card, pulled out her chair to sit next to me. She immediately said, 'Oh I recognise you.' I was just about to say, 'Odd socks,' to give her a clue, when she continued, 'No, don't say anything... you were on... I have it on the tip of my tongue...' I thought I would be more helpful and raised my middle finger.

'Up yours Delores.' However, my helpful hint didn't provoke the response I'd expected. She recoiled, turned quickly, looked back at me and then shot off towards a nearby waiter. After glowering at me, the waiter showed her to a vacant chair on another table. I was confused and lent over to have a look at her name card. 'How was I supposed to know her name was Delores?' I directed my comment to Reggie, who rolled his eyes. The waiter came over to grab the name card, rather too aggressively for my liking, and headed off.

I decided to break an awkward silence by conversing with my fellow entrepreneurs from Angels. Reggie informed me that Reggie's Sauce was flying off the shelves in all the major supermarkets and Egg Man said the egg boiler was currently the best-selling item in Harrod's Electrical Department. I could hardly believe they'd wangled any investment out of the Angels, let alone managed to sell anything. I told them about the exponential sales of Odd Socks.

As a networking opportunity, the event was turning out to be a waste of time but at least grub was provided. However, that bloke, Heston Services, has a lot to answer for. Nouvelle Cuisine, it's a scam! For starters, we had snail porridge. The only thing that resembled a snail was the pace of the service. The main course was 'Sound of the Sea'. The only sound I heard was from my rumbling stomach due to the fact I was still famished at the end. The egg and bacon ice cream did little to assuage the hunger pangs and my mind turned to real food; food of the Gods: avocado and prawns, steak and chips and Black Forest gateau. What is there not to like about the seventies? The wine provided, though a little on the dry side for me, was very acceptable and I decided to make the most of the copious amount on the table.

The after-dinner speech was made by Gordon Bennet, the Governor of the Bank of England. Eschewing the conventional dinner jacket, he was pointedly wearing the uniform of the meritocratic part of the establishment, a dark grey lounge suit. But, as he sported a purple tie, he obviously wanted people to know that underneath this bland carapace was a rebel – what a radical! He came onto the stage with about as grumpy a visage as I'd ever seen. However, he had obviously been coached on how to woo an audience. As he reached the microphone stand, his face became suffused with the fakest of alligator smiles and he looked towards a roving cameraman.

Gordon Bennet spoke very well, even though he had a strange habit of starting his sentence as if his words were chewy and the content was the normal, self-congratulatory drivel. In a light, educated Welsh accent, he started by praising the city folk, then he praised politicians for eradicating boom and bust and for providing the conditions for this time of great wealth generation. He talked about bankers being wise sages and said, 'We've never had a better period of sustained wealth generation. There is a virtuous cycle of investment and repayment.' Obviously, that sentiment hit a raw nerve and I had to have another glass of wine to retain my sangfroid.

Gordon Bennet wasn't finished and the more he carried on, the more annoyed I became. He went on about politicians creating a fabulous ecosystem where everyone wins. 'Trickling fabulous wealth into the hands of the masses,' I think were his words. I have never received the faintest of trickles and said under my breath, 'Central Banker,' or at least something similar. However, it must have been louder than I intended as the heads of everyone on my table shot around to stare at me. I consoled myself with more of the '97 Mouton Rothschild.

I could hardly believe my ears when Gordon, referring to entrepreneurs, said, 'You make wise investment decisions. You are modern day Time Lords, time travellers who are able to see into the future and pull value from the future to the present.' This was the same claptrap spoken by Nicholas De'Ath. I doubted that they were in league and put it down to them reading the same dumbed-down magazines like the Harvard Business Review. The really annoying thing was that everyone started to clap loudly. After a short pause, he carried on, 'Above all there are the Hedge Fund Managers. You are the modern-day alchemists.' Everyone cheered. Amazing!

Finally, and thankfully, Gordon Bennet allowed my blood pressure to return from off the scale by shutting up. A great round of applause followed this and he vacated the floor. The female host who was on the hefty side and wore a skin tone dress accentuating her bright red lips replaced him. She droned on at some length about the awards, and it was clear this was simply a vehicle to promote the sponsors, as she mentioned their name every five seconds.

I actually considered leaving before I became irredeemably bored, but I hadn't finished the wine. After more guff, the hostess announced a 'Special Category Award', which was for the companies promoted by the celebrity investors on Angels. I sat up straight when she said, 'And please, a big hand for Odd Socks, Reggie's Sauce and Perfect Egg.' We were encouraged to stand and make our way to the front. On the stage, the sponsor's Managing Director presented us each with a glass plaque with the name of the company on it. I'm not sure if it was the effect of the Bri-Nylon shirt, but as I grasped his hand, there was a powerful electric shock that made him flinch and put his hand under his armpit.

On stage, under the bright lights and with cameras rolling, I decided to seize my chance to get some free publicity. I hitched up my trousers to reveal the odd socks in all their glory and took the microphone out of the hostess's hand. Full of wine-instilled confidence, but lacking a script, I started, 'On behalf of Odd Socks and my fellow awardees, I'd like to thank you for this honour.' I could see to my left that the bright red lips were about to cut me off, but I deftly turned away and carried on. 'Luck is when preparation meets opportunity.'

195

Then, with microphone in hand, I felt the need to kick, hit and hur
as much as I could.

To the best of my recollection, this is what I said, 'I want to
dedicate this award to bankers and other lenders. You are the wise
sages, the Masters of the Universe, the rainmakers.' I paused and
listened to the polite applause. Then, a clear image of Nichola
De'Ath came into my mind and his words came back to me a
easily as if reading an autocue. 'People think bankers act a
intermediaries between savers with no immediate use for thei
cash and borrowers - with bankers earning a modest, but wel
deserved, profit by paying less interest to savers than they charg
borrowers. Well, that might be how it once was, but the modern
banker generates money in a completely different way. In fact
there is no effort at all. Yes, they simply type a figure into a
computer followed by noughts – plenty of noughts. Tap, tap, tap
here's half a million for you, another for you. Any more for any
more? The process is so easy that it is almost unbelievable. By
continually creating money in this manner, with a few strokes of
keyboard, they keep on lending, lending, lending.'

There was a general intake of breath from the audience. 'You ar
the wise sages because you have found the easiest job in the world
You type noughts on a computer and, hey presto, you lend, lend
lend…' Then I went completely off-piste, 'Money, money
money. Always honey in the rich man's world. It's a rich man'
world.' I was pleased with my original choice of words.

There were a few boos from the audience and the hostess made
grab for the microphone, which I sidestepped. Now I was in ful
flow. 'But, and there is a 'but', the wise can be foolish and th
foolish can be wise. And you, wise people think you contro

money, but the reality is that money controls you. You are like conditioned rats at a laboratory lever, pull, pull, pull because money has programmed you.' I was encouraged by the gasps from the audience. 'Pull, pull, pull. Any more for any more, and debt keeps on rising.' With my recent experience of getting into debt at the forefront of my mind, I said with feeling, 'You lend to the nearest schmuck who takes the risk and bears the consequences when the market turns against them. When he can't pay, you screw him.'

On that stage, at that precise moment, I experienced total clarity and could see what would happen if no one was able to pay back their debts. I had to share it, despite hearing the beginnings of a slow handclap. I glared directly at Gordon Bennet. His face had lost the fake smile and assumed its natural look, like its owner was chewing on a wasp. 'Bust follows boom as night follows day. And a bust there will be. The noughts are running free like an unstoppable river, ready to burst its banks. What happens when the black magic no longer works? What happens when bankers realise they have bought liabilities rather than assets? You have no idea? I'll tell you; ordinary people will suffocate from the stink of the debt piled up around them. And don't be fooled by the fancy names. You can package up debts to look like assets and call them securities, but they are still debts. A pig is still a pig even if it wears lipstick.' I looked across to the hostess, standing there pink and pig-like, and she rushed off the stage, clearly offended and upset.

Then, I was grabbed under both arms and ushered back to my seat in non-too gentle a fashion. I knew I had shocked the audience, but I felt proud of what I had done. If only Nicholas had been able to see it, I am sure he would have approved of my presentation skills.

197

I hardly paid any attention to the stage after that until the hostess, seemingly recovered, announced, 'And now we turn to the winner of the Business Start Up of the Year. Usually, this goes to companies operating for more than one year, but on this occasion, there has been a sensation that cannot be ignored. I am pleased to announce the Business Start Up of the Year goes to *All About You.*' I spat a mouthful of red wine across the table.

I hadn't seen New Guy in the crowd, but there he was getting up to accept the award. I sat back and decided to bide my time. After the small, linen suited figure had been handed an impressive gold shield by the sponsor, he started on his acceptance speech, 'I am very pleased to accept this award and I dedicate it to my hard-working designers and software developers.' He pointed towards a group sitting at a table towards the front of the room. I was disturbed to glimpse, of all people, my I.T. consultant as he raised a thumb in return. *Ramdeep Parkavakar,* I muttered to myself, *you jolly well will be when I get hold of you.*

New Guy continued in his self-congratulatory manner. 'Matching people and jobs has made *All About You* a household name that sits alongside Facebook and Myspace. People are building their profile online and being offered suitable jobs that match their interest and capabilities without the intervention of expensive specialists. It simplifies the recruitment process and eliminates discrimination and bias. In our first year we are well set to achieve over four million pounds in revenue.'

I slowly raised myself and, like a cat pursuing its prey, stealthily made my way past a few tables towards the stage where I intended to throttle New Guy. But, I never made it that far. Security must have been watching me because I was picked up, escorted to the main door and tipped out into the City night.

Numb, without thought or feeling, I staggered around the corner to where I had parked the Jaguar XKR to find it had been wheel clamped. 'Up yours.' I addressed these words to the world.

The Future is Imagined

I couldn't bear to think about how I'd been ripped off by New Guy. I focused on what I would do to him if I ever met him in a dark alley.

Like a beaten animal, I retreated to my lair and licked my wounds. Gradually, the idea gradually came into my mind that I should give up on being an entrepreneur and throw myself at Susan's feet, begging for a second chance. What did I have to lose except a shabby vestige of pride? But, at the back of my mind, there was more than a nagging doubt that she wouldn't have me back.

Over the following days and weeks, as the pain of betrayal dulled, I became convinced that making a success of a book was the only way to salvage something out of my life. Following my usual pattern of obsessive, compulsive behaviour, I devoted more and more of my attention to writing the best seller.

I was still struggling to come up with an idea when, one night, Corvid arrived. I clung onto her feathery back as we shot out into the midnight blue sky. It was wild and windy. We were not entirely at the mercy of the mighty gusts, but nor were we able to follow our chosen path directly and easily. Eventually, we managed to navigate to a clearing in the forest to join an unkindness of ravens.

Corvid introduced me to her family and friends and the elder statesman of the group welcomed me as a special and honoured guest, taking me under his wing – metaphorically speaking. He had a deep and croaky voice, commanding respect despite a slight stammer. I listened intently as he compared ravens to other creatures. 'We are the caw, caw cleverest animals on the planet.

Oh, you think you are smart, but you humans are simply rapists of nature and her dominions.' He looked at me with sadness, not anger or annoyance.

'Caw, caw, couldn't agree more.' Even in my dreams have the unfortunate habit of unconsciously taking on other people's accents and idiosyncrasies.

'Whilst other species don't measure up to us, they are still caw, caw, clever; all are moving around and making choices within their own limits.' I begged to differ and, remembering something from 'O' level biology, put an awkward question to him.

'Surely you are not suggesting the humble amoeba sets off with a plan?' The elder laughed. If you have never heard a raven laugh, I hope for you sake that you never do. It's a very creepy sound, conspiratorial and with a quality that makes your blood run cold.

'Especially the amoeba. It even has an awareness of probability. It caw, caw, constantly asks itself, if I pass this un tasty food am I likely to caw, caw, come across, with a bit more effort, something I like better. And it doesn't spend time trying to eat something too big for it. No, I can assure you all living things move and choose.' I had to agree as the trees towering above us moved in a little and murmured, 'Yesss, yesss, mmoooovvving chooosssing.'

I awoke with a feeling of amazement; what a journey I had been on? Corvid, I reasoned, had visited to reinforce Biella's message about writing a book and had given me the idea about the freedom of choice all living creatures have.

I am pleased to be able to report I eventually finished a manuscript for the book, which I called *The Future is Imagined - a Treatise on Time, Uncertainty and the Nature of Being*. I can't say it was easy to write. Certainly, after completing the first draft, it wasn't easy to read back to myself as the untamed handwriting was difficult to decipher and reviewing it made my head ache. It included a lengthy, insightful tract on the pathogenic nature of power structures and how the fake, 'Call me Tony,' informality at work hides the fact that the fat cats are feathering their nests – if you know what I mean. This was the hardest part to decipher as the paper was scored and ripped where the pencil lead had broken through. Some of the text is still seared into my memory and I can quote you key paragraphs. However, the act of writing it feels so distant, so long in the past that it would be as if I was quoting from the work of other people.

Of course, the major theme related to the nature of time. I even defined a second dimension. However, I have to admit that I did leave out Kairos's ramblings on the space-time dimension.

It is philosophical but also positive. Time's arrow is not directed at a predestined point, rather the future is what we imagine it to be.

The book was written as a kind of autobiography. Not so much a personal history, more of a journey through a set of ideas. As you are an educated reader, I will summarise the argument; nothing ever quite repeats. That is it. Nothing ever quiet repeats.

I'm not quite sure how I managed to fill five hundred pages with my insights, but I can assure you it was transformational stuff.

I managed to bring ideas of free will into the business world and explained the flawed thinking that underpins most of what we read about in books on strategy. It was a fairly lengthy critique, which, on reflection, can be summarised as, 'The first casualty of war is always the strategy.'

I even wrote a critique on I.T., at least its inherent dangers. I painted a vivid picture of a dystopian world of big-data, algorithms and artificial intelligence running a digital dictatorship. I even quoted the traitorous Ramdeep and warned of the dangers of augmented humans reaching the powers of ancient Gods. After all, Gods that really don't know what they want are truly terrifying.

I drew on my in-depth personal experience. But, I'm not sure on what basis I had the right to question Darwin's theory of evolution, unless of course you count my 'O' Level in Biology. To be honest though, I think it is the best chapter in the book. Evolutionary forces and random gene mutations cannot explain the almost miraculous emergence of the human intellect and language. What is more, being clever, doesn't always confer competitive advantage. Ask Plato, or Galileo, or even myself, whether it helps to be clever.

I have often been told, 'The trouble with you (Billy, Bill, Wills) is you don't like change.' In putting pen to paper, I realised that my numerous critics were right. I don't, and why should I? After all, I have experienced the height of the jet age, grown up in the space age, worked through the digital revolution and entered full speed into the Internet era. Surely that is too much change for anyone in a lifetime?

However, it is not so much the advances in technology that I'm against. It is more the slow descent to the baser level of human nature. Even I was surprised about the length of the list I compiled of things I didn't like about our modern, open, egalitarian, non-discriminatory, non-judgemental, digitally enslaved world. It was a cathartic release to have them out of my head and down on the page.

With the last full stop in place I sat back with my co-collaborator, H, and enjoyed a sense of immense fulfilment. I also let my mind wander and began to contemplate on how I would splash the cash when the book topped the best-sellers list. *It was*, I was sure, *only a matter of time!*

My bubble of wellbeing, consisting of a heady mixture of self-congratulation and a satisfaction that could only come from knowledge that I had a secure future income, was not even burst by the arrival of a 'sharp' letter from Susan's solicitors. This detailed divorce proceedings and came together with a tome specifying the 'simple' process. I admit to being shocked as I had rather assumed that absence would make the heart grow fonder.

The first step, the letter informed, was to meet up with her solicitor to agree the value of the joint assets. They suggested I bring my own representative. A voice from a distant TV programme came back to me and, as I put the letter on the teetering 'to do' pile, I said out loud, 'I didn't get to where I am now by paying for someone to hold my hand.' I was adamant, *What could be easier in any case than halving the value of what we owned?*

In the dead of night, the prospect of losing Susan seemed harder to bear and, to comfort myself, I thought, *I just have to face it. This time we're through. Breaking up is never easy, I know. But you have to go. Annoying me, annoying you, it's the least I can do.* I got up, walked heavily around the room and jumped up and down to annoy Bruce. I even shouted out, 'Aha.'

At the appointed date and time, I toddled off to the solicitor. You could tell by the name of the firm that I was in for a beating; Ditch, Hyme and Hyde. You just couldn't make this up, could you? I met Mr. Hyde. Such an apt name. It was entirely possible he had a nice side that Mrs. Jekyll saw but all I got was the hideous creature without compassion or remorse. He said I had fifty thousand pounds of equity in the jointly owned property. After fees, he offered me thirty-five thousand; evil, self-indulgent, and utterly uncaring to anyone but himself.

I told him not a penny less than sixty-five thousand and he had the nerve to knock me down to thirty-six thousand. *Sod him,* I thought, *and sod Susan. Let her have the damn property.*

If that wasn't taxing enough, some weeks later I had to go to some infernal meeting with a judge about my divorce. I was told it provided some sort of opportunity for arbitration but it looked just the place for a shootout. Doors either end of the room gave it away and I nervously waited for Mr. Hyde to burst in through one of them pistol at the ready. I admit to being distracted, but the Judge was quite sweet really as she repeatedly asked whether I'd properly accounted for all the assets of the partnership. I simply asked whether future earnings would be taken into account and, when she said they would not, I decided against trying to prise out the last penny from Susan. *After all,* I thought, *when my book is published, she isn't got to get a sniff of the royalties.*

206

Pride is a deadly sin. Oh boy, did I pay for it.

With every page I wrote of *The Future is Imagined* my self-esteem grew a little more. With each little pearl of wisdom laid down in black and white, or whatever colour depending upon the writing instrument at hand, my sense of self-importance was fluffed and puffed. With each dragon of convention slayed, my chest swelled. In the end, my ego must have been the size of the Hindenburg. And I'm not exaggerating when I tell you its deflation was as catastrophic as when the zeppelin, like a huge fireball, fell burning from the sky, killing most of the people on board.

I was informed of the decree absolute at the very worst possible moment. The previous day, I realised I had lost the manuscript. Can you imagine the scene when I discovered it was not in my Asda carrier bag? I doubt it.

I remember reading somewhere that there are seven stages of grief. I can't remember what they are all named, but I certainly know that they start with shock and denial. *It must be in here somewhere*, I thought and turned the flat upside down, quite a feat as it was already in, let's call it, an unstructured state. Every five minutes I returned to the Asda bag somehow convincing myself that it was still in there, and that I had missed it. Gradually it sank in that the masterpiece had gone and I started to beat myself up. If I had a 'cat of nine tails' handy, I really would have given myself a flogging. Instead, I had to make do with a tongue-lashing but even that was pretty brutal stuff. At least I had H for company; she took the edge off the depression that came in the wake of the pain and guilt.

Don't ask me how I lost the manuscript. My memory is hazy at the

207

best of times. The last time I remember having it with me was when I was returning from the library and had popped into a Costa Packet Café to shelter from a heavy shower. This is not one of my usual haunts as it's full of the pretentious university lecturers and TV producers who now live in my part of town.

I actually ventured back to this coffee emporium to see if it had been found. What an ordeal!

There were only three people ahead of me at the counter and imagined I would be able to quickly ask about the book and be off hopefully clutching the tome. Well, I don't think I've ever stood about for so long for such little result. It took the young man working single-handedly, almost all day to toast two paninis, boil extra-hot milk and take the money for the orders. I don't understand how and why these coffee shops are sprouting up overnight like mushrooms in a damp forest. There must be millions of people who have nothing better to do with their lives than queue endlessly for something that can be made at home instantly. And, by the way, when did a toasted cheese sandwich become quite so expensive?

Anyhow, by the time I was face-to-face with the harassed worker I was not best pleased. However, with a trained smile, he addressed me with, 'God Moaning.' I honestly thought I was on the set of 'Allo, 'Allo.'

'He's not the only one.' My reply elicited a queer look and I carried on, 'I left my book here the other day, has it been handed in?'

'I check.' He replied, nipped out of the back and came

back with two books. One of them was *Mr. Greedy and the Gingerbread Man* and the other was a Sudoku puzzle book.

'Silly barister.' I mumbled and left without further comment.

With the realisation that my future was not to be as I had imagined, all I could do was to sit wrecked and smouldering. If I did make it to bed, my dreams tended towards the fantastical but were always frightening.

I once dreamt that I was hanging on a crucifix next to two common criminals, surrounded by a crowd of happy spectators. Struggling to draw breath and unable to move because of the nails in my hands and feet, I found myself enduring the fierce, baking heat of a middle-eastern midday sun with flies swarming around my face and body. After a seemingly endless period of torment, I heard a gruff voice and, cracking my eyes open, saw a Roman centurion standing in front of the furthest cross whose occupant had lapsed into apparent unconsciousness, his raggedly turbaned head drooping. As a result, mosquitoes and horseflies had settled on him so thickly that it seemed like a black heaving mask covered his face.

It was disturbing to see what happened next. The centurion used a short wooden ladder to clamber a little way up the cross and then swung a long truncheon at the prisoner's shins. The sound of breaking bones and the shock waves dispersed the flies to reveal the prisoner's face, puffy-eyed and swollen with bites. His mouth was set forever in a silent scream.

The centurion moved to the man on the middle crucifix whose face was clean-shaven and largely clear of flies. But his groin, stomach and armpits hosted groups of bloated horseflies sucking at his naked skin. This man had clearly been driven out of his mind as he was croaking out nonsensical phrases like, 'Oh think twice, it's another day for you and me in paradise.' He also mumbled incoherent words referring to a son, mother and forgiveness. He noticed the centurion and asked, 'What do you want? Why have you come?' The centurion didn't say anything but placed a sponge soaked in wine and myrrh on the end of his lance and raised it to the criminal's lips. After he had wetted his parched lips the man said, 'They think it's all over.' I thought, *It is now*, just as the centurion took away the sponge and pierced this criminal through his side with the tip of his lance.

I wasn't offered even this measly refreshment and thought, *This is the story of my life, not the slightest bit of help!*

A little while later, I heard a man's singsong voice saying, 'Come with me, trust in me.' Looking down from the cross, I saw Nicholas De'Ath standing there with a huge syringe in his hand, the foul content of which promised immediate relief.

I did, at the time, wonder whether this dream was Jesus calling me, giving me an opportunity to repent and follow Him? However, lying in the arms of H, I decided that it wasn't Jesus I'd met. After all, the man on the next cross was clean-shaven and wore no crown of thorns. I also recognised the words he was saying about paradise and realised Jesus wouldn't have quoted Phil Collins on the cross.

The Descent

5th March

Thick flakes of snow are blowing against the windowpane and settling like big smudged thumbprints. People walk by looking like snowmen with mud showing through. It's one other reason to hunker down.

9th March

I keep thinking other people will find out about my vice. Even though there's nothing to give me away. The pupils of my eyes only betray me in the evening and I never see anyone then, except perhaps Leon.

But why, after all, should I have to hide and feel afraid. I'm behaving as if 'drug addict' were branded on my forehead. Whose business is it any way, besides mine? In any case, have I really gone so far downhill? I cite this diary in evidence. The entries are fragmented, but then I'm not a writer by profession. Do they sound unbalanced?

10th March

Had a most disturbed night's sleep. I heard a constant tap, tap, tapping on the window pane, but every time I got up to investigate there was no one there, not even a twig in sight.

I think I am jumpy because I'm running low on money and supplies.

Only two wraps remain, for emergencies only. A trip to see Leon is essential.

11th March
Nothing much to report. Supplies topped up.

22nd March
As I think about the book I find it all rather ironic. I wrote about freedom to make decisions. Who am I kidding? If free, it was only to make a terrible mess of a life that had once promised so much. It seems too painful to consider this a possibility.

1st April
I remember the dream I had when Corvid took me to her unkindness, and I feel very alone. Even the humble amoeba the elder had talked about, with his moving and choosing, is having a better life than me. God forbid, with his calculation of probabilities, he might be better at maths than me.

Everything is turned on its head. I started Dynamic Link because I have an overwhelming belief in human freedom and individual agency. But how am I using my freedom? What am I choosing? Yes, to lie here and wait for my next fix. What is my life? A complete absurdity!

2nd April
Have been trying to recall all the motivational speeches given by Biella. She extolled the virtues of positive thinking. I must simply believe in something and smile.

3rd April
Smile or die.

4th April
Made the mistake of going to social security today. The miserable

unsmiling paper-pusher who, eventually, saw me couldn't give a damn. She sent me home to get bank statements and didn't appear hopeful I would get any money from the State. Clearly, a middle-aged man, living in his own house (albeit hanging on by a thread) doesn't need a handout. Sod it, I'm not going back there, cap in hand.

1st May

Weighed myself today. A bit of a shock as I've lost three stone.

17th May

The rain is terrible and has persisted all day and into the night. The soiled clouds spilling their sulphurous rain, onto the sodium-soaked pavement stop any thought of venturing out into the urban jungle. Not that I want to go out but needs must on occasion.

18th May

Spoke to Leon about rehab. He almost frightened me to death with his strange answer. It was something like: 'If they try to send you to rehab just say, I won't go, go, go. Lest you be in any doubt, you'll end up in a padded cell and be left to scream to your heart's content. Even if the hour is your last, they still won't give you any. Jackson strangled himself eight times one night by tying da bed-sheet around his neck. Mercy, mercy me, did he get any succour, any help? Not a bit. They still didn't give him nuttin'. The spirit may be strong but da flesh is weak. I beg of you, follow this brotherly commandment, if dey try to send you to rehab say, no, no. No!'

19th May

Susan arrived today, probably wants to make sure I'm packed and ready to go. She looks well, even younger than I remember her, although her hair is shockingly short. Tomorrow, the flat becomes her property. Bitch! Doesn't she understand that entrepreneurs often start and fail and start again and succeed!

Susan said I look terrible. It's true, I've lost even more weight and I am pale. I didn't bother to reply. I packed some of my stuff in silence. So what if I'm leaving the ABBA albums. Let them go, let it all go. I did have a little cry when she left. *When you're gone* I thought, *how can I even try to go on, when you're gone?*

Later, I felt stronger. Good riddance to the woman who failed to love me enough to prevent this, but I felt so down.

I was shocked to find I only had a small amount of H, and after I had boiled up the powder and drawn it into the syringe, it only filled a quarter of it. I shuddered; what if Leon could not immediately re-supply me?

23rd May
Moved out of flat. Left it in a right state, I have to say but what the hell, Susan wanted it back, she can deal with the mess.

It is quite a relief to be away from the demanding letters. Bankers and creditors; let them whistle. Even though I will get some money for the house, these bloodsuckers aren't going to get a penny. I wonder what unpaid debts do to Nicholas De'Ath's firm? Not that I give much of a damn.

I don't like leaving the B&B during the day, but the landlady insists I'm out for a couple of hours so she can clean my room (She really means inspect as there is never any obvious signs of any cleaning having taken place when I return). Such a pain, as have to hide my paraphernalia.

25th May
The landlady started talking to me today. Out of nowhere, she blurted out that a friend of hers had become addicted to cocaine. I wanted to say, 'What's that got to do with me?' Instead, I made my escape. I don't want to start getting chatty with some old busybody like her.

A moonlit night. My mind is calm and serene. For a few hours I am so happy. Soon I shall sleep. Nothing upsets me after an injection but I had a weird experience

A distant, fuzzy, celestial light disturbed the infinite dark. It grew in intensity and coalesced to resemble a moon and penumbra.

Slowly, the penumbra shrank and the image transformed itself into a bare, light bulb.

I spent a good deal of the rest of the night looking at the naked bulb hanging forlornly from the ceiling.

29th May
Susan. Had I ever even loved her? Maybe, but not the same way I love H.

H, it is time again.

'Aarghh…'

'There…'

29th May
Susan, Susan, isn't life beautiful!

You were my sweetheart, but I have a new one now. She has a harsh side and makes my life a misery but also rewards me beyond the dreams of avarice.

Susan, I once believed I had reached you, but I realise these were shallow sensations. This girl really gets under my skin. She fills my head with intoxicating light and takes me to a different level of living. I'm no longer a primitive beast with basic desires. No, I am a sophisticated man and woman conjoined in perfect harmony, wedded at the point of a needle.

I lift my left arm and let it fall again so the renewed rush of H into it, briefly interrupted by my movement, can immediately affirm the presence of my possessive sweetheart.

Now, diary you must be put aside, whilst I savour my love, my life.

1st June
Saw Susan in Budgens today. She was in the frozen section (entirely appropriate) and was leaning into one of the freezers to get something. I could tell it was Susan by her characteristic bobbed haircut and look of disdain. I was about to turn away but on second thoughts, I decided to be civil and to wish her good day.

However, by the time I'd walked over to the frozen food section she had obviously picked what she needed and had headed off. Then, on coming to the end of the aisle, I saw her by the bakery counter choosing a loaf - organic of course. However, by the time

216

I had walked over to this part of the store, she had again disappeared. *Never mind,* I thought, *she must be in a hurry.* I made my way to the cashier to settle up for my Cuppa Soup and Pot Noodle and saw her floating out of the shop. I really mean floating as she seemed to be head and shoulders above everyone else and I don't think that all shoppers in Budgens are midgets.

I hurried to the exit but couldn't make her out in the busy crowd thronging the High Street. I shouted, as loud as I could, 'Susan.' Three women and one man turned around, but not one of them was my wife.

I was disappointed not to have at least said hello and was thinking about heading home when the shop security guard grabbed me by the arm. He asked, 'Are you going to pay for those?'

Seeing Susan has made me realise I'm not in a good place. Where did it all go wrong? I had a normal childhood, went to university, married a beautiful woman and created a system anyone would be proud of. How come I have ended up like this?

Looking back, maybe my problems started when I was made redundant and put too much time and money into Dynamic Link. No. Thinking about it, I'm sure it all started to slide when I met that gangster, Nicholas De'Ath. What sort of coach was he, with his advice to say brush and for me to ask for more? No, I have a few things to say to that man, if I ever have the misfortune of bumping into him again.

3rd June
Had to get supplies. I don't like venturing out – people disgust me and my waxen pallor might scare them, but in my jacket and hat,

217

I can pretend to be invisible.

The hat partly obscured my vision and, when crossing Camden High Street, I was nearly run down by, of all things, a bright red Jaguar XKR. It wasn't a good start and the day got worse.

Before going to see Leon, I read the Financial Times in the library. The market is on a bull run and Gorgo Industries is shooting up the FTSE100. I had an image of Nicholas De'Ath in his office counting huge piles of fifty-pound notes. How could I have been so foolish as to ignore an invitation to talk? It appears the offer letter was genuine, and it looks like people are getting rich from investing in his company. I couldn't help screwing the paper up and disturbing the hushed library with a bellowed, '--- King marvellous!'

On the way back to my lodgings after meeting Leon, I tried to be a little more vigilant with regard to traffic. However, I was taken aback when I looked up at a line of buses in the High Street and saw that all of them had bus side adverts that read, 'Socks Appeal.' This showed a man sporting odd multicolour socks and it was captioned, 'Part of the Individuated Products Range.' After that, I noticed that every other advert seemed to be for one of these products. The smug face of John Lewis advertising his scent collection and the now sexy figure of Delores Headon advertising her 'individuated lingerie' were too much to bear. I rushed, as quickly as I could, back to the cold welcome of H.

5th June
Everything is gloomy. Looking out of the window at night, the street lamps shed orange tears of pity as the chillingly damp rain falls on London. H is failing to lift me up tonight.

My forearms and thighs are a mass of unhealed abscesses. I don't know how to properly prepare sterile solutions, besides which I have injected myself with an unsterilized syringe on about three occasions when I was in a desperate hurry to get a fix.

This cannot be allowed to go on.

6th June
Googled, 'symptoms of H withdrawal'. This is what it says:

'Feelings of depression, anxiety or irritability. A weakening of the memory, occasional hallucinations, aches and pains and excessive bodily fluids. Fever. Restlessness and sleep problems. A mild impairment of consciousness.'

Actually, it doesn't sound so bad. I am resolved to fight the addiction.

7th June
Woke at 9.30am. Not feeling too bad. Slightly shivery but can cope with that. Decided on a period of abstinence.

8th June
Don't want to recall the horrors of a day without H.

12th June
(Illegible scrawl).

13th June
Nonsense. The last entry was nonsense. It's not as bad as all that. I can give this up

14th June

Sooner or later I will give it up… but for now, I need a syringe.

A deep breath and another.

Feeling better. Ah… there it is… a state of cold in the pit of my stomach, a taste of peppermint.

To sleep, sleep.

22nd June

I looked at the calendar and realised that today is my birthday. Had a sit down for a while and a little cry to myself.

The landlady knocked on my door and entered, but I didn't interrupt my crying and just tried to wave her away. She carried on talking, and gradually, I understood I had burned holes in my sheet (cigarettes do help calm my nerves). Handing her some money seemed to solve the problem; I assume it was enough because she went away.

When I feel well enough I will complain to her about the dirty pillowcase, the lack of hot water and mould in the bathroom. The rest of the complaints are minor as I'm not usually up early enough to eat her greasy breakfast.

23rd June

I wrote the last entry during a period of abstinence and much of what I said was unfair. The landlady is kind and the lodgings are comfortable enough, although the breakfasts actually are inedible

27th June

I'm lying down feeling weak after a fit of vomiting. I can hardly move. I am writing this diary using a crayon (God knows how I came across it) as I can't be bothered to cross the room to retrieve the pen.

What to put?

My hands are almost transparent.

2nd July

I went to the library again. For some reason that tart, Gloria, said that I'm not welcome anymore. Well, I walked out that door. I must say, it took all the strength I had not to fall apart. Turning back, I shouted, 'You think I'll crumble, you think I'll lay down and die?'

Gloria even had the temerity to shout back something like, 'Go on now, walk out the doorrr, just 'eff off, because you are not welcome anymorrrre.' Charming!

21st July

I will break myself of this habit. This will be my last injection – followed by no more, I swear.

23rd July

I congratulate myself. I haven't had an injection for fourteen hours! Fourteen! Unbelievable!

I will break myself of this habit, but now I need to reward my self-control with just one more injection, my very last and then no more.

24th July

I've managed to bag a large supply from Leon, which has relieved me of my worst fear, running out.

I have a plan. I am going to get really high, utterly in orbit, no half measures and then make a clean break.

It's a bit like being an astronaut. With sufficient fuel onboard I will lift-off, gather speed and then be airborne, never to return to the launch point again. Piercing the stratosphere, I will leave my past behind, propelled through the point of no return and beyond the compressing tug of gravity. Then I'll be free, carried along by the fuel on board.

I can feel the elixir trickling into my body and the lovely secret warmth. My brain is strong and free. When my sweetheart is on board, I am strong. The strongest!

T minus one. We have lift-off.

Tomorrow is the day. Geronimo!

25th July

I'm in no state to make the clean break today.

The Blue Plaque

I picked up the phone and called Leon. I'd had his number for a while; just bumping into him at the pub was far too risky a way of maintaining a constant supply. My call rang out and cut to voice mail. Although it was only just past eleven o'clock, Leon being already ensconced in the pub was my only hope. Getting dressed was particularly hard; my joints were quivery and weak. Once I was sufficiently attired, and as quickly as my shaking legs could manage, I set out to find him.

When I saw Leon sitting in his usual place, the anticipation of the enjoyment to come took the edge off my suffering. He was talking to three of the most dissolute people I had ever seen in my life. When he saw me, he heaved his big frame off the velvet bench and herded us all into the gents. As soon as the door shut I asked, 'Have you got any? Hurry, I'm dying.' His answer made my body cramp up.

'Billy man, Billy. I can't supply today. I haven't even got any ting for me self.'

'What? No!'

'Da Feds is clamping down in Camden. Just take it easy for now.'

'Take it easy! What the hell, I'm going out of my mind.'

'When I get some more, you'll all be da first t' hear.'

'One wrap Leon, just one.'

'But, I've told you man, I'm out.'

'Leon, I've been without since seven last night. What am I going to do?' I didn't care if I sounded like I was whining. The others cut in with similar pleas.

'Tell you what bros, I'll go and get some f' us all, but I'll 'ave to go to a different manor. It will be dangerous and expensive You come too Billy dey won't be expec'ting a whitie.'

'What are you talking about Leon? You are a whitie!' As ever, his blue eyes shone like little sapphires but his pale skin seemed to have blanched even more with the thought of undertaking a dangerous mission.

'Erhh, yeh, well, I know. Two of us are better than one, I suppose.' For a moment, Leon sounded like the English public-school boy I always suspected he once was.

'Where are we off to?

'The Longworth Estate.' I didn't like the sound of that, but my need was great.

Outside the pub, we hailed a taxi and headed off on our journey However, the warm feeling of reassurance had already dissipated my body no longer believed I was able to re-supply it. And when we arrived at the decrepit 1960's housing estate another feeling arose, that of fear. I had only seen such estates on the TV. Now standing by the decaying and cancerous concrete council flats, started to sweat profusely. Even Leon had lost his genial countenance and was looking edgy and scared. He told me where we had to go and what I had to do, but I started to shake so violently that he soon realised I would be unable to help him.

Leon headed into enemy territory, a completely anachronous sight in his second favourite burgundy-red velvet smoking jacket. I tried to look as unobtrusive as possible, leaning against a fence at the edge of a tarmac play area. This area was equipped with a badly bent basketball target at its far end, around which a bunch of feral looking kids were huddled.

I felt so weak that I just wanted to die. But, I knew I couldn't. No addict will kill himself, except inadvertently through neglect or an overdose.

Drug addicts are often described as weak characters but I can tell you we are some of the strongest willed people around. We'd rather go through atrocious suffering than give up on the smallest chance of getting another fix. No, I had to stick it out. In fact, I'd no alternative other than to prostrate myself in front of fate and beg it to be lenient.

I tried to keep positive by focusing on a sweet reunion with H in ten minutes time or so. High time too, as my body was feeling weaker and weaker. I had terrible pains in my stomach, which was crying out for my mistress. As I leaned against the playground fence, I was thinking how lovely it would be to feel the stab of the needle. In a matter of minutes, I told myself, a few tiny instants in the grand scale of things, no time at all.

For some reason, I remembered my treatise on time. 'The living present is a circular interaction between the future and the past in the present.' How right I had been. Except that my living present was dependent upon Leon returning as soon as possible.

Then, I wondered, if the past can affect the future and vice versa, could I, somehow, change my past? If only Kairos was here, he could place effect before the cause to put a kink in time's arrow and I would miss the inevitable and truly awful future target. I concluded that, given the chance to revisit the past, I definitely would ignore the letter from the charlatan who calls himself Nicholas De'Ath.

When I opened my eyes, I was dismayed to find the bunch of feral kids now surrounded me. My first thought was, *Shouldn't you be at school*, but I didn't vocalize this. 'What do you want?' I asked nervously.

'Wadja got for uz?' The nearest and ugliest asked.

'Advice.' I said the first word that came into my head.

'Advice!' The ringleader's eyed narrowed.

'Never trust a Chinaman.' If I had given it more than momentary consideration, I would have realised that this was no time to start repeating Nicholas' racist remarks.

A kid at the back of the pack with a round face and almond shaped eyes raised himself to his full five foot, three inches and tried to look threatening. 'Don't you mess wid uz. I iz not asking again. Wadja got?' The leader of the group started again and his words and attitude were acutely menacing.

'Nothing.'

226

'Nuffink! What about that watch?'

'Time! You can have what I have left.'

'Iz you mezzin' with me?'

The thought came into my head to correct his English but I knew that might not help. I wasn't feeling brave, only scared and my heart banged against my chest as the pack closed in. Suddenly, there was a booming voice from my left.

'By their acts be they known.' All heads flicked left and it was wonderful to see Leon's big frame appear. The kids vanished as if they had never been there. They obviously didn't want to mess with a dandy who sounded like a priest and looked like he could handle himself in a fistfight.

'What did you get?' I brought myself back to the really urgent question. Leon showed me his huge empty palms. 'Nuffink!' I said and was again amazed at how quickly I assimilated other accents.

We headed for a boozer just outside the estate and, once there, Leon explained that he was lucky to still be alive. Apparently, the dealers operating on the estate get jumpy when strangers turn up out of the blue. After one glass of beer, I needed to go to the toilet as I couldn't keep anything down. After vomiting, I sat for a short while on top of the toilet seat in a grim cubicle, dark, cold and damp, and cried. My withdrawal symptoms were almost insufferable and I realised that they were only going to get worse. Once I had recovered a little, I returned to Leon, who had come up with a plan involving a cash machine and a trip to Kings Cross.

227

We arrived in Kings Cross after a short ride on the tube. I felt so tired I gave Leon my credit card and pin number to take out sufficient funds. Leon told me to sit and wait on a bench near to the station complex and I sat down in a space next to a couple of office types and watched the city go by. In fact, it swirled by. I was already feeling giddy and this sensation was accentuated by watching the teeming buses apparently pirouetting around me. Pictures of John Lewis and Delores Headon, advertising their individuated products, seemed to constantly rush past me on their big red steeds. I even thought I heard Delores whisper from one of them, 'You are a financial imbecile, so I'm out.'

I looked at the people spewing out from the station and thought about them hurrying to meetings, friends, or lovers. Whereas I was alone, abandoned and washed up, lost in my victimhood and despair. A silent sob welled up in my throat and forced my mouth to gape open. The office types cast contemptuous sideways glances at me, then quickly stood up and headed away.

When Leon eventually returned, he was as high as a kite. He slumped next to me and said, 'Cocaine only today. Let da retribution of heaven fall on da heads of da Feds for screwin' up da supply chain.'

'You liar.' I was sure his blissful smile was not cocaine induced.

'Take it or leave it.' He dipped into his pocket and his palm contained a phial. I took it as I had paid for it.

'What about the rest of the money?' I said.

228

'Man, you is one big warrior.' I didn't understand what warriors had to do with it, but further questioning was useless as he had slumped back on the bench into what must have been blissful dreams, his face radiating contentment.

Cursing Leon, I went to the toilet in the station, clutching the phial in my hand. I entered a cubicle and sat on the toilet seat. The usual sad graffiti was etched into the door, but one effort made me smile. Just below a 'Jesus Saves' sticker, someone had written, 'God Shoots,' and above that someone else had added, 'Up'. I smirked, just briefly, as an image came to mind of an old man in white robes shooting up in this grimy cubicle, but then I felt incredibly sad. My mind drifted back to the time when I had seen the light and had chosen Jesus. Was he able now, in this moment of need, to extend his hand, as he had done in my teenage years, and help?

No! Not even divine intervention could save me from the consequences of my actions.

My whole body was painfully jittery and my hands were shaking wildly. I had a crazy thirst and every cell in my body was screaming for H or annihilation.

I hurriedly filled a syringe I had with me (I was in too much of a state to worry about whether it was sterile or not) and leant back fearfully. I knew what cocaine could do but what the hell. I just needed to block out the craving, the desire, the burning yearning for my darling H.

I was no longer a slimy, dissolute addict, whom young boys can threaten or office types look at disapprovingly. I was a calm, man of the world observing himself objectively. I sat up straighter than

229

I had in months. I didn't care about being unfaithful to H, I consummated my relationship with C by bringing her into me. I looked up at the bare light bulb hanging above my cubicle and I heard an orchestra playing outside. Later, I danced a tango together with Corvid in a huge ballroom under a starlit sky.

This time, cocaine was being gentle with me, supportive even. My blood sang and surged. Then lighting flashed in my brain and I was transformed. I was with God. My thoughts soared - *I am everyone and everything. I sit on the right hand. In the beginning is the word and the word is I. I create and everything i magnificent. I forget and all fades.*

I stood up in the grimy cubicle and stammered, 'Jesus Saves. Then, I was almost startled out of my skin by the attendant banging on the door, rattling the handle and shouting, 'Mister, you been in too long. Time to go!' The shock upset the cocaine. Then, I injected myself with more cocaine, why, I cannot say.

The attendant hadn't gone away and he banged and rattled the door once more. However, this time his voice had a singsong quality to it, 'William, come with me, trust in me.' I threw open the door thinking to confront Nicholas De'Ath, the author of my downfall only to find the turbaned figure of the attendant looking disapprovingly at me. I rushed out of the toilet and headed the devil knows where, but everywhere there were bodies, walking dead, city detritus going nowhere. I dipped my shoulder and punched a hole through the human wall.

I have no recollection of where I was or how I had got there, but the next thing I knew, I was talking to Susan. Although words o apology formed in my head, instead, out spewed random utterances, 'I would have been successful, but you left me, deserted me, bitch. You ruined me.' I must have mixed her up with my landlady as I also shouted, 'Filthy sheets, tasteless sausage, you filthy slob.' A wild fury built up in me, and I leapt at her and, using a large blue and white scarf, started to throttle her. Susan's head made a vulgar, sagging movement, and she collapsed in a soft pile. I stared at my murderous, transparent hands.

Seconds later, I was alert and looked around to find that I was sitting in the squalor of some hotel room that, judging by the state of the sheets on the bed, was clearly rented out by the hour. Thankfully, Susan turned out to be a filthy duvet, which was now piled limply by the wall. The blue and white scarf had disappeared.

A few synapses had fired correctly and informed a sensible me, burrowed in the depths of my brain, of my dangerous predicament. This sensible me knew that I would be irrevocably lost if I couldn't use this moment of clarity to save myself. But, if Jesus couldn't save me, then the sensible me was completely helpless set against the craziness of my mind and the cravings of my body. This sensible me saw it was madness to inject myself again, but I did, twice in the thigh.

I had the urge to go home to my wife and ask her forgiveness and help. God knows how I found my way back, I cannot remember the ride, but I have an image of coming to the converted Victorian semi, ringing the bell and banging on the door. Eventually, it was opened by Bruce. His watery eyes bulged stupidly and offensively, but he slammed the door in my face before I could even open my mouth. I stumbled back along the path, then turned and looked at the door. I was heartened to see a blue plaque beside it and could just read the words, 'Willie Fidler, Founder and CEO of Dynamo

231

Blink, lived here.' My heart sank and I shouted back, 'It's ---King
William.'

The only thing that would subdue this crazed excitement of mind
and body was H or, I reasoned, its closest equivalent, morphine
and I headed towards the High Street to find a chemist. I rushed
along the road all the time getting wilder and more desperate.
People flung themselves out of my way as blood flowed from the
injection punctures and stained my clothes. Madness entwined me.
I giggled slightly as I imagined bazookaring the local gasometers
incinerating the whole city with its pointless chemists stocked full
of morphine but not prepared to dole it out to the needy.

The last thing I recall about that day is standing in Boots screaming
like a wild beast, 'Let the devil take me.' as I barged people out of
the way in my haste to get to the prescriptions counter. I demanded
morphine, good, green morphine as I recalled being given in a
different lifetime. To emphasise the seriousness of my demand, I
picked up a handily placed can and hurled it at the display of
apothecary jars on the wall. The mirror behind them exploded
spectacularly.

Several security guards then laid their hands on my shoulders and
I was spent. Up to then, I had the strength of ten men but in an
instance the madness was over. I took small, placid steps as
rationality returned and I realised that the torture of withdrawal
had now begun. My parting words to the clearly shaken chemist
were, 'Do you take Boots' loyalty card?' I then passed out.

Judgement

St. Peter shut the laptop with quite a bang and it brought me back to the reality I faced. I detected a slight shake of his head that would have sent a shiver down the back of the sternest of people. I simply folded in like a rising soufflé in the face of the icy blast of his unvoiced criticism.

In a direct and accusatory manner, he said, 'There is a rather long list of charges. Do I need to go through all of them?' It was clearly a rhetorical question as he continued, 'Before making a judgement, is there anything you would like to say in mitigation?'

'Yes…' My mind whirled trying to catch hold of a viable reason to be saved. All I had to fall back on was the weak argument that I was a victim. 'It is all my mother's fault.' I blurted out. If only, it had been Professor Dixon and not St. Peter whom I had to convince, as I was sure that the professor would have been amenable to the unworthy suggestion that it was my mother's entire fault.

'Go on.' St. Peter muttered and raised his eyes skyward.

'Yes, she would offer custard or cream with the homemade apple pie and I would reply, 'both'. What sort of parent is it who gives their child both? Surely, I would have been a stronger adult and capable of dealing with loss if my mother had actually loved me enough to force me to choose. As it is, I can now see how my early life experience of having it all and not having to make choices shaped my future. What hope did I have? I am a victim.'

'Victim? I don't think that applies at all. Was it not you who chose to go on the course and to answer the call from Nicholas De'ath?'

St. Peter seemed to take on the tone of an irritated schoolteacher, 'You talk of being a victim, but you already knew that the whole situation was entirely dodgy when you ventured into the offices of Nicholas De'Ath; why didn't you just get up and leave? On reflection, don't you think, instead of fantasising about The Raven, you should have gone home and taken stock of your life? Could you not have asked yourself simple questions such as, why has Nicholas De'Ath taken an interest in me? Or what is this about poor souls and debtors? Had you bothered to take a copy of the contract, you could have scrutinised the detail. After all, everyone knows the devil is in the detail.'

These were good question and at that moment I didn't have good answers, so I tried to distract him. 'Dodgy! I am surprised about the choice of your wording. It's not very biblical.'

'We need to keep up with the times.'

'Ah, hence the pager.' People say I lack social skills, but I realised that referring to the pager as, 'so last century' was not going to help my case so I didn't verbalise this.

St. Peter continued. 'I hope you see clearly that it was your choices that led you to here, to your day of judgement. You wanted worldly success with the red jaguar and other trappings and you asked the devil to help you achieve it. You simply made the wrong choices.' I have to say that at this point my mind was empty, but my body was filling with a sense of doom as quickly as a water

234

butt on a rainy day.

I wanted to stop this interaction, to at least delay the inevitable judgement, so, clutching at straws I asked for a cup of tea. It must have been a case of old habits die hard as I also requested a pot noodle. If this was to be my last supper I might as well make it one I had come to enjoy.

St. Peter let out a prolonged exhalation but nevertheless then got up and vacated the room. I was left alone for a long time. Alone. Completely alone. I felt like a deep-sea diver cut off from his support craft and left to look out of his brass and glass helmet at nothingness. No plankton of thought floated by that provided any succour, any hope that it could be used in my defense.

St. Peter eventually returned to the room. When he opened the door, I thought I detected the faintest of mists around him, like he had just walked through a fog or got off a cloud for that matter. He carried a tray and on it were a mug of tea and a plate of sandwiches. I suppose it was customary to provide a condemned man with a little nourishment. He placed the tray on the table and I took hold of the cup, which bore the motto, 'Jesus Saves.' I considered highlighting the difference between the marketing message and reality, but decided against it. Instead, I asked, 'And the pot noodle?'

'Right out of it.' In a way, I was heartened to detect that irony existed in the afterlife.

The sandwiches were so curled at the edges they looked like they were smirking. Nevertheless, I took an egg and cress one and looked over at St. Peter. His eyes had the look of an old Labrador about them. I wanted to know what was really going on. He had the sort of face on him I could only attribute to him having been on the receiving end of some sort of poor appraisal. I obviously knew how he felt and offered an amiable, 'You look like a bloke who has just lost a bob and found a tanner.'

'Are all your sayings and jokes pre-decimal?' The comment was rude and beneath him, even if the answer was, 'yes'.

I was just about to give him the old lie of, 'You can trust me, I'm from HR,' when I realised it was unlikely to help.

St. Peter's voice, surprisingly, had a conversational quality to it when he said, 'It is clear you need to be careful what you ask for; Red Jaguar, Industry Award, Blue Plaque... and from whom.'

'Can we focus on something positive... I did at least finish a book.' Again, I was on shaky ground.

'Ah yes, *The Future is Imagined*. Remind me, did you use the premise that there should be no female managers?' I was taken aback that he was using an off the cuff comment in a personal diary to make me sound sexist. I wasn't going to have that.

'Have you ever had a female boss?'

'No.'

'Well, until you do...' I was not sure how to end the sentence, but I think he got the point. After all, he pre-dates the feminist movement even more than I do and even saints are products of their environment. Wickedly I thought, *I do hope he one day, has the joys of a female boss. Just wait until he has to up his workload and improve his quality levels. He won't even have time to buff his nails.*

St. Peter cut across my train of thought with, 'Even in your darkest hour, help was at hand. Do you remember your dream of being on the cross?'

'How could I forget? I replied. 'It was so vivid.'

'What do you think this meant?'

'Too much cheese for dinner?' I had a horrible idea where this was going, but I hoped my flippancy would distract him.

'Praise The Lord. Do I have to spell it out? You met Jesus on the cross. Even then, you simply needed to ask Him and he would have provided.'

Despite the reality that H was a very demanding mistress, despite everything in fact, even if it had been Jesus next to me I honestly would have chosen H over Him. I didn't say this to St. Peter of course but from my actions it was clear that this was the case. However, it does show that I had no control of my actions, for whom in their right mind would choose another injection over eternal life?

Have you ever felt like a recently vacated diving board? Well I did in that interrogation room when St. Peter looked at me and shook his head. I can tell you, nobody wants to see that. He didn't need to say anything, I just vibrated uncontrollably. I felt doomed, and his next comment added to a sense that I was about to be tipped into the abyss. 'Oh dear, oh dear.' It wasn't the sort of fulsomely compassionate summary I was hoping for now he had reviewed my whole life. But, it was what he said next that really worried me. 'With all you could have done in the Garden of Eden, you chose pollution.' His use of the word 'pollution' was odd and feared I was going to be faced with some trumped up charge of singlehandedly filling the seas with empty pot noodle jars.

I imagined I was going to be made to answer for modern man's sins. That would have been harsh, as I'd done my bit to help the green agenda in the past. *Surely*, I thought, *I cannot be held responsible for the depletion of the ozone layer, destruction of rain forests, acid rain and over-fishing.* I was about to tell St. Peter that I had once earned a Blue Peter badge by sending aluminium milk bottle tops into the programme, but he stood up and towered menacingly over me.

'What are we going to do with you?' His Whiteness tugged on his beard as if genuinely pondering on his question. What would you have answered in my position to plead your case for redemption?

'What are the options?' That was all I could come up with.

After a short pause, and having given his beard another tug, he said, 'Well, I am in a quandary here. You are involved in an interesting scenario that I am rather keen to see played out.'

'Do you mean…?' My question was interrupted.

'I want you to return to the land of the living and continue your interactions with Nicholas. When we next meet, and somehow think that this will be soon enough, I want you to report

238

on what has come of the individuated products. I am sure that there is something more to this than meets the eye. And while you are about it, keep your ear to the ground. Listen out for any talk of biological weapon development, artificial intelligence, Big Pharma and crypto currencies – stuff like that?' I hadn't a clue as to what he was referring. I thought *Crypto what?* However, I didn't want to highlight my ignorance about what was probably the sort of everyday chat served up on Breakfast TV, so I didn't ask for details.

I recollected the time I sat in Nicholas's office in front of a man who barely knew how to charge his mobile phone. I replied, 'I think you have the wrong idea about Nicholas, but I am very happy to oblige.'

'Good.'

I suddenly found myself in a psychiatric hospital.

Psychiatric Hospital

I can't say I recall everything about the psychiatric hospital, but what I do remember is clearly engrained in my memory: the barred window, shiny oil-painted walls… and the distant sound of whimpering and whining like being in some dogs' home.

I didn't sleep at all during the night-time; that was when grey apparitions appeared with hunchbacks and limbs hanging at odd angles. They came slinking over and gathered around the foot of my bed, muttering and keening. Only by banging the bedstead was I able to keep them at bay, and it wasn't until the first rays of weak sunshine found their way into the room that they finally floated away.

As the morning light strengthened, I tried to go to sleep, but the moment I closed my eyes Leon's face leaned down towards me brazenly laughing and hissed, 'Confess.' All I could do was keep repeating the same thing. 'I want to tell the truth, the whole truth. sh, sh, sh!' I found that my lips dried out exceptionally quickly and I had difficulty even swallowing.

Each morning, waiting for breakfast to arrive each morning, I would feel a chill run across my back. I would then huddle up tight and pull the blanket right over my head. This offered some momentary relief, but I would immediately start feeling hot and then cold again, so cold my teeth started chattering. This seemed worse than the torments Leon had talked about when he tried to put me off going into rehab. For some reason his words had a sing song quality to them and kept going around my head, 'If they try to make you go to rehab, just say no, no. No.'

241

Other than the night-time apparitions vanishing, daytime provided no respite. Despite being awake I never felt like I had re-ascended from the chasms and sunless abysses of sleep. My sense of space and time were powerfully affected.

Space swelled and was amplified to the extent of immeasurable infinity. This did not disturb me as much as the vast expansion of time. I sometimes seemed to have lived eighty or a hundred years in one day.

Each day offered just one mildly positive occurrence. Shortly after a tasteless breakfast had been served up and cleared away, the nurse, an ugly old woman with a hag tooth like an old-fashioned tin opener and a Woodbine voice, administered a wretchedly small injection of methadone. How can anyone stay alive on a dose of that size? It didn't seem to do anything to assuage the torments and anguish of withdrawal, which continued to weigh me down like lead.

If there is a benefit of a forced stay in a psychiatric hospital then it is the opportunity to reflect on one's life, death and rebirth. Often, I thought about my meeting with St. Peter and how lucky I was, despite my very blemished soul, to be given the chance to redeem myself.

Having been returned to the mortal coil, I resolved to change. Big time. Root and branch. The whole six yards as our American cousins would call it. I doubted whether few others had had such a clear wakeup call and I intended to repay St. Peter's trust in me.

I even reflected on my old school reports, particularly Mr Duffield's comments that I needed to be able to self-reflect. If only

242

he could have seen me in the psychiatric hospital; he would have been impressed. I reflected a great deal and understood that my miserable escapades were due to the entanglement with Nicholas De'Ath. I resolved to have nothing more to do with the charlatan and give him a piece of my mind if I ever had the misfortune to meet up with him again.

In the evenings, I sat in front of the bleak, barred window in my room expecting some figure to appear. The suspense was intolerable, but no one came. This pattern was repeated for a number of days and nights, which I cannot enumerate. Then, one evening, after the shadows of the bars of my window had mirrored and timed the sun's westward move across the sky, I came out of a doze with a start. Sign Man was sitting on a chair in the corner of the room. He was immediately recognisable and wore his customary style of outfit; on this occasion in a bright green colour. He had his sign with him, which bizarrely, now read, 'Children Crossing', so I assumed he must have mugged a passing lollipop lady.

I asked Sign Man how he had got in and had Nicholas De'Ath sent him? He didn't answer my questions; instead, he stood up and opened the barred windows, which was surprising, as I assumed it was permanently locked. After a struggle, he forced both himself and the sign through it. I jumped out of bed and looked out of the window. Sign Man was standing on a ledge beckoning to me to follow him.

The opportunity to escape was too good to miss. I tightly fastened my dressing gown and followed him through the open window. After making an easy climb down a drainpipe, we soon disappeared into the gloom of the late evening. We walked in companionable silence for what seemed like mile after mile in silence. The surroundings were burnt out, drained and dead. The black road narrowed away towards the horizon, but the scenery seemed to be unchanging. I felt like I was treading the rim of some sort of great donkey wheel, kicking it behind me step by step but not advancing at all. At first, I believed that my desire to eradicate everything had actually turned into reality. But, eventually, we approached the outskirts of a town where the tangled remains of a gasometer standing out of the landscape broke the monotony.

I had no idea of the town's name or where it was; in truth, I had never seen anywhere like it before. After passing thatched bungalows and terraced houses made of straw, we arrived at its centre. Here, the narrow streets were jammed with wooden fronted shops, catering more for entertainment and personal services than for tangible goods and provisions. In fact, setting aside its unusual buildings, it presented the appearance of a typical modern town centre. There were tattooists, ear piercers, nail bars, tanning salons, betting shops, dubious herbalists, various shops selling mobile phone paraphernalia, fancy-dress shops with skeletons in the windows, pet shops selling coiled snakes and the usual array of charity shops and coffee emporiums, all of which were empty. Especially the windows of the charity shops were universally grimy and covered with hand-written 'sale' signs trying to shift the tired, dusty tat on display.

Bizarrely, for a town notably completely absent of any kind of transport, we passed a used car lot squeezed between two ancient looking warehouse or factory buildings. There were a few rusty cars out on show and, with its rear-end tucked half way into a small workshop at the back of the lot, I thought I saw a Jaguar XKR, but in the darkness I couldn't make out its colour.

244

We turned into a side street where there were a number of old-style taverns that reeked of smoke, stale beer and pickled eggs. We had seen no passers-by up until then, but here people lay sleeping in doorways like bodies washed up in the tide.

It wasn't long before I felt the need for a drink and no sooner had I registered my thirst than Sign Man walked into the middle of the road and raised his 'Children Crossing' sign as if to stop the non-existent traffic. I crossed the road and found myself in front of a tavern, the likes of which Long John Silver might have frequented. I stooped and entered through the low entrance door formed of ancient timbers. To my wholehearted surprise and delight, Corvid was standing behind the bar, seemingly glowing. Conscious I was still in my pyjamas and dressing gown, I looked down to make sure nothing untoward was peeping out.

I desperately wanted to spend a few minutes in her company, but she was determinedly business-like, saying, 'Good evening, Nicholas is expecting you. If you would like to go through.' She directed me to a door at the back of the room and in passing by I inhaled her particular scent.

Pushing open the door, I entered a room bathed in light reflected from a huge log fire burning in an inglenook fireplace. In the gloom, I could just make out De'Ath's green-lit bureau with its ship's compass, which I now reasoned must be a sort of mobile office. Sticking out of a typewriter was headed paper embossed with the same gold font as that on the first letter I had received from Nicholas De'Ath and Partners.

After acclimatising to the light for a little while, I made out the shape of De'Ath sitting in a Windsor chair in the shadows. He wasn't in his normal dollar green pinstripe suit but, instead, wore a red velvet smoking jacket, edged with black brocade over what looked like royal-blue silk pyjamas. Next to him, a fat cigar was smouldering in an ashtray, shaped like a grasping hand, on top of an Arabic style coffee table decorated with arches and mother of pearl motif inlays.

He beckoned me over and invited me to sit next to him on a Moroccan leather pouffe. After sitting down, I made out that the walls of the room were covered with a red baize fabric and that a dark sheepskin rug, almost two inches thick, covered the oak floor together with cushions and a Turkish hookah. Not surprisingly, the room smelt of leather and cigars but is also had an underlying aroma redolent of the forest floor on a hot day.

Then, I noticed Corvid sitting at the desk. She had somehow followed me into the room without me noticing. Nicholas eventually asked, 'How are you William? I can't imagine the accommodation is up to much.' I tried to put a brave face on it.

'Oh, it's not too bad. At least the bed is comfortable. And you?'

'Business is booming. It's a record year for noughts.'

'Is there no limit to the noughts you provide?' I decided would be sociable for a while until a suitable opportunity arose to confront him with the fact that he was personally responsible for my decline and fall.

'It's simply a bottomless pit.' Nicholas answered.

246

'There is something I would like to know about your business.'

'Go ahead.'

'What happens if nobody can pay back the noughts? If there is a crash, surely you lose all your noughts when debts go unpaid and banks lose money.' I hoped I'd found a fatal flaw in his business plan.

'William, don't worry about me. That's what I'm looking forward to. When all the poor sods like you can't pay back their loans and the banks stop lending, even to each other, Governments step in. Central Bankers are the real experts at tap, tap, tapping. And, oh boy, when they start they will never stop. Strings of noughts so long it is almost impossible to count them. And who do you think supplies their noughts. Yes, you've guessed it.'

I wondered if there was any limit to the amount of noughts Nicholas could provide, but changed tack, 'And what about the individuated products?'

'When you ignored my letter, I assumed you weren't interested. But, since you ask, the individuated products are fuelling a boom of unprecedented proportion. It's a pity you didn't respond, I could have cut you a great deal' I was reminded of the dodgy second-hand car salesman, then, maybe because of the association with being ripped off, my blood boiled and I went on the attack.

'You promised success.' I almost spat the words out.

'And you had it.'

'For such a short time.' I snapped back.

'It seems it was for the best. Some can handle it, others can't.' The surge of blood through my temples had already abated and all I began to feel was self-pity.

'What am I going to do now?' I almost whimpered.

'If the path you are on is leading in the wrong direction, then take stock.'

'Can you help me?' My voice sounded so weak and piteous.

'Did you read the contract?'

'Er… no.'

I looked towards Corvid for some sort of support but she didn' meet my gaze. Nicholas continued, 'I promised you success. Did you not have the red Jaguar, an industry award and a Blue Plaque' I delivered. Now you are in my debt.'

'I had the red Jaguar for a few days, the industry award was just to humiliate me further and the Blue Plaque had the wrong company on it.' Tears were already forming.

'Didn't you tell the Angels your company was called Dynamo Blink?'

A shiver ran down by back as I suddenly, and hopelessly belatedly realised the nature of the contract I had signed and who I was actually dealing with. I exclaimed with some force, 'If this is some sort of Faustian pact, I've been robbed.' I was heartened at how easily I recollected the story of Dr. Faustus selling his soul to the devil.

'How do you mean?' Nicholas replied with feigned innocence.

'As I recollect the story, Dr. Faustus had an extra twenty-four years of service from Mephistopheles before he had to give him his soul. What did I get?'

'Now you remind me, such a nice man. But he was a doctor.'

'What...?' I was lost for words. After the pool of silence became too deep I mumbled, 'And what about me now?' My voice sounded like it was being dragged up from the deepest of wells.

'Oh, I still have some work for you.'

I then recalled that I had been given a mission by St. Peter and particularly the instruction to keep my ear to the ground. Understanding that I had a chance of being favourably received by St. Peter, even if that were to be a long time in the future, I tried to bring to mind the topics he had highlighted. However, I have to admit to not remembering them exactly. 'Does this have anything to do with biological products?' I asked and Nicholas cocked an eyebrow.

'Such as?' I actually had no idea what St. Peter had in

mind so I just blurted out the first thing I thought of.

'Yoghurt?' I realised I had better move on. 'Or what abou artificial limbs... or was it intelligence?' Nicholas furrowed brow indicated he didn't know as to what I was referring, so I hit him with what I considered was the big question. 'Have you com across a big farmer?'

'To whom have you been talking in the psychiatri hospital?' I decided not to raise the issue of cryptic crossword Nicholas continued, 'I think you are addressing the wrong person. From his blank look, it was clear that he had no idea as to what was referring.

'Completely the wrong person.' Corvid chirped up fror the darkness.

The conversation was interrupted by the arrival of Kairos, th Time Manager. He was in his usual demob suit and was swingin his pocket watch around on its chain. 'Time.' He called and sounded like 'last orders', given that we were in a taverl However, instead of saying, 'Drink up,' he launched into some so of lecture. 'Time is a force as well as a dimension. Have you nc felt its force just the same way as it eases uranium's journey t lead? Haven't you felt its tug? Time is not only a force, it' precious; especially when it is up.' I felt like I had at the end c one of my company appraisals, utterly deflated and now, death tired. I immediately fell asleep. I have no recollection of the lon walk home, but the next thing I remember I was back in my cell.

The rain beat down for days afterwards, shrouding the worl outside from my sight. *Long may it continue*, I thought, *I don need the world anymore... and no one in the world needs me*

250

However, despite my wish simply to cease to be, a regime of sorts had been established for me that involved some social contact – albeit of a very institutionalised kind.

Firstly, there was the daily visit of the nurse who I found out was called Hazel Knut and I came to quite like her. Setting aside her protruding tooth, she reminded me of the hostess at the entrepreneurs' awards especially as she had stumpy, trotter like hands. Strangely, her smoker's voice hid a soothing and pleasant manner. Then, there was the occasional visit of the psychiatrist. He was a bearded man with small round glasses and a pointed beard. He reminded me of a famous psychiatrist, possibly Austrian, but his name slips my mind.

I found it odd that his nails were bitten to the quick and understood that he must have entered the profession to work off his own neuroses. Not that I had a shred of sympathy for the man who was effectively my gaoler and I took pleasure in playing the difficult patient. I remember one particularly amusing conversation. It started by me asking, 'What do you propose to do with me now?'

'What would you like me to do?' His innocent questions obviously hid a cruel and spiteful character.

'Send me back to my flat; I could continue the treatment at home.'

'It's not as easy as that. You are sectioned.'

'Well you cure me then or at least get me well enough to be un-sectioned. You invented morphine, extracting it from the dried, rattling seed-heads of that divine plant – so you can damn

251

well find a painless cure for it.' Actually, I meant that and said it with some venom.

In the endless hours of confinement, I often replayed Google's description of H's withdrawal symptoms. I didn't experience any hallucinations, but I must say that the rest of the description is dull pedestrian and completely inadequate.

What the addict deprived of H, even for a mere hour or two experiences are not feelings of depression, dejection or even low mood. This is not where the suffering lies. It is a state of indescribable irritation of the stomach, unrequited thirst accompanied by intense perspirations that feel like you are sweating out droplets of fat.

There isn't a cell in the body that doesn't thirst. But thirst for what? Being wrapped in wet palm fronds and having cucumber segments placed over my eyes whilst drinking India's monsoons, or lying naked on sea sponges whilst swallowing the winter mists of the Emerald Isle, or sitting on succulents in the Amazon rainforest whilst absorbing the incessant rain would not have slaked my thirst. There is not enough water in the Scottish lochs to prevent a dry, slow, suffocating death. That's what lies behind the academic and anodyne phrase, 'a depressed condition'.

One day, I was lying on my bed in this, so called, depressed condition when in walked Leon with a trolley load of books. immediately assumed I had slipped into a dream state and was about to say, 'I confess,' when his booming laugh confirmed that he was real. It was a sweet reunion, and I asked, 'How come you're here?'

'Da Feds caught me with a stash of uncut cocaine. I tried to argue it twas for me own use but dart didn't cut da mustard.'

'Yes, but this is a psychiatric hospital. You're not mad.'

'No, I is not stayin' in hospital. I is ordered to serve on a community programme and as it 'appens I ain't complainin'. In, fact I can't believe me luck, business is good here too. Praise da Lord. If der is any ting you need, just let me know!'

'Surely, not H!'

'H, grass, C, E, you name it.'

'But, I have no money.'

'For old friends, it's on account.' For me, the clouds passed, the sun came out and the birds started to sing.

It was only when Leon had left that I realised he was still in possession of my credit card and pin number so I was sure I was going to pay for my sweet reunion. But what is money? I had no other use for the stuff.

Each daily visit from Leon, with his trolley of books, allowed me a few hours of calmness and serenity, delayed until after 'lights-out'. For these few miserly hours I was happy. Nothing upset me when I was with H. However, the time with H was so limited, her visits were over too quickly and, for the rest of the long day and night, all I could think about was her return.

Another inmate I was surprised to see was The Stage Manager

from the recording of Angels. I bumped into him during a daily exercise session, which consisted of a miserable couple of circuits around the quad of the Victorian pile. It was only later, that I chillingly remembered Nicholas' comment to the Stage Manager about schizophrenia. I quite often saw the Stage Manager at these sessions, but, quite frankly, he was rather a bore as all he went on about was his impending heart attack. But, at least, he provided a link to the outside world. Also, if I felt down, seeing him made me think of David Evans's head rolling around on the helipad, which soon cheered me up.

The Awards Ceremony

Sleep continually eluded me in the psychiatric hospital and I would often look out into the stygian night. Somewhere, beyond the scary forest and the icy river, was the strife-torn city with its multitudes rushing to keep heads above water by frantically chasing the next dollar. In contrast, I was able to let my thoughts go wherever they wanted. In my solitary cell I was almost happy. Nothing concerned me. I needed nothing and had nowhere to go. No one was calling me, but then, one night, I heard my name and a gentle tap, tap, tap on the barred window.

I moved closer to the window and was surprised to see the figure of Kairos, the Time Manager, standing outside. I tried the window, which to my astonishment was unlocked and I let him in although it was a struggle for him to squeeze his round frame through the small aperture. Once inside, he complained of being hot and took his jacket off. Instead of a checkered waistcoat, he wore a tank top with thin, garishly coloured hoops around it. I could hardly believe this style faux-pas and asked him, 'Why the change in attire?'

'Oh this, I have just come from the opening of another bierkeller and these tops are all the rage.' I didn't want to hear any more and simply offered him a chair, which he settled in as if he was preparing for a long stay.

I got back into bed and Kairos said, 'You'll never believe, old fruit, what is happening out there.'

'I'm not that interested.' Genuinely, I felt 'out there' was a different world, and one that didn't include me anymore. However, my response didn't stop Kairos from filling me in.

255

'The stock market is on a bull run the likes of which ha never been seen before. I don't recall anything being this crazy And the public can't get enough of the individuated products. Th Angels are becoming super rich and shares in Gorgo Industries ar going through the roof.'

'I hope not all of the Angels are getting rich.'

'Especially So Su Mi. His *All About You* is blazing th trail.' My throat constricted so violently, it felt like someone ha grabbed it from behind.

'My *All About You*.' I was very sharp.

'Don't take it too hard. Nicholas did warn you.'

I was already tired of Kairos and was rather curt with him, 'It lovely to see you but why are you here?'

'Oh, I have an invitation for you.'

'Me!'

'Yes, you. Nicholas De'Ath has tickets for the *My T Awards* and wants you to be one of his guests.'

'I don't want to be reminded of my humiliation.'

'Don't worry about that. It is time for retribution.'

'Retribution?'

'Yes, and you wouldn't want to miss that would you?' I didn't know what he was talking about the word had appeal.

'When is it?'

'Tomorrow night'

'I don't have anything to wear.' It didn't occur to me to think I was also in a psychiatric ward and couldn't just walk out.

'Don't worry about that. Be ready for Nicholas at six o'clock.'

I didn't feel sleepy but must have dozed because when I opened my eyes Kairos had disappeared.

True to his word, there was a tap, tap, tap against my window at precisely six o' clock the next evening. I walked over and to my delight, both Corvid and Kairos were waiting there to be let in. Kairos carried a large suit bag, which I took off him as he squeezed into the room. He then helped Corvid hop through the window. In the gloaming, she looked more radiant than ever in a dark dress with narrow shoulder straps. These only partially covered dainty, silk bra straps, holding up her impressive breasts. I had before failed to fully appreciate the scale of her décolletage. Kairos, on the other hand, looked his normal seedy self and still wore the check suit but now sported, as well, the clashing tank top.

The bag contained a dinner jacket, trousers and dress shirt on a hanger. In her silky, hard to place voice, Corvid told me to hurry up and get ready and I took off my dressing gown and pyjamas without any embarrassment. After all, she had seen everything before.

Once I was suited and booted, I was disappointed the trousers were the right length and that I hadn't been supplied with odd socks. However, I realised it was probably best that I didn't draw any attention to myself at these awards. As the finishing touch, Corvid tied my bowtie for me, and standing near to her, I smelt her wondrous scent. I thought we must look quite a matched pair, as her dress was made of the same velvety, midnight blue material as my jacket. I felt a fluttering sensation and wondered if it was too late for me to fall in love again.

With me appropriately attired, and feeling excited for the first time in a long while, we started to walk towards the door. I was beginning to understand how Kairos operated and wasn't surprised that we instantly found ourselves outside the hospital gates standing by a large, jet-black coach and four. The hooves of the shiny, shimmering, black-coated horses were clopping impatiently on the road, and the plumes on their heads jittered in the light of the rising moon. The coach's door flopped open, and a hand was extended towards Corvid who rose and disappeared into the coach without obvious effort. I struggled to follow her and needed the help of Kairos pushing me up by my bottom to get me in. Considering that he was very squat and looked like physical exercise would be a health hazard for him, Kairos nimbly followed me into the coach without assistance.

Inside the coach, a candlelit interior revealed Nicholas, sitting back on a padded leather seat, wearing a very similar outfit to my own. I was reminded of just what a handsome fellow he was. Sitting next to him in a new, canary yellow and black, hazmat suit was Sign Man. Once Kairos had plonked himself down next to me

Nicholas gave two sharp knocks to the side of the coach and it started off with a jolt.

Nicholas offered us drinks from a crystal decanter and, despite the rocking of the coach, poured us all rather large measures of green liquid without spilling a drop. I firmly clasped the fine crystal glass, hoping it was the elixir of life I had been given at A&E in Camden all that time ago. Alas, it wasn't morphine, but as I drank the unfamiliar, bitter-sweet, curiously alien-tasting liquid, I had a feeling of being filled with helium and becoming weightless. Nicholas made a strange toast, 'We've begun to drink from the cup of retribution. Now let's drain it to the very bottom.' Whether or not it was the effect of the strange beverage, I felt the sensations of normal life returning to my body and looked across at Corvid. I avoided her eyes and stared, instead, at her remarkable décolletage.

The trip by coach and four was surprisingly quiet and comfortable. After a few more glasses of the liqueur, which was rapidly acquiring a taste like newly gathered nectar, I even had the sensation of flying. Nicholas adopted an avuncular tone as he engaged me in conversation, 'Tell me William, what are your ambitions?'

'I don't have any.'

'But when you get out of hospital?'

'I'm happy there. Everything is provided for me. I don't need to make plans.' Corvid leaned forward revealing more of her soft, cushion-like breasts.

259

'Even the humble amoeba makes plans.' She whispered and I didn't know what to say.

'Think about it.' Nicholas instructed.

All too soon, we were soon trotting along The Strand heading towards the Royal Opera House, where the awards ceremony was being held.

Do I need to describe a TV awards ceremony to you? I don't think so. Who hasn't sat watching one of these because there was nothing better on? What you might not appreciate, though, is the pecking order that applies; India's caste system is less rigid. Take for instance the queue to get into the Royal Opera House. When we arrived, there were masses of smartly turned out 'C-list' people, some vaguely familiar, who were standing patiently in line, hidden out of the view of the cameras. They were periodically released from this queue, in small batches, to walk along the red carpet and into the Opera House. 'B-list' celebrities were similarly corralled in a smaller queue, but they had a longer walk along the red carpet, allowing them more time to linger and attract the attention of the photographers who waited patiently to hook the bigger fish. The 'A-list' celebrities got to wait in a smoky huddle of limousines but were called for in strict order. The megastars simply arrived at a time of their choosing.

It was strange that our coach and horses didn't cause a stir in the waiting crowd as we rocked up and joined the A-list huddle. This must have been because the husband of David Varnish, wearing his customary oversize spectacles, chose this moment to breeze past the onlookers and all attention was focused on him. I was surprised that we were soon called forward and realised that

260

Nicholas's celebrity stock must be high indeed. On the red carpet, Corvid put her arm through mine as we walked along whilst camera bulbs epileptically flashed into our faces. I was particularly pleased to see we were ahead of John Lewis who was being allowed in as part of the current release of A-listers. Possibly because of the effects of the green brew I gave him a cheery wave but, luckily, he didn't see me. I certainly didn't want any further interaction with a man who had gone out of his way to humiliate me.

Before taking our seats in the stalls we congregated with other A-listers in the VIP area and sipped champagne. I'm sure we presented quite a sight standing there, Nicholas looking sharp and dapper, Corvid awesomely beautiful, Sign Man hip and Kairos out of place in his demob-style suit and ridiculous tank top. However, no one even seemed to notice us, let alone came over to chat. I, for one, was pleased, as I had tired of the, 'Up yours,' greeting that had become the normal way people spoke to me.

Instead of chatting, we watched TV's finest arrive. Beetle and Dick, the Saturday Take-Off hosts, were there brimming with confidence that they would win *The Best Show* award for the seventh time. Then, there was a celebrity businessman who wafted by smelling of fudge or burnt sugar. Soon after this, there was William Woss, the presenter who couldn't pronounce his W's so he was known as Big Rilly. If you don't know who I am referring to, he is the one who fronted Top Goat, as in Greatest of All Time, and fell from grace after being found guilty of tax evasion. I was surprised to see him looking so slim, as I'm sure that the last time I had seen him on the telly he had developed quite a paunch.

I couldn't be bothered to celebrity spot after that and decided to

try and get to know Corvid better. I chatted about how nice th
surroundings were and then asked her where she was from. He
reply was rather abrupt, 'Why do you ask that? You have bee
there.' Initially, I assumed she had meant that strange town I'
walked to with Sign Man and then realised she meant the forest
had dreamt about. I wasn't able to quiz her further as there was a
announcement for us all to take our seats.

Big Rilly turned out to be the host for the awards. He wa
obviously on some sort of rehabilitation programme for falle
presenters working their way back up the slippery media pole. Fc
some reason, the audience found him moderately entertaining. H
had an easy repartee with the people called up to receive an awar
and despite being rude, and sometimes completely vulgar, h
somehow didn't cause offence. It was a trick I had yet to pull off

The other thing you don't realise when watching an awarc
ceremony on the TV is how long it goes on for and how man
ridiculous awards there are; *Best Clapper Loader* for instance.
almost seemed as if the whole process was designed so that ever
one of the attendees left with something - however insignifican
Thankfully, as the ceremony progressed the awards became mor
meaningful. The award for the *Best Reality TV Show* went to *Th
Garden of Eden.* Watched by millions, but I don't need to tell yc
how stupid this is. When they played a clip on a giant screen c
scantily clad women and men with tattooed torsos cavortin
around under a pretend apple tree, all I could hear was the ta, t
ta of Nicholas' laugh.

The awards seemed to go on longer than a day with nothing to d
in my hospital room, but at least I was sitting next to Corvid ar
could occasionally look sideways at the fold between her breast

This was a sight to behold, and it had a stimulating effect on me.

Finally, may da Lord be praised as Leon might have appositely put it, there was the award for *Best Show*. The short-listed nominations were read out and included Angels, Jungle Fever and Saturday Night Take-Out starring the serial winners, Beetle and Dick. When the announcer provided details of the final nomination on the short list, it was as if life had suddenly taken a big swing and hit me right in the solar plexus followed, as I fell forward, by an uppercut to the chin.

This nomination was for a science programme called, *The Future is Imagined – Time, Uncertainty and the Nature of Being - Revealed*. Big Rilly informed us that the BBC's series had wowed the nation, rocked academia and had been such a success that the hardback book sold over ten million copies. I could hardly focus but realised my lost manuscript must have been picked up by some academic or TV producer after I left it in Costa Packet.

I didn't have time to think about the loss of royalties from my book before Big Rilly announced, 'And the rinner is…' As current practice dictates, he paused for twenty minutes or so before adding, 'Angels.' Beetle and Dick triumphantly jumped up and immediately sat down again, trying not to appear crestfallen.

Out of nowhere it seemed, John Lewis and the Angels entourage materialised on stage. There was kissing and tears, but in the mêlée, Delores Headon came to the fore and turned, posed and generally showed off her hourglass figure. The whole production team seemed to be up there obscuring the celebrity investors and, try as I might, I couldn't see New Guy. Eventually, I leant across to ask Nicholas if he knew what had happened to the absent Angel.

263

His answer heartened me no end. 'Oh, So Su Mi has other concerns. Hackers have stolen all the personal data on *All About You* and the bank details of the recruiting companies. A class action will be taken against him and he will be made bankrupt. He'll never work again.' I couldn't help myself, planted a kiss on Corvid's cheek and said out loud, 'So Su Mi. Yes, you will be. If that's not Karma, I don't know what is.'

Big Rilly invited the audience to watch a clip of the funniest moment on the show when an entrepreneur had made a pitch to the Angels to sell a worthless company for one million pounds. This unnerved me, although, interestingly enough, so far no one had identified me as Odd Socks, nor had they given me the finger. Nevertheless, I feared I was being set up for further humiliation.

As I anticipated, my pitch, shown on a huge screen, was accompanied by gales of laughter from the audience. Later, when I was seen giving the finger to Delores, I feared the vibrations from the clapping would loosen the massive crystal chandelier dangling precariously above us from its fixings. Then, the scene on the video changed to the pitch made by Nicholas, specifically to the film of the Angels trying the perfumes. As soon as this started, Big Rilly looked around and wrinkled his nose as if someone in the group had farted. Then, I found that I could also smell something disgusting like a combination of cabbage and rotten fish-heads, and it wasn't just coming from the stage.

The video clip moved on to when Delores Headon tried on the corset. At this moment, on stage, it seemed as if an invisible person had grabbed the live Delores around her waist and was squeezing her tight. She buckled over, her face went bright red and her eyes looked like they were about to pop out of her head. The video

264

continued playing, but everyone's eyes were focused on the live Delores as she clawed at her dress, ripping open her buttons as she tried to release something. All around the auditorium, other ladies were, similarly, ripping at their garments and trying to discard them as quickly as they could.

As ladies rushed out of the hall madly undressing as they went, the video clip changed to show the Angels trying on the individuated jewellery. On stage, John Lewis immediately grabbed his hand as if it had been bitten or scalded. Jimmy Bannaman did the same and Delores Headon clutched at her necklace, the jewels of which had turned from red to black. Around the auditorium many women, and some men, were trying to rid themselves of rings and necklaces that seemed to be burning into them like hot coals.

Not even Big Rilly could prevent the awards descending into a complete disaster. He too had started to undress, and it soon became obvious that he was wearing one of the Angels' individuated, and now highly ill-fitting, corsets. Much to my delight, a large hairy belly suddenly popped out over of his straining trousers.

I had never seen anything quite so entertaining.

The auditorium quickly emptied because of the stink from the fetid perfume, ladies fleeing to release themselves from their strangling corsets and people rushing out to put burning rings under cold taps.

Of the few people present who weren't fleeing from fetid smells, fighting with corsets or burning jewellery, most of them were on their phones shouting out instructions like, 'Gorgo Industries. Sell the shares. Yes, the lot.'

Our small party was left alone to its own devices. I tried to say something to Nicholas but could not get past his ta, ta, ta. Eventually, he stopped laughing and said, rather enigmatically, 'How I love to see the Angels fall,' then announced, 'come on, let's go, the Debtors' Ball awaits.'

The Debtors' Ball

Outside the Royal Opera House, the coach and four was awaiting our return. The horses stood still, apparently unruffled by the sight of half-dressed women sitting on the nearby pavements and men angrily stomping about waiving their fists amidst a plethora of flashing blue lights and distant wailing sirens.

Back in the coach, once everyone had stopped laughing, Nicholas turned to me and said, 'I'd like you to be the Master of Ceremonies on this occasion.'

'Me?' I was flattered but couldn't hide my surprise.

'You.'

'Me...why?'

'I have business to attend to.'

'But I have no experience.' Corvid squeezed my hand reassuringly.

'All you have to do is welcome the guests, announce the entertainers and hear confessions and repentances.' Even in the candlelight, I could see he was focusing on me with his kindly eye. 'William, if you conduct yourself well tonight, you can make one further request.'

'One further request?' I asked quizzically.

'Yes, one request.'

'Oh. Thank you… By the way, where is the Debtors' Ball

'The Longworth Estate.'

'The Longworth Estate!' You can imagine my surprise.

'Do stop repeating me.'

It didn't take us long to arrive at the Longworth Estate. The coac
stopped near the sad looking basketball court. I was afraid the fera
kids would be there, but luckily, they must have been mugging ol
ladies elsewhere. The estate appeared deserted, unlit and unlive
in, but I could make out a distant thud, thud of techno musi
Nicholas stepped down from the coach first. Then, he, ver
gentlemanly, gave Corvid a hand down. She was followed b
Kairos and Sign Man (strangely sans sign). I was the last to vaca
the carriage and, being unaided, almost tumbled out.

Burning candles, set in red glass vases, lit a path leading to th
entrance of Philip Brown House. The 'Sir' preceding the name ha
been scratched out on the faded nameplate. Corvid noticed m
looking at it and said, 'Yes, he had his knighthood revoked after
was found he had molested young girls and raided his companie:
pension funds to pay for his lavish lifestyle.'

'But why is the Debtors' Ball here?' I asked.

'Oh, Nicholas has a very ironic sense of humour and find
it amusing to have the Debtors' Ball in a building dedicated to suc
a villain. He's someone who Nicholas is particularly lookir
forward to meeting in the future.'

268

Nicholas obviously knew where he was going. He confidently strode into the concrete monstrosity of a building and then turned into a stairwell and up a foul-smelling staircase. Nicholas, almost gliding up the stairs with his entourage following on behind, must have presented any onlookers with a very odd sight. I focused on Corvid's shapely calves and ankles as I immediately followed behind her.

On the first floor, as we turned onto the connecting corridor, the thud, thud of heavy-duty speakers, now blasting out some terrible rap music, was palpable. In fact, the walls of the flats seemed to vibrate with the colossal noise.

Some people wearing hoodies loitered close by the flat from where the music seemed to be coming from. As we approached, I became alarmed as I noticed this 'welcoming party' included the intimidating ringleader who had threatened me on my previous visit to the Longworth Estate. I tried to attract Nicholas's attention so to warn him, but Corvid turned to me and put a finger to her lips. Surprisingly, as we drew near to this group, they all turned and bowed and waved us through into the flat.

The door opened straight into a small, grimy hallway, which led into an ordinary front room with a big settee and chairs, upholstered in soiled red Draylon fabric decorated with greasy looking antimacassars draped over their seatbacks. Three ducks flying up the wall vibrated violently in tune with the blaring music.

My attention was drawn to some scantily clad women wearing feather boas standing around a couple of dodgy looking guys who were ostentatiously handling wads of fifty-pound notes. I concluded that these must be the dealers who had so scared Leon.

Standing behind this group were three men. One of them, a younger man wearing a tight pair of trousers, stood erect, his chest pushed out to show his manliness – all vim and Viagra. The other two appeared to be politicians or some other corrupt officials like CEOs of pharmaceutical companies. They were hunched shouldered and sad looking, giving the impression they had just returned from the funeral of a close friend.

The dealers were too busy counting their loot to notice us. But the others looked up as we came in and Nicholas acknowledged them. 'Nice to see you Astrid, Zenaka, Faisal, Mr. Smith and Mr. Klein. Sorry to hear about Claxso.' They nodded deferentially and thought, *strange name.*

At the back of the room, I saw none other than the guru who had extolled the secret of success, sitting at a table with her glamorous assistant.

I was speechless with shock to see Biella and Stan at Nicholas' party and stood stock-still with my mouth wide open. Now cannot quite understand why, on seeing Nicholas for the first time at his office, I didn't immediately recognise how closely he resembled Stan. Indeed, Biella and Corvid were also almost identical. I suppose I was confused by the fact that they were exact copies but in the negative. The reversal was so complete that even the power balance had flipped.

Nicholas and his body-negative obviously knew each other as they shared a complicated series of handshakes with each other and even body pumped. The greeting with Biella was more business like and I thought that she even gave the faintest of curtsies. With the reunion complete, Nicholas turned to me and asked, 'Do you recognise Biella Zebuv?'

'Yes.' I said turning towards her.

'I trust you've put the secret to good use?' The striking, evangelical intonation of her voice was just as I remembered it. By way of an answer, I simply twirled around showing off the new suit and the lack of holes in the bottom of the trousers.

'And Stan?' Nicholas asked before I could add a verbal response to Biella's inquiry. After Nicholas' greeting, I tried to be cool and offered a palm for a high five. It is embarrassing when that sort of gesture is not reciprocated.

Leaving me with my hand in the air, Nicholas escorted Stan and Biella to the back of the room and engaged them in conversation.

I felt numb. Had my seemingly voluntary attendance at Biella's course been part of a plot to get me involved in Nicholas' enterprise? Was I the victim of some well-planned scam? It almost seemed too elaborate and fanciful to be true. I eventually regained my composure and asked Corvid, 'Are they Nicholas' partners?'

'They are part of the franchise.' Corvid's answer didn't make complete sense.

'Part of the franchise?' I asked incisively.

'Yes, the world turns on entrepreneurs developing new businesses to entice people to continue to spend money on items they can't afford and don't really need. Of course, most of them go straight into debt. It all helps keep the noughts flowing.'

271

'Did Nicholas arrange for me to go on the course with Biella and Stan?'

'Haven't you understood anything about how Nicholas works? He simply provided the opportunity. You chose to go.' Corvid's reply intrigued me, but I didn't have time to ponder on it as Nicholas beckoned us both over, and then conducted us into a backroom. And what a room it was. Initially, I assumed it was some sort of 3D holographic projection, but soon had to accept that this council flat had the characteristics of the Doctor's Tardis. We were standing in a tropical forest where scarlet-breasted parrots with green tails, hopping from branch to branch, produced deafening screeches of, 'Ecstasy, ecstasy.' Mandrills swung from lianas creating darts of red and blue under the shimmer of the canopy.

The forest with its hot, steamy air soon gave way to another, cooler room, the amazing grandeur of which was difficult to take in. We were standing at the head of a vast red-carpeted staircase that cascaded down in front of us. At the bottom of the staircase, a huge ballroom stretched out with marble columns so high that they appeared to support a starlit sky. I couldn't get my head around how this was possible but decided that, as so many fantastical things had already happened, I would just accept what I was seeing and leave further reflection until after the ball.

Appearing to be rather out of place, a DJ's deck stood against one wall. By its twin turntables a thin white man with earphones on, wearing a tank top of all things, stood swaying in time to an unrecognisable piece of rap music being blasted-out of the stacked speakers. Competing with the noise, I shouted to Corvid, 'It's shame about the music.'

272

'Why's that?' She shouted back.

'Because it's trash.' Unfortunately, the song ended suddenly and I heard my voice shouting out 'trash' echoing around the vast hall. It reminded me of my time in front of the Angels, and I was embarrassed when Nicholas turned to look at me. I was thinking about the reward he had promised if I did a good job, and hoped I hadn't already screwed-up the opportunity. As we walked past the DJ, Nicholas shouted, 'Norman, nice to see you.' Norman in return blew him a kiss. Kairos, who had somehow appeared at my side, whispered in my ear, 'Finboy Fat, we're very lucky to have him. He's huge.'

The ballroom was empty of guests but a row of men, wearing black trousers and starched white shirts with trays in hand stood ready to attend to them when they arrived.

I felt splendid; privileged even, to be part of Nicholas' entourage.

We went through into another hall that was bordered by walls of red, pink and milky-white roses, which also gave way to a starlit sky ceiling. In this room, a one-hundred-and-fifty-piece orchestra were making a squeaky racket. I hoped this was them warming up rather than being 'New Music'. Close to the orchestra, a small group of men and women were standing around. The men were small and swarthy, whilst the women wore red tops, short skirts and black fishnet stockings. I assumed they must be pimps with their prostitutes until Corvid, who was next to me, said, 'I see the tango dancers have arrived.'

We walked past the orchestra and Nicholas called out, 'Herbert, so pleased you could make it.'

273

'Herbert Von Carryon.' Kairos whispered in my ear as the tail-coated conductor raised the whole orchestra to its feet with wave of his baton. Herbert then turned away from the orchestr and gave a low bow with his left hand placed on his heart.

We carried on into a banqueting hall with a roof lit by, what looke like, thousands of bunches of illuminated crystal grapes. There Nicholas, turning towards me, told me he needed to attend to som business with Biella and Stan and that I should ensure all wa prepared for the evening ahead. He then strode off with th business gurus followed by Kairos and Sign Man. I wasn disappointed as this left Corvid and I together, but I wondere what I could add in the way of preparation, as everything seeme to have already been organised to the last detail.

Tables heaved with oceans of fresh seafood arranged in dishes, c splayed out on great blocks of ice. I say fresh, I mean aliv gasping oysters, grasping crabs, beckoning calamari, twitchin lobsters on layers of salad, a feast of feathery shrimps, piled plate of pouting pike and a stunning selection of sturgeon, salmon an sea trout. All ingredients for the biggest and best barbecue I'd eve seen. A bare-chested man of the deepest ebony colour, wearing a elaborate headdress including two gazelle horns, tended the rec hot coals.

Also, on offer were sizzling saucers of sautéed sparrows, snail snake, spiced sausages and steaming saucepans of stewed stea next to what looked like horses' hooves heaving with a greas; gelatinous gloop. Corvid must have seen my look of distaste an said, 'Yes, Nicholas likes to cater for all ethnic tastes.'

The floor was covered in glass and below us, I saw semi-nake demonic-looking men with pampas-wide chests and washboard stomachs preparing more food in boiling cauldrons and frying pans set over intense, fiery flames. I was just wondering what had happened to the Chippendales when Corvid slipped her arm through mine.

I had never felt so good, especially as I could feel the pressure of Corvid's left breast against my right arm. She escorted me to the other side of the hall, where there was a vast selection of drinks. Together, there was enough booze to float a battleship. A centrepiece was formed by a fountain of champagne emerging from a Nebuchadnezzar and then cascading over what looked like diamond-encrusted rocks before decanting into waiting flutes that never seemed to overflow.

Close by was a large table piled high with candy jars full of pills of different colours and shapes. Each was labelled with a letter and, together, they made up a substantial part of the alphabet, although I suspect 'B' for Beta-Blockers was there just for effect. There was even H but I had no desire for her. Corvid, it seemed was providing a sufficient high. C was there in its powder form, great, jars full of the dreadful snowy white stuff. Next to the jars was a pyramid of brown phials simply labelled Morphine, possibly for the older age group, and in front was a tray holding a pile of syringes. The label said, 'single use only,' and I thought, *It's good that Nicholas should think so much about health and safety.*

On another table, woven baskets brimmed over with a fabulous fullness of freshly foraged fungi. I had never seen such a variety of magic mushrooms. Even those seeking a vegan high were catered for!

275

We walked over to a table that bore teetering piles of crockery. Each item was decorated with a gold embossed crest in the shape of a raven and a goat together with a monogram of ND. I picked up one of the plates and looked at it closely; the shiny porcelain reflected the lights that hung from above. By some trick of the light, when I returned the plate to the pile, the raven fluttered its wings and the goat jumped.

Corvid also fluttered, unlocked her arm from mine and said, 'As you have to announce the tango dancers later on, why don't you go and speak to them now. I will see you back at the entrance.' I didn't like being separated, but went over to the tango dancers and, to my frustration, found that they only spoke Spanish. As my Spanish is limited to, 'Dos cervezas por favor,' and, 'donde están los servicios,' I found that communication was helped by raising my voice and asking, 'Where – are – you – from?'

'Argentina' The leader seemed to understand when I was slow and loud.

'What is your group name?'

'Qué?'

'Your-name?'

'My name, Carlos.'

'No, not your name. Name – of – troupe?'

The leader answered and I was going to comment that the name of the band seemed inappropriate but had no time for any further

276

interaction as Kairos had come up to me and said, 'Two minutes to midnight. Please be ready for the guests.' I was amazed how late it was and ran swiftly up to the top of the stairs leading from the ballroom where Corvid was waiting.

The first guest arrived a few minutes before the stroke of midnight. And what an arrival; a man half undressed, with his braces undone and his bowtie missing, shot into the room. He looked about him in a suspicious way, as if he was expecting to find someone up to no good. When he saw us, he calmed down, came over and shook our hands. Once he had moved on and was making his way down the stairs, Corvid explained, 'He murdered both his wife and her lover, after coming home early from work one day to find them in bed together. He now arrives early at all events.'

A couple, arriving right on the stroke of midnight, followed the cuckold. At first, I assumed they must have come in fancy dress as they appeared at the top of the staircase as two filthy, decomposing, mummified figures. I was about to say something to Corvid, when the bandages and wrappings started to melt away to reveal a handsome man with a beautiful consort on his arm. He wore a black dress suit with diamonds for shirt buttons and she wore a full-length, sequinned gown, topped off with a fox draped around her neck as a collar. Corvid welcomed them, 'Madame and Monsieur Coupes De Pied, what a pleasure.' As they descended the staircase, she turned to me and said, 'A great chemist. Poisoned his first wife.' The fox fur collar winked at me just before they disappeared from view.

After the shock of these first arrivals, the remainder of the first wave of guests was disappointingly run-of-the-mill. They mostly comprised black marketeers, prostitutes, tattoo artists, body piercers, cabaret dancers and estate agents. It seemed that Corvid read my mind, as she said, 'Nicholas respects all his guests especially these, the true entrepreneurs.'

The slow trickle of guests turned into a stream of people of all races and creeds that blurred into one. No sooner was I told someone's name than I had forgotten it. Corvid, however, was able to provide a running commentary, explaining who the guests were and what they had done. She showed no fear or favour, treating stellar 'big hitters' like Caligula and Messalina the same as all of the procession of traitors, poisoners, gallows-birds, procurers, hangmen, card sharps, informers, spies, rapists, brothel-keepers, bankers, hedge-fund managers and time-share salesmen. The attendees were a cross section of society with a surprising number of Lords and Ladies, Peers of the Realm with the odd Knight of the Garter, plenty of judges, JPs and a disproportionately large representation of HR Managers.

I didn't worry about remembering names, I simply welcomed the guests, smiled, invited them to eat, dance and drink and to generally let their hair down. The last instruction also applied to David Evans, who arrived carrying his head under his arm. The snazzy cravat, he had been wearing on the evening of his demise was draped over his severed neck, and the overall effect was to make him look like a shop mannequin. Although the people in the queue jostled behind him, I managed to have a brief conversation despite my opening remark being a little insensitive. 'Just flown in?'

'Not exactly.'

'How are things?' I was quite enjoying talking down to

278

him.

'Actually, not too bad. Interesting people here.'

'Really!'

'Oh yes, I've struck up quite a relationship with casino operators and Ponzi scheme billionaires.'

'Good, catch you later.' But, I had already decided I wouldn't.

Actually, David Evans was not the only person with a displaced head. When I had a moment, I asked Corvid about a ragged looking man who also carried his unsmiling bonce under his arm. She said he was once a priest who had been unfrocked after a regrettable incident involving a butternut squash. He had taken the injunction that he should forever hold his head in shame very literally.

People began to arrive in a torrent that swept past me and flooded down the stairs at such a rate I feared the vast hall would soon overflow. On every step there seemed to be a tail-coated man, accompanied by a semi-naked woman. I was worried that one of the guests, at least, was likely to break her neck walking downstairs, as she was wearing manacles. The buzz of the voices even seemed to drown out the thud, thud of the rap music that hadn't stopped for a moment.

It wasn't long before the party was in full swing. The champagne fountain was in constant use with everyone carrying a flute. Guests with itchy feet had already begun to gyrate on the dance floor. I even made out Messalina twerking up against Caligula.

As the flow of new guests began to dry up, I had time talk to som
of the latecomers. I welcomed a Russian with the strange name o
Nobby Chock who, Corvid informed me, had been a Soviet spy
He had been ordered to kill a defector in Salisbury with a powerfu
nerve agent decanted into a perfume bottle. However, his wife ha
rifled through his bag before he left and had tried on the scent.

Another guest was a good-looking man with a youthful face th
contrasted with a shock of white hair. Setting aside the hair, b
reminded me of myself prior to losing too much weight. Befo
coming towards us, he stood back and, pulling out a blue and whi
silk scarf, patted his brow as if hot and then, surreptitiousl
dabbed his sad eyes. Looking towards the new guest, Corv
explained, 'Every day this man, Rupert, burns his blue and whi
silk scarf in a stove but in the evening finds that it has bee
returned to his bedside table.'

'Why's that?' I asked.

'He strangled his wife with the scarf.'

'Then he deserves his eternal reminder.' I said, but the
remembered the cocaine-fuelled hallucination in which I ha
tightened a blue and white scarf around Susan's gizzard.

'Don't be too judgemental. His wife had a pernicious typ
of bone cancer and was in the utmost agony. He loved her so muc
that he could not bear the thought of her experiencing any mo
pain.'

'Oh.' Uncharacteristically, I felt a flood of sympathy for the man and, as we shook hands, I asked him whether he liked champagne. When he said he did, I invited him to get drunk and forget about everything. I can be quite sensitive at times.

Once all the guests had arrived, I took the opportunity to draw breath and rub my hand, which was sore and limp through extensive hand shaking. For some reason, I asked myself, was it fate that had brought these people to the ball or had their free choices in life earned them eternal unrest? Clearly, this was too difficult a question to answer, but it prompted me to ponder for a short while on where everything had gone wrong for me? I so wanted to blame Susan or Nicholas, but at that moment I realised that the only person in the dock for my car-crash of a life was me. 'Guilty of gross negligence.' I imagined the judge saying and I mouthed, 'Send me down.' Corvid looked at me and said, 'It's time for us to go.' A chill ran down my back as I feared she was going to add, 'Hell and damnation awaits.' But, instead, she said, 'You need to announce the tango dancers.'

We headed down the staircase together, then through the heaving mass of drinkers and dancers and on into the room holding the orchestra. I stepped onto the rostrum, and looked out at a mass of faces stretching the length of the hall, I felt nervous but said, 'brush' to myself and smiled; this did the trick, dispelling my nerves. The last notes of the orchestra ebbed away and I announced, 'Ladies and Gentlemen, now for your delight and delectation, please welcome, all the way from Argentina, The Buenos Hairys. Please vacate the dance floor.'

Redemption

The Buenos Hairys might have had an odd name, but the dancers were magical. From the very first bars played by the orchestra, flashes of heels and legs whirling and entwining entranced the audience. It was stunning and, sadly, too soon over. To wild applause the dancers retreated from the floor, but the orchestra carried on playing fiery tango music.

Corvid came up to me and said seductively, 'I love tango, do you dance?' As I have two left feet, I fell into paroxysms of laughter and laughed so heartily I felt old once I had finished. Nevertheless, Corvid took hold of my hand and led me onto the floor. 'Just relax.' She said and held me in a warm embrace with her soft, welcoming breasts pushed against my chest. Relaxing was hard to do but from somewhere, devil knows where, I had a sense of being able to tango and, after taking her hand and returning her embrace, took a step forward. Corvid stretched a leg back and we set off around the floor with long, even strides, swept along by our own momentum. Then, without separating at all, she was around me and seemingly through me, and yet our feet did not clash nor our knees collide.

Just as the dancers had done, Corvid flicked her heals and caught me with powerful snaps, hamstring to hamstring. The faster the orchestra played, the better I danced. Walking, then whirling and wanting, we were one entity in two bodies. Even our breath came as one. On the final note, I flicked my eyes to meet hers and felt young and strong. It defies explanation, but this was the best experience I had ever had.

I thought of the philosophy that underpinned Dynamic Link and realised that dancing tango perfectly illustrated the second dimension of time. I had been completely in the moment. The music surrounded us and time was compressed. Without thinking about it, hours of dancing felt like it had taken place in minutes.

Fleetingly, I thought about Susan, who had hated dancing, and then I contrasted her with Corvid. I don't think I had ever felt as connected to another human being as I did in Corvid's arms. She must have felt the same as, when I placed my hand around her waist and led her off the dance floor, she said, 'Shouldn't life be more like this? A couple connected and responding together, so that two becomes one.' I felt warmed by her sympathetic tone.

'Indeed.' Then I thought, *That's odd, as surely she would have to be tough minded to work for Nicholas De'Ath.*

'You don't have to be evil.' She said and I realised that must have verbalised my thoughts.

I reluctantly relinquished hold of Corvid to continue my role as master of ceremonies. I made my way through the throng of merry revellers back to the rostrum to introduce a succession of fire eaters, magicians, jugglers and a very odd act, consisting of three fat, naked men holding balloons and trying to move them, in time with the music generated by a small band, so as not to reveal their manliness. Possibly because the band had to compete with the overwhelming sound of the orchestra in the next hall, the act was only partially successful, and the more the men messed up their timing, so revealing their less than impressive genitalia, the more the audience guffawed. Amidst all this debauchery, I noticed one face stood out, that of Rupert who was now completely drunk but retained his immeasurably sad eyes.

284

I felt the presence of Corvid next to me before I felt her touch my arm. All I wanted to do was stay close to her, basking in her increasing radiance and inhaling her unique aroma, but she had joined me to pass on an instruction, saying, 'You are needed in the main hall.' Then, she put her hand through my arm and led me through the main hall to the bottom of the staircase where Nicholas was standing.

Nicholas signalled Norman to stop the dreadful noise. To my blessed relief, he immediately complied with this instruction. At that precise moment, a figure appeared at the top of the stairs and the eyes of all the assembled company looked towards him. Outwardly, he was no different from the thousands of other male guests, except in one respect, he was literally staggering with fright. Bright red blotches glowed on his cheeks. He was stunned, and I was too, because this was Gordon Bennet, the Governor of The Bank of England.

Nicholas first pointed towards Gordon and then crooked his finger to beckon him down the staircase. His wobbly legs looked like they could easily buckle and send him toppling down. I noticed for the first time that he had a glass eye. As he stood before the assembled crowd, which despite the generally high level of intoxication had become completely silent, Nicholas addressed him, 'Gordon Bennet, so pleased you could make it.' He pointed to me. 'Don't you recognise my emissary? Gordon's good eye now swivelled in alarm to look at me.

'I do.' However, he didn't look or sound too sure of his answer.

'I sent him to tell you of the dangers of neoliberal

capitalism. What was your response? Oh, yes, to ignore him completely.' Gordon turned paler than I considered any ashen face could be and gibbered, 'I remember.' I was momentarily taken aback as I hadn't realised that I'd been sent to the award ceremony as an emissary. As I recalled, I hadn't mentioned anything about neoliberal capitalism and had only warned of the dangers of the unrestrained noughts.

I wondered whether Gordon had died, along with the rest of the assembled guests, but Nicholas made it clear he had not by saying, 'You may carry on now, but forever you will be remembered as the man who could have forestalled the crisis. Let it be on your head. Now you must have a drink.' Nicholas led the frightened man towards the banqueting hall and I just caught him saying, 'We aren't here to ruin people. We just give them the opportunity to do that for themselves.'

The wall of sound returned as Norman fiddled with his decks and restarted the music, if you can describe such a dreadful cacophony in that way. I quickly made my escape to the next hall, away from the chorus that largely featured 'muvvas' for some reason.

With my duties fulfilled, I went in search of Corvid and located her in the concert hall, where the orchestra was playing proper music. I slipped my arm around her slim waist and steered her onto the dance floor. I found myself floating in a fairy-tale pool of happiness, breathing a sweet, dreamlike mixture of revelry and rhythm. The champagne and Corvid's unique, intoxicating fragrance, with its notes of freshly foraged fungi, manifested long-forgotten stirrings in the trouser department. My soul had dissolved like salt in water. I was the crowd and the crowd was

286

We danced a rumba, then a waltz and then a quickstep. Each of them, I performed with amazing skill, never wavering or losing balance, even when performing the most complicated of lifts. Finally, the conductor announced the last number and, predictably, it was a slow, smoochy one. This was the sort of dance I always used to miss out on at school discos because, by the time I got up the nerve to ask a girl to dance, some other blighter had nipped in ahead of me. Now, I was being recompensed in a way I could hardly believe. I had the most beautiful woman in the world in my arms and, what is more, I could report the return of normal functioning to my most vital of organs. I was still swaying gently to and fro when I realised the orchestra had packed up and left.

A large grandfather clock, which I hadn't previously noticed, started to strike. I counted twelve chimes, which was odd because it surely couldn't be midday. All of the guests who were capable of walking had disappeared, and the remainder looked like flotsam that would be washed away on the next high tide. Corvid and I walked around, hand in hand, in search of Nicholas. We found him sitting together with Kairos and Sign Man in a room that was remarkably similar to the one in which I had met him in the unknown town. The strange bureau was there and Kairos was sitting at this slowly typing a letter with one finger. There was no sign of Biella and Stan.

Nicholas sat with his unshod feet resting on a small stool. I was amused by the fact that he wore a pair of odd socks that matched his eyes, one being olive coloured and the other like pale ashes. He beckoned us over to sit by him.

'Have you enjoyed yourself?'

'Completely, it has been the best night ever.'

'I'm pleased you liked it and were able to do such a good job. Frankly, I have been to too many of these.' I actually did feel I'd done well and wondered whether it was time to ask about the reward suggested by Nicholas in the coach. The image of lying down with Corvid came to mind, as did the words of Nicholas 'Ask for more, you are worth it.' However, uncharacteristically, held back.

'Thank you,' I said and then added, 'it is time for me to return to my room in the hospital.'

I wasn't sure why I wanted to go back to my hospital bed but was surprised by Nicholas's chirpy reply. 'Excellent, the right answer. You should never simply ask for anything, especially from those more powerful than yourself.' It was if he had read my mind about desiring Corvid. 'When they want, they will make the offer and give of their own accord. Now, I am making the offer, what one reward would you like for being our host tonight?' For some reason, the imploring face of Rupert came into my mind.

'One thing?'

'Demand it.'

'I demand that Rupert is never again given the scarf he used to strangle his wife.' I surprised myself by making the request, but realised that I had been moved by the recollection of my cocaine-fuelled hallucination. The one in which, I had also used a blue and white scarf to strangle my wife.

288

Nicholas sat back, put his hands behind his head and laughed, 'Ta, ta, ta. Are you asking me to offer forgiveness? Despite being in this windowless room, compassion strives to creep in through the narrowest of cracks. I think you have come to the wrong department.'

'Completely the wrong department.' Kairos chipped in. Nicholas ignored Kairos's comment and continued.

'Although the scope of my department is very wide, wider in fact than some ever thought possible, it is a case of each to their own. What sense is there doing something that is the business of another department?'

'Is it not possible?' I asked dejectedly.

'I won't do it, but you can.'

'Can I?'

'Of course.' Nicholas put his forefinger to his lips, 'Shhh, shhh. Don't tell everyone, but we all can.'

Unexpectedly, the door burst open and Rupert, dishevelled but now apparently completely sober, walked in. I stood up and turned to him. 'As tonight's host I have it in my power to forgive you.' Rupert gave a shriek and fell spread-eagled, face down on the floor. When he tearfully said, 'Thank you,' I had never felt so overjoyed and, somehow, it was if I had forgiven myself. So, redeemed, a great weight fell from my shoulders.

After Rupert had got up and walked backwards out of the room, bowing slightly as he did so, Nicholas said, 'That, I must admit, was a trifle unsettling.' Kairos looked directly at me and commented.

'Time is a terrible thing, it can make you go quite soft. Nicholas shot Kairos a glance with his cruel eye. However, when he returned his gaze to me, the pale ash predominated.

'I have been a little unkind to you.' Nicholas continued 'You're not a bad sort. Tell me what you would like? One more thing is possible, because I didn't do anything myself in that last case.'

I recalled being with St. Peter and the opportunity he had given me of a second chance. Then I thought of Corvid and spending more time with her. In the end, it was a simple choice. St. Peter could whistle if he imagined I was bothered about spending time in his company or that of his ilk.

'What I really want is to join Nicholas De'Ath and Partners.' I don't think I had ever said anything quite so true in my life.

'Ta, ta, ta,' Nicholas burst out laughing and, when he had controlled himself, added, 'you are already on the firm. But, as I have come to like you, I'll think about a promotion.' I had no idea I was already part of his operation and put it down to the contract I had signed.

The Reunion

At the first opportunity, once back in the safety of my hospital room, I asked Leon if he could give me an extra dose.

Leon, my ever-obliging friend, readily supplied me with the extra dose, which I took in full anticipation that H's nightly visit would be very special. Indeed it was, my heart beat fast and there was a return to the old intensity. But, the reunion was ruined by someone shouting, 'Quick, he's arrested.' Although intrigued as to who had been arrested, I wanted to point out how grammatically incorrect the statement was, but couldn't summon up the energy. Then I heard the word, 'Clear,' but it was spoken as if it came from the end of a long tunnel. The last words I remember hearing were, 'I'm afraid that's all we can do for him.' In the same way that TV screens faded when switched off, in the days when they were powered with valves, the light faded to an intense dot and then that too disappeared leaving an infinite blackness.

I don't know how many days had passed since Leon had been overly generous with his extra allocation of H, but a distant, fuzzy, celestial light disturbed the infinite dark. It grew in intensity and coalesced to resemble a moon and penumbra.

Slowly, the penumbra shrank and the image transformed itself into a bare, light bulb.

This single bulb hung over a small wooden table, and I found myself sitting back on a plastic chair looking up at the bare, unshaded light.

A shiver started in my scalp and worked its way quickly down to

my toes. When I looked around, I wasn't surprised to find that
was back in the interrogation room. My blood temperatur
dropped at least a few degrees when I saw St. Peter sitting nea
me, rocking back and forth on his chair. I felt so much like a tyr
with a slow puncture that I wouldn't have been surprised if I wer
hissing as well.

I looked into St. Peter's chestnut coloured eyes and waited for hir
to speak. I didn't have to wait too long. 'Back so soon?' H
accompanied this welcome with a hollow laugh that had all th
humour of a truncheon bearing down on a soft, yielding skull.

This was one of his, now familiar, rhetorical openings. H
continued, 'Well, I was not expecting that. The Devil excelle
himself this time. I didn't have time to ask him to explain th
comment as he quickly followed up with these doom-laden word
'Now, what are we going to do with you?'

'What are the options?' I was sure I would regret askir
this question, but it just popped out. St. Peter sat forward, claspe
his hands, turned them inside out and cracked his knuckles as if I
were some weightlifter getting ready for his lift.

'I am sorry, but there is no choice.'

'No choice!' I didn't like the sound of that at all.

'Yes. Heaven is out of the question, of course!'

'No, not hell, Surely not?' I experienced a terrible feelir
of panic, as intense as anyone could imagine. I didn't want to I
some mummified figure whose only opportunity of escape was

attend the occasional debtors' ball.

My heart rate spiked and the room seemed to tilt to starboard as if HMS Findler had just been caught amidships by an enemy torpedo.

Eternal conscious torment was going to go on for a long time. I hardly heard St. Peter say, 'No. Not hell…'

St. Peter shifted about uncomfortable on his chair and then stood up. He started again, 'Not hell…' but stopped again. I could not help but think he was struggling to say something he was embarrassed about. 'Hell…,' he began again, 'hell has been rather over advertised.'

'How do you mean?' I was confused and sought some clarity with a further question, 'You mean, it's full?' The burbling brook of St. Peter's laugh told me that wasn't the case.

'Constant conscious torment these days is reserved for a very few souls.' I struggled to take in the implication of this unexpected, revelatory remark.

'Do you mean that all this talk of hell and damnation has been over-done?

'Possibly.' St. Peter sounded sheepish. 'HR has come up with the crazy idea that hell for the masses is discriminatory.'

Now I understood why St. Peter had looked so miserable during the time he had spent with me. It was now blazingly obvious that his role as head gate keeper had been rather scaled back in size and

scope. I must say I smiled such a smile that my face seemed to cu
in two.

I sensed that I was somehow in a position of advantage and neede
to press home with it. Although no longer bothered about singin
Kumbaya My Lord for eternity in the company of the selected few
nevertheless I said, 'Well in that case, are you offering a place i
heaven?' There was the burbling brook again.

'No, we have annihilation for you.'

'Annihilation!' This word has very nasty connotation
especially when it refers to your own being.

'Yes.'

I was almost too nervous to speak and hoarsely whispered, 'B
that sounds worse.'

'No, it is as if you have never existed. You will not b
bothered about the silence and blackness of eternity ahead an
more than the eternity that preceded you.' I was immediatel
reminded of my old professor, and what he had described all thos
years ago.

Despite the professor taking comfort in the idea of annihilation,
didn't like the sound of it at all. If Kairos could provide a kink i
time's arrow I would have been able to return to the Professor'
study and categorically tell him he was wrong. There is n
immediate comforting, black, eternal nothingness once you sli
the mortal coil. You still have to endure the final appraisa
However, that is something he will have already learned by now

I'm not sure I've had many great 'aha' moments during my life, but I experienced one then. 'But my book.' I stuttered.

'What about it?'

'It lives on. It is I. I am in people's minds, and, from what I have heard, it is a huge success and a force for good. I will continue to live on through my book, annihilation or not.'

St. Peter furrowed his brow and said, 'Hmm. I am a busy man and haven't got the time to discuss this now. However, I accept that the book is useful. It does help people to realise that they are the architect of their own lives and cannot blame others for the path that they are on.' After this favourable comment, I couldn't bring myself to admit that I had lost faith in my own ideas, and so I kept quiet. It looked like St. Peter was softening and might even pardon me and allow access to the VIP lounge.

St. Peter's eyes filled with pleasure, and his voice had a light airy tone as he said, 'You can wriggle all you like, but there is one specific reason why I have taken a personal interest in you.' I didn't like the sound of this because it chimed with a question I had been harbouring for some time; why was this right-hand man of all right-hand men interested in a junky like me? He continued, 'Yes, I was intrigued as to what my old friend was up to.' The penny well and truly dropped. His only interest had been in finding out what canny little scheme Nicholas had up his sleeve.

I felt used. To be honest, I lost a lot of respect for St. Peter when he made this admission. All this reviewing and making me feel bad was a cover for wanting to find out what Nicholas De'Ath was up to. How cruel!

295

At that point, I wished I hadn't been so cooperative in the investigations as it was now clear that his interest was clearly not focused on me.

Despite being miffed with St. Peter, I nevertheless was becoming desperate to be given the celestial equivalent of the keys to the management toilets. Even if hell had been rebranded or given a makeover, I wasn't keen to give this eternal nothingness a try. I was quite surprised with my assertive voice when I demanded 'Surely, I have to be charged with something before I get sent down!'

There was a sharp knock from the other side of the two-way mirror and St. Peter hastily departed the room without a single word. I suddenly realised that the mirror must be for third parties not so much to observe me as to monitor the performance of St. Peter. HR must have come up with some crazy new way of providing peer reviews.

When St. Peter returned he had even more of a hangdog expression. I was thinking about making another last-ditch attempt to bond with him when he said, 'The list of charges is very long but I am advised that your sexist and racist attitudes alone are sufficient for the punishment that awaits.'

I was about to complain. I haven't a racist or sexist bone in my body. I thought, *even if I do find Benny Hill funny, surely the punishment does not fit the crime.* I even smiled at the trivial nature of the charge. I thought I'd show my conceit by asking for my unpaid BBC licence to be taken into account. However, I realised that irony was likely to be unhelpful at such a critical moment. Rather, I said, 'Whoa, Pete, just before you scatter my soul across the cosmos, don't you owe me something? I feel degraded, sordid even. You used me!' I could feel myself welling up like the second-rate actors had done at the TV awards.

St. Peter looked at me with his big brown eyes and said… 'Look this is very irregular but…' He didn't finish the sentence and, just as I was thinking, *I ain't seen nothing yet,* he raised his hand skyward. I assumed he was going to make the sign of the cross but instead of doing that he jabbed his finger and pointed at me. 'For services rendered. Go.' This sent a chill of cold fear down my spine.

The Georgian Villa

My home office is located so that it looks out from the south-facing aspect of my Georgian villa over a classical English country garden. As I sit at my desk, looking out past the garden to the driveway where my red 4.2 litre Jaguar XKR - with grey leather interior of course – is parked, all of these recollections seem very unreal, like half-remembered dream fragments.

I no longer crave for H. My obsession for her has disappeared. Now that I am clean, it would be all too easy to explain my experiences as the product of an overactive, drug-fuelled imagination. But, I can't accept this explanation, given that my diaries and other personal documentation sit on the library shelves next to me, in the very same boxes used by St. Peter. Proof!

I am busy, far more so than I ever imagined I could be, but I do have time to dwell on my interrogation at the hands of the Head Gatekeeper. Certainly, with the benefit of hindsight I can see the case I should then have mustered. But that's me all over; the bright idea or riposte to a sarcastic comment comes to mind too late.

The argument for the defence in the case of *William Taylor Findler versus the Crown (of thorns)* has the same simple foundation as I put, unconvincingly, to St. Peter, namely: it wasn't my fault - but this time it's backed up by the facts.

There is no better way of gaining a perspective on life and death than having your soul weighed in judgement. With the benefit of having gone through the process twice, there are certain facts that stand out.

Let's start with the fact that free will is a hoax. Choice is a con and personal agency is a sleight-of-hand card trick. Just because we have words for things like freedom, choice and free will for example, this doesn't mean that they exist. It's a trick that language plays on us and is used by the powerful to ensure that we, the proletariat masses, don't rise up and accuse them of buggering up our lives.

The only real decision I made in my life with heartfelt commitment was to join Nicholas De'Ath and Partners. But, as I have just described this was never my decision to make. It had already been made for me, I was already on board.

In fact, when I review my early life experiences it is clear that I was at the mercy of events even then.

I would ask you to review your own life experiences and observations. I am sure that we can all agree that the early steps taken towards the world of work largely determine the end result. Certainly, when I look back I see how small nudges, seemingly insignificant events, completely determined my future career. The entry in my diary for 20th January 1974, reads, 'Received a letter today from Kings College Hospital. *Dear Miss Findler, thank you for your interest in physiotherapy, I enclose a leaflet.*' I'm sure I made it clear my name is William.'

I'd written to the teaching hospitals, because I was stupid enough to follow some random careers advice provided by my PE teacher Mr. Kharna (we called him Jim behind his back). I don't think he had any qualifications to be a PE teacher, let alone a career advisor. Nevertheless, all those unlikely to go to university had to dutifully spend time with him having our future career mapped

300

out. In one of these sessions, Jim asked if I had any interests, and I told him I'd developed an interest in the human body (is there a teenager who hasn't). But, he didn't have a sense of humour and took my quip as being a serious reply. As a result, he suggested that physiotherapy might be of interest as a career. To show willing, I duly sent letters to the teaching hospitals asking for course details. All the replies I received were addressed to me as a girl. This was in the seventies; sexism had yet to be invented, and I just took it as a clear indication that physiotherapy wasn't for boys.

I often wonder how different my life might have been if I'd challenged gender stereotyping. Would I have ended up where I am now? No! It's almost impossible to think that a diligent physiotherapist would be sitting where I am now, wondering what the hell had happened. However, I might be wrong. Perhaps we end up at the same predestined point in life whatever initial path we choose to follow?

After what has happened, I am now left with the distinct feeling that the thoughts shaping my life were not actually my own. I even doubt now whether the idea for the award-winning sock business was mine. Oh yes, I twisted and turned in the face of events, but like a fish on a line, I was captured by a higher power. That is the only sound conclusion I believe to be possible.

Didn't Nicholas clearly demonstrate the hand of fate in peoples' lives by predicting the early demise of David Evans?

Nicholas revealed the fact that Jason had already set the conditions in train that made the separation of David Evans's head and torso inevitable. Surely, a similar cause and effect sequence occurred

301

that led to my demise. Unfortunately, I can't blame Jason for my predicament.

Despite what Kairos tries to do with his little distortions, I am convinced now that the arrow of time flies in a straight line and is aimed at a specific point. And, I might add, not a very pleasant one.

In the unlikely event I do have an independent mind and free will, what sort of free will is it to choose to give it up and let the chemical compounds of H and C take it over?

Any investigator of an accident, worth his or her salt, will want to go beyond the fact that a car hit another car or a helicopter decapitated a well-known TV personality. To get to the root cause, apparently, you have to ask seven why's. Such as, why did the helicopter cut off the David Evans's head? Answer; because the rotor blades sliced it straight off. Why did the rotor blades do this? Answer; Because the aircraft slewed around - and so forth to the seventh 'why'. In this way you go back from the incident, along its cause and effect trail, to find that Jason had been out the night before he serviced the helicopter's rotor blade and had consumed a skin full. Mind you, if you ask more than seven why's you end with generalities like; Because Igor Sikorsky invented the single antitorque tail rotor - so it's a fine balance.

When I undertake the 'seven why' analysis, it is far from clear as to why my gravy train hit the buffers. However, it is clear that Jason was a supporter and friend, even co-collaborator. The same cannot be said about Nicholas De'Ath. The diary clearly shows how despite my misgivings, he 'recruited' me to help him unfold his masterplan.

302

Even Biella and Stan Zabuv, as Corvid had revealed at the Debtors' Ball, were somehow in on this conspiracy.

I've had the opportunity to think about what I had learnt on the course and how, in fact, I had suffered through going down the entrepreneur's rocky path. What a gilded picture Biella and her ilk paint of it and to the pot of gold at its conclusion.

I can almost hear Biella's imploring voice, 'Be the master of your fate, be the captain of your soul.'

In a sturdy craft, I had metaphorically left the safe haven for the new world with a strong following wind in my sails. However, what Biella had failed to mention is that once launched there is no way back, especially if you have followed the mantra, 'make, massive irreversible decisions.' What those who are selling the secret of success don't tell you is that once you are out to sea the wind changes direction and the sturdy craft springs a leak.

The only, so called, free choice I had was to continue and hope that, at best, I would land shipwrecked on a desert island.

What they don't tell you about at business schools are the real demands put on the entrepreneur. What they don't tell you about are the sleepless nights, the worry and, in my case, the fact that nobody understood a word of what I was saying.

And now I am talking of powers greater than myself, I must refer back to St. Peter. When I think about him, it is always with a tinge of sadness. How the mighty fall! His role, with the ultimate power to send people upstairs or downstairs, has been limited, through the exercise of political correctness, to keeping an eye on his archenemy. With the use of hell as a final destination having bee[n] essentially banned, I do wonder whether the massive an[d] unrestrained spread of evil across the world is due to there bein[g] no ultimate sanction. But that is taking my attention away from m[y] principal concern; namely, me.

In a story with many odd occurrences, there is one aspect th[at] stands out above all else. How come I feel saved by the Devi[l] When he allowed me to stop the perpetual recurrence of Rupert[']s scarf at the end of the Debtors' Ball I felt redeemed. I suppose, [it] doesn't matter. The most important thing is I'm not carrying [the] burden of guilt like that suffered by most of the other attendees [of] the Debtors' Ball. In any case, I wouldn't have trusted bein[g] redeemed by St. Peter. I can't get over how used I was by that ma[n]

Once upon a time, and it feels like a fairy tale as it was so lo[ng] ago, I used to think that life was like London's Underground Ma[p] It held out the prospect of so many choices, points of entry a[nd] destinations all at my beck and call. However, in reality, life ha[s] become more like an out of control tube train careening through [a] series of flickering stations with the driver, for some reaso[n] unable to take his hand off the deadman's handle.

I imagine myself sometimes summing up the case for the defen[ce] of yours truly. 'I put it to you, members of the jury (for a jury [of] your peers it should be, not some suit who has been in his role to[o] long) in my train crash of a life, it is clear I wasn't the driver at t[he] wheel (well, technically I was in the illustration I just gave, bu[t I] hope you understand the sentiment).

As I say, I wish I'd put a stronger argument forward when I m[et] St. Peter.

Now you have had the warts 'n' all version of my sorry tale, I need your expertise and objective analysis. If you can categorically come to the same conclusion that I have arrived at, then that would certainly be useful corroborating evidence, should I ever again be hauled in front of St. Peter. Although, I suspect that he will be leaving me to my own devices now I am twice dead.

I can't say I am proud of much of it but I hope you don't think I deserve any worse an outcome. God Forbid, I hope you don't think that I was harshly treated by St. Peter! I had a lucky escape there. Heaven by all accounts these days, with HR effectively running the show, is no fun at all.

In the final analysis though, I certainly can't complain. I have plenty of time and I am turning my attention to the follow up of *The Future is Imagined*. It's going to be called *It's About Time*. I have only penned the introduction so far but I already know what the last line will be, 'The future is imagined but it won't turn out how we imagined it to be.'

If you have any helpful thoughts, or even useful contributions to the next book, please send these to me at the address of my eternal employer:

William Taylor Findler
Consultant | Coach | Author
C/O Nicholas De'Ath and Partners
66b North Colonnade
Canary Wharf
London

Epilogue

It's now sometime since I finished telling you about my life and asked for your help in reviewing it. I'd like to thank Dermot O'Logical for taking the time to personally reply. Interestingly, he also took the opportunity to advise about the potential of cryptocurrencies for generating untold noughts. I told him to forget it - Cash is King.

Such a lot has happened since the awards ceremony and after being released from the psychiatric hospital.

Thinking about the awards ceremony still makes me laugh and I have kept a few of the press cuttings. The clipping I like best includes a photograph of a largely undressed William Woss trying to rip off his own underwear. The headline ran, 'Liar, Liar, Pants on Fire.' Typically, the press got it wrong, as it was the jewellery on fire.

Soon after the ill-fated ceremony, a major investigation was instigated with a report on its findings rushed out. It concluded that a magician or hypnotist had managed to fool the Angels into placing unwise contracts with Gorgo Industries. The hysteria at the awards was also explained away as 'mass hypnosis'. Although searches had been undertaken to find the mysterious character in the luminous green pinstripe suit and his weird entourage, they were never found. However, that didn't stop people reporting a range of misfits who only vaguely matched the descriptions published in the press. These included anyone wearing a light green pinstripe suit. Bizarrely, a number of road workers were hauled off for questioning for the simple 'crime' of holding a Stop/Go sign.

At around the same time, the long-awaited air acciden[t] investigation report concerning the unfortunate meeting of Davi[d] Evans's head with the rotor blades of an Agusta 109 was finall[y] published. This confirmed the speculations of the expert cras[h] investigator reported at the time. I expected there to be a heav[y] fine or sanction for the operating company, but no such action wa[s] taken and the company continues to fly a fleet of helicopters. Poo[r] old Jason took the hit! I suspect the investigators used the inferio[r] American 'four why' methodology as all the blame was put on th[e] apprentice, who, one evening, had gone out with friends and th[e] following day failed to assemble the over-locking mechanis[m] correctly. As a result of not using the 'seven why' system I talke[d] about earlier, no one seemed to go on to consider whether Jaso[n] had been trained properly or ask why he was not being supervise[d] whilst he worked. It is a safe bet that Jason's life is ruined.

All of that pales into insignificance in comparison with wha[t] happened in the financial markets on the day after the TV awar[d] ceremony. Only then did it become clear that Nicholas had, a[ll] along, being planning to break the banks.

On September 15th 2008, due to having bought tens of millions [of] shares at bubbled-up prices in the now worthless Gorgo Industrie[s] Lehman Brothers collapsed. This precipitated the onset of th[e] Global Financial Crisis. Soon after this collapse, the U[S] government introduced the Troubled Asset Relief Scheme makin[g] available seven trillion dollars for bailouts of the banks that ha[d] financed the Individuated Products bubble.

I could go into detail about the effect the crisis had, but you live[d] through it and know how deep and difficult it was for some. N[ot] me though, because I had become a partner in Nicholas De'A[t] and Partners.

I now work for Nicholas De'Ath and Partners in a nice office at 66b North Colonnade, which has a fabulous view of the city skyline that always attracts favourable comments from my clients. The only downside is that my office is next door to the HR department and the walls are thin. I'm often disturbed by the sound of wailing and sobbing.

I was with Nicholas at 66b when Gordon Bennet, as Governor of the Bank of England announced the introduction of Quantitative Easing. This is when the central bank buys government securities from the market in order to lower interest rates and increase money supply. Do you see how knowledgeable I have become in this area of high finance?

Ahead of Gordon's announcement, I had been given a rare opportunity to sit with Nicholas in his office. Kairos dragged in a huge transit box marked up with the words, 'Sixty Inch Large Screen TV'. This reminded me of the time I was in Lee Wang's Import and Export Emporium, but the connection was so tenuous I didn't ask whether he supplied TVs to Nicholas De'Ath and Partners. Anyhow, once Kairos had unpacked the TV and set it up, we were just in time to watch Gordon on the BBC news. He had regained his fake smile and, with the TV lighting behind, it looked like he had a halo around his head. He even sounded like some sort of Messiah as he proclaimed, in an evangelical tone, 'I have saved the free world.'

Nicholas couldn't have been in a better mood and I took the opportunity to ask him, 'But is there no consequence to this endless creation of noughts?'

'To everything there is a consequence.' He replied 'Today, people are enjoying themselves in the present without care in the world. They forget that they're effectively asking pitiful future generations to pay off their debts.' However, he didn't show the slightest hint of remorse as he burst into a rendition of, 'Debt glorious debt.' After that he said, 'Let Gordon and the other Central Bankers think that they have established a new world order where the red tooth of capitalism no longer holds sway and that their printing presses keep everyone fed and watered. We know better, don't we?' I didn't like to admit that I hadn't a clue what he was talking about, so I kept quiet.

What I do know is that the crisis provided us with our best year on record. The banks were refloated owing to Gordon's largesse and the demand for noughts rocketed.

I'm incredibly busy. Doing what? I hear you ask.

Do you recall the speech I gave at the Entrepreneurs' Awards night? Well, luckily, others remembered it too. When governments, the media and people in general asked, 'Why did no one see the financial crisis coming?' I stood out as someone with great prescience. I was even interviewed on Breakfast TV and was able to put the boot into the bankers. By the way, I was wrong about the people who work on Breakfast TV. They are a lovely lot and I even managed to meet Carol Churchwood; she does have a toothsome figure. By good fortune, the TV series, *The Future Imagined* had already educated the presenters on the nature of time and I was able to explain that, to their cost, Governments and Bankers had forgotten how profoundly uncertain the future without getting strange looks.

I now act as a business coach and consultant and have a long waiting list of bankers and investors (including the odd celebrity Angel) who are seeking to restore their wealth and happiness. My job is to provide them contracts they don't properly read.

Busy as I am, I still have a great deal of time for myself and I use it wisely. I spend hours in a sexual reverie longing for Corvid. I think back to our time together at the Debtors' Ball and imagine taking the dancing onto a horizontal plane.

Of course, that is no longer possible.

I recollect the last day I spent with her with absolute clarity.

In the morning, a series of visitors arrived at 66b North Colonnade. This was unusual, as Nicholas normally didn't come into the office during the day. Through my office window, I watched Corvid take a group of them into Nicholas' office. The men were wearing either grey suits with garish ties (probably politicians) or polo shirts and chinos (probably CEOs) and the women were all in power suits. I thought I recognised a few faces.

It was just before lunch, and as I was unable to stand any more whining sounds from the HR Department, I felt I needed to spend a little bit of time gazing upon Corvid, so I made my way to the reception area. Unfortunately, it was full of important looking people and Corvid was busy answering questions. I decided to wait until she was free and so took a seat. A small group were seated close by and I was amazed that a member of the party looked like one of the richest men in the world. *What could he possibly want in the way of noughts from Nicholas De'Ath?* I mused.

I was not quite close enough to hear the full conversation, but definitely heard Corvid's name being mentioned plus, 'nineteen' They clearly were talking about the love of my life and speculatin on her age. I felt like going over and defending her honour bu restrained myself. Then I realised I had no idea how old sh actually was.

Shortly afterwards, Corvid directed all of the people through to se Nicholas, and I sauntered over to the reception desk once she ha returned. I casually asked, 'What's going on? It's been very bus today.'

'Nicholas has been giving briefings on the next project.'

'Oh, that sounds interesting. Was that the leader of th MFI and Ted Ross from the NWO I saw earlier?'

'Anybody who is anybody has been here today. Nichola is going to do something that will make the financial crisis loo like a tea party.'

'Really! Can you say more?

'It is not all planned yet but, in outline Nicholas is movin from greed to fear as the ultimate motivator. Driven by pharmaceutical, bio-security agenda, apocalyptical forces ignorance will be running people's lives and ruining the lives future generations robbing them of the freedoms and liber parents wanted to bestow on them. It is simply brilliant.'

'Sounds scary.'

'Oh yes, people will be made to feel frightened. Under the pretext of saving the planet from global warming there will be a health scare. This will involve a biological weapon and forced lockdowns of the world's populations.'

'Did you say biological weapon?' I immediately recalled the conversation with St. Peter. 'And Nicholas has come up with this?' I asked, furrowing my brow. It seemed implausible that Nicholas was behind anything involving high technology or science for that matter.

'No, not all of it. But he has some very clever advisors. For instance, I have a PhD in Virology.' I was speechless and realised that I had rather under-estimated Corvid's role in the Nicholas De'Ath enterprise.

Corvid continued, 'Anyhow, the environmentalists will be happy because it will be end of mass travel and cause a massive reduction in the use of fossil fuels. But debt will be so enormous that Nicholas will have complete dominion. It is beautiful.'

The word 'dominion' resonated with me. I remembered how masterful I had been with Corvid whilst dancing the tango at the Debtors' Ball. I rested my elbows on the reception desk, placed my head in my hands and looked at Corvid's lovely features and marvelled at how the rays of light from the crystal chandelier glinted on her hair. However, the talk of a new project brought niggling doubts about what had happened to me back into my mind.

'Can I ask you a few questions?' I enquired, standing up and making my way over to the leather chair I had sat in when first visited the office. Corvid followed me and, once we had settled ourselves down, I asked, 'Why me? I'm still puzzled as to why Nicholas chose me.'

'Such vanity! Do you think you're the only person whom Nicholas contacted?'

'Not exactly.'

'He talks personally to anyone who calls for him.'

'Really!'

'Yes, and what's more, everyone, at some time in their life, will have a letter with a gold embossed address land on their doormat. It's up to them whether or not they choose to respond to Nicholas's invitation.'

'But I had two letters! I ignored one of them.'

'Did you? But, you still went into the sock business.' It was clear I had somehow drawn Nicholas' particular attention to me and that powerful forces were at work way beyond my comprehension.

Feeling rather weak and insignificant, I tried to big myself up, 'At least I was useful. After all, I was sent as an emissary to warn Gordon Bennet.'

'You were a minor player in Nicholas's plan to break the banks.' Corvid's tone was sharp and then she softened, 'But, you have been well rewarded. Nicholas is not often so generous if allowing self-forgiveness and granting wishes is really very rare. At least you can continue without the eternal remorse most attendees of the Debtors' Ball have to endure.'

Corvid's revelation that I was a bit player in a much bigger drama confirmed what I had always suspected, but they hit me with some force that manifested itself as a physical sensation of being firmly pressed on the chest. Rather defensively, I managed to ask, 'But, I was the Master of Ceremonies, how come I had such a privileged position?'

'I'll tell you if you promise not to be big-headed.'

'I promise.'

'Nicholas wanted to reward you for getting *The Future is Imagined* published.'

'He did?' The pressure mounted on my breastbone. This I didn't understand and wondered, *How come both St. Peter and the Devil liked my book?*

I brushed over the fact that, whilst I wrote the book, someone else got it published. I was confused and asked, 'Why?'

'Haven't you learnt anything?'

'Seems like no.'

'Haven't you noticed that Nicholas hates technology?' Of course I had, it explained why he always used a typewriter, but I let Corvid continue without interruption. 'He is concerned that free will is being undermined by computerised systems and processes together with an increasing belief that humans are programmed to act. People seem to use their freedom, only for the purpose of denying its existence. He wants to defend the idea that humans are moving, choosing beings.'

'Whatever for? That hasn't got much to do with investments or disposals.'

'But it has everything to do with the collection of souls.'

'The collection of souls?'

'Nicholas is right, you do have an annoying habit of repeating what people say.'

'Sorry, go on.'

'There is simply no challenge or fun in dealing with automatons.'

'Automatons?'

Corvid gave me a sideways glance indicating she thought I might be deliberately annoying her, then she carried on, 'Yes automatons, those without free will, those programmed to act, those simply on the track of cause and effect, cannot be judged and found wanting. Damnation awaits only those whose choices have led them there.'

'Wow. Sorry for being thick but how has my book actually helped?'

'Your book, if I can remind you, explains that in a world where nothing repeats, free will is essential. If I can quote you directly, *we are all moving, choosing beings, where events don't simply happen. We are responsible agents.*' The trouble was I didn't believe my own ramblings anymore

'But, I'm not sure why I'm caught up in the drama of Nicholas breaking the banks. And, why did he want to do that in any case? Surely, there's a limit to the amount of noughts he needs to amass?'

'Debt, including huge national debt, provides the best environment for evil to flourish but people still need to choose to act.'

I was in a reflective mood and Corvid also seemed happy to chat. I continued and asked, 'I've seen a kindly side to Nicholas, is he getting soft in his old age, as Kairos seemed to imply?' Corvid looked at me with her yellow eyes, hesitated, as if unsure as to what to say, and then replied.

'Good and evil have been set as polar opposites, but life is messy and is never just black or white. For evil to flourish there needs to be an attractive quality. And what can be more attractive than philanthropy? As you saw today, Nicholas is using some of the world's most famous philanthropists to further his cause. And, even our good characteristics, if pushed too far, can lead to problems.' I tried to think of my own good points I'd pushed too far but couldn't bring any to mind.

This was all too much for my weakened brain to handle and my thoughts returned to the enjoyment of sitting next to one of the most beautiful women I had ever seen. I decided I needed to tell her how I felt. 'Do you know, if Kairos was here and I could get him to reverse time, I wouldn't do it.'

'Why's that?'

'I would choose to live my lives exactly the same. Without all these twists and turns we would never have met and I would not be here now, sitting with you. I feel very close to you.'

I was just about to fully declare my feelings and desires toward Corvid when the foyer turned light green and Nicholas appeared wearing his usual attire. What was odd though was that I'd never seen him anywhere other than in his office before. Gathering us together, he took us to the lift and pressed the button for the top floor. From there we went up a flight of stairs and, after pushing open two doors with 'Restricted Personnel Only' signs on them, made our way onto the roof of 66b North Colonnade. It reminded me of the rooftop where David Evans lost his head. I smiled; happy days.

For a moment I wondered why we had ventured out onto the roof but understood that Nicholas was probably expecting a helicopter. 'Any travel plans?' I enquired, in a light-hearted, conversational manner trying to hide a worry that they were about to leave me.

'There is work to be done in China.' Nicholas replied. I was taken aback given the warning he had once provided.

The conditions on top of the skyscraper were not ideal. The day had been plagued by thunderstorms and, with the sky blackening by the moment, it looked like another one was about to hit us

Without a word, Nicholas, Sign Man and Kairos strode off to the far side of the roof leaving Corvid and me standing by the door. I glanced at her and noticed that tears had welled up in her yellow eyes.

At that point, lightning cleft the sky, momentarily enhancing Nicholas's light green pinstripe suit with a phosphorescent glow. The thunder crack was almost instantaneous, and when I looked back, Nicholas and the others had disappeared. I turned towards Corvid. Where she had been standing were a few black feathers already scattering in the breeze.

I was in a state of shock as I drove home to my Georgian villa in St John's Wood in my red, 4.2 litre, Jaguar XKR.

It is as if a huge void has opened and I am suspended above it. I know, more than likely, I won't see Corvid again, yet I have such a longing to be close to her. I should have told her my feelings before.

Regret. Interminable, perpetual, abiding, relentless, recurring, eternal, regret. Maybe this is what hell is?

Other Relevant Publications

It's About Time
By William Taylor Findler

A journey into the territory of *time*, *uncertainty* and the nature of *being*.

Reviews

Revealing and possibly revolutionary! Time, uncertainty and the nature of being are dealt with in an extraordinarily relevant way.

Anon.

I always said that he could do better.

Mr. Duffield
Ex Teacher

About the Author

Russell John Connor was born in Altrincham, Cheshire. After his family moved south, he was educated at Charters School, Sunningdale and University College London. On gaining a diploma from the London School of Economics in Industrial Relations and Personnel Management, Russell entered the business world and worked for a range of companies as a manager and consultant before starting his own business.

Russell lives in Windsor, England. He is the author of twelve books and, unusually, these span both business and fiction.

Lightning Source UK Ltd.
Milton Keynes UK
UKHW021257060722
405457UK00009B/1786